PODCASTER FROM GOA

RAJEEV NALAWADI

DEDICATION

This book is dedicated to all the divine manifestations around the world as we spend our brief moments on this beautiful planet together.

CHARACTERS

Hugo De Carvalho – Host of "Veritas Unveiled"

Veronica De Carvalho – Wife

Miguel – Wise old man visiting Hugo

Rodrigo Esteves – Executive producer

Ana Da Costa - Receptionist

Ashley Fernandes – Research team lead

Vishal Sen – Audio & Sound lead

Priscila Silveira – Marketing manager

Rebecca Silvestri – Social media manager

Sunil Gupta – Visual editor lead

Antonio Batista – IT Team lead (Local & Cloud)

Olivia Posada – Guest Booker

Akash Tripathi – Senior Detective in India

Alfonso Cunha – Inspector in Goa India

Julian Sanchez – Detective in Spain

Table of Contents

PROLOGUE

J ulian, the detective from Spain, would soon find himself on
the brink of becoming intricately entwined in a story that
would unravel the profound mysteries of human faith,
offering glimpses into the very essence of hope itself. This is a
story that would reach deep within Julian's soul, leaving an
indelible mark on his heart and mind.

In the sun-kissed shores of Goa, a place where the azure
waters whisper tales of the old world weaved with Portuguese
ancestry, the story of Hugo De Carvalho unfolds, a name
whispered and celebrated in many corners of the digital world.
Known fondly as Hugo, his roots delve deep into Portuguese
soil, a lineage tracing back to nine generations, a rich tapestry
of history woven into his being.

The quaint streets of Goa, with their colonial echoes, saw
the birth of an icon. For a decade and a year, the steady hum of
activity around Hugo's channel, "Veritas Unveiled", resonated
with voices of the past and promises of the future. A staggering
1,359 episodes, each one a masterpiece, filled the voids of
countless hearts and minds, reaching an astounding 20 million
subscribers. His tireless dedication was evident in the prolific
release of over 100 episodes annually, a rhythm that found its
tempo in the heartbeat of millions.

Hugo had his roots in this coastal paradise, Goa, where the lives of two dedicated educators, Hugo's parents, intertwined in the pursuit of knowledge. His father, a man of numbers, was a math teacher in the local public high school, while his mother, a woman of words, taught English to eager young minds. Together, they painted the canvas of countless students' futures with vivid hues of learning and aspiration. They labored tirelessly, sharing wisdom and nurturing the young saplings of Goa's intellectual garden until they reached the age of retirement.

Hugo's parents had cultivated not only the minds of their students but also a dream for their own son. With unwavering determination, they invested their hopes in him, urging him to tread the path of engineering. They saw the potential for greatness in him, a beacon of academic excellence that could illuminate their family's name.

And Hugo, as their beloved son, carried their aspirations as his own. He embarked on a journey through the labyrinth of electronics and communication, dedicating himself to unraveling the intricate threads of technology. He navigated the sea of complex equations and circuits with a mathematician's precision and honed his linguistic skills with the finesse of an English scholar. His professors marveled at his ability to bridge the gap between the intricacies of science and the beauty of language.

In time, Hugo emerged victorious, having completed his engineering with flying colors. His insatiable hunger for knowledge led him further into the realm of computer science, where he delved deeper into the digital cosmos. This dual expertise bestowed upon him a formidable advantage, an edge that set him apart from the rest. He possessed the rare gift of understanding technology in its intricate detail while being highly proficient in the art of weaving words, a perfect blend for the modern world.

But the wheel of fate turns without mercy, and at the tender age of 23, Hugo faced a loss that would forever change the course of his life. His parents, the pillars of his dreams and the architects of his ambition departed from this world, leaving him orphaned. It was a cruel twist of destiny, a moment when he was bereaved of their presence just as he was on the cusp of presenting them with the tools of his own success.

With a heavy heart, Hugo continued his journey. He embarked upon a career in engineering, working diligently in the bustling city of Mumbai for six long years. Yet, amidst the cacophony of the urban jungle, he could not escape the call of his ancestral roots. Goa beckoned him with its tranquil shores, whispering promises of a different path, a new calling. Just the brief visits to Goa during festivals would not be satisfying enough.

Around the age of 29, Hugo heeded that call. He returned to the land where he had spent his formative years, to the sanctuary of his ancestral property. It was here, amidst the whispers of palm leaves and the caress of the sea breeze, that he found solace and inspiration. Here, he decided to embrace his true passion to become the architect of his destiny.

In Goa's serene embrace, Hugo embarked on a new venture – podcasting. With his deep understanding of technology and his eloquent command of the English language, he found his voice in the digital realm. His podcasts became a platform for insightful conversations, a canvas where he painted the hues of knowledge and wisdom, just as his parents had done in their classrooms.

In this tranquil haven, Hugo found a way to honor his parents' legacy. Through the power of his podcasts, he continued to inspire, educate, and connect with the world, a testament to the enduring influence of his parents' unwavering belief in him. As the sun dipped below the horizon, casting golden hues over Goa's shores, Hugo knew that he had finally found his true calling, a calling that echoed the dreams of his parents and the rhythm of his own heart. His face, a canvas of time at the age of 40, bore the delicate strokes of Portuguese artistry intertwined with Goan warmth. A global beacon in the vast ocean of the internet, Hugo's influence stretched far and wide. As the digital age thrived, so did he, carving out a niche, a sanctuary of deep thought and relentless truth-seeking. The distinct timbre of his voice, the magnetic allure of his presence, and the depths of his curiosity made "Veritas Unveiled" a haven for minds that thirsted for knowledge, information, and enlightenment across a myriad of topics.

Despite an academic path paved with circuits and codes, with degrees in Electronics and communication and a master's in computer science, Hugo's heart pulsated beyond technology with stories, questions, and revelations. A modern-day bard, his gift was to untangle the intricate webs of knowledge from across the world & universe, presenting them as threads of simplicity, making the esoteric accessible to the masses. Each episode, with its poetic eloquence and fervor, became a fireside chat, drawing listeners into its warm embrace.

The episodes of "Veritas Unveiled" paint a vivid tapestry of human experience. One moment, Hugo delves into the sprawling digital forests of emerging technologies, deciphering the language of AI, and the next, he's meandering through the intricate pathways of the human psyche, unveiling the mysteries of the mind. His episodes on self-transformation echo the age-old teachings of Eastern sages, reimagined for the modern soul, while personal improvement becomes a dance of discipline, motivation, and reflection. Spirituality isn't just confined to ancient scriptures; Hugo weaves it seamlessly with contemporary philosophy, offering fresh perspectives on ageless questions. And as he speaks of the body, mind, and soul, it's clear that for Hugo, these are not isolated entities but a harmonious trinity. New-age problems, from the existential anxiety induced by social media to the struggles of finding purpose in a hyper-connected world, are untangled with grace and wisdom. Each episode is a journey, a bridge connecting the external world of tech and trends to the internal cosmos of thoughts, beliefs, and emotions.

In the luminous studio of "Veritas Unveiled," the brilliance of Hugo's dialogue with his esteemed guests became the very tapestry of enlightenment for his vast audience. Each conversation was a deep dive into the recesses of human knowledge and wisdom. With tech moguls, he navigated the intricate labyrinths of artificial intelligence, questioning not just the how, but the why and the implications for humans. Philosophers found in him a worthy sparring partner, as they dissected existential conundrums and explored the ever-evolving definition of consciousness. When conversing with spiritual leaders, the discourse soared to ethereal heights, juxtaposing ancient dogmas with contemporary spiritual evolution. Industrial tycoons shed light on the balance between profit and ethics, while psychology experts and Hugo together untangled the complex webs of human emotion and cognition. Every dialogue was an intricate dance of question and insight, as Hugo, with his characteristic fervor, steered these luminaries to reveal not just knowledge but wisdom, transforming each episode into a mosaic of profound revelations.

In a world where the flicker of a screen could ignite ideas and catapult unknown faces to stardom, Hugo's odyssey from a visionary engineer to a global digital virtuoso showcased the alchemy of grit, innovation, and the symphony of a team working behind the curtains.

In the heart of Goa, amidst the balmy breezes and the tales of yore, Hugo De Carvalho emerged, not just as a storyteller, but as a beacon of veracity, guiding millions towards their quest for knowledge.

Chapter 01

HUGO'S SLICE OF GOA

Nestled along the azure shores of Goa's fabled coastline, Vagator emerges as a veritable haven for those who seek respite in nature's opulent embrace. Here, the world slows to a languid, tropical pace, and the very air seems infused with a heady mix of salt, sun, and serenity.

Vagator's pièce de résistance is its resplendent beach, a sandy crescent bathed in the soft caress of the Arabian Sea. Stretching languorously for what seems like an eternity, it is a tableau of dreams come alive. The sand, kissed by the dawn's first light, glows like golden silk beneath the ever-watchful gaze of the sun. Crystal-clear waves, as if sculpted by a celestial hand, playfully rush to the shore, their gentle symphony echoing through the hearts of those who tread upon this hallowed ground.

Yet, it's the red rock cliffs that stand sentinel along the beach's edge, like ancient guardians of a sacred realm, that truly define Vagator's enchantment. These vermilion sentinels, weathered by centuries of monsoons and sea spray, jut defiantly into the sky. Their rugged façades tell stories of time's relentless march, etched in the very texture of the rock. Here, time seems to move both swiftly and serenely, an eternal dance between life and stone.

Vagator, with its beautiful beach, resolute red rock cliffs, and Villa Carvalho perched upon the precipice, is more than a destination; it is a testament to the timeless allure of nature's artistry and the eternal appeal of Goa's coastal splendor.

Amidst this natural wonderland, nestled on the edge of the cliff, like a jewel in nature's crown, is Villa Carvalho, Hugo's ancestral home. A sanctuary of luxury and refinement, it offers a vantage point to behold the grandeur of Vagator in all its glory. Its whitewashed walls and terracotta-tiled roofs blend seamlessly with the landscape, a testament to architectural harmony.

Villa Carvalho emerges as a resplendent testament to bygone eras, a sanctuary steeped in the rich tapestry of Old Goan Portuguese design. This architectural jewel, perched upon the red-rock cliffs, stands as a venerable portal to a world where time has woven a tapestry of nostalgia and elegance.

As one approaches Villa Carvalho, its whitewashed walls adorned with bougainvillea and ivy, a whispered echo of colonial grandeur whispers through the salt-scented breeze. The structure, meticulously preserved in its historical glory, boasts the hallmark of a bygone era, high ceilings adorned with ornate cornices that lend an air of majestic grandeur to the living spaces within.

Villa Carvalho unfolds its grandeur over two enchanting floors. Each space, meticulously designed and curated to pamper the senses, promises an embrace of comfort and refinement reminiscent of home, if not surpassing it.

Arriving on the ground floor, one is greeted by a vestibule of opulence. A hall of generous proportions, graced with high ceilings and adorned with tasteful artwork, invites guests into an atmosphere of understated elegance. This hall serves as the gateway to the villa's myriad treasures.

Further on, the dining room unveils itself, a place of communion and feasting. A grand table, capable of seating nine, stands at the center, promising convivial gatherings and sumptuous banquets. The ambiance is set aglow by soft lighting and the gentle hum of conversation.

The kitchen, a culinary haven, beckons with its modern appliances, a testament to the villa's dedication to convenience and functionality. A bar counter, sleek and stylish, awaits the mixing of cocktails and the creation of culinary masterpieces. Every necessary utensil and implement stands at the ready, making the act of cooking a delight rather than a chore.

On this first floor, a single bedroom stands with its own allure, a sanctuary of solitude and reprieve. The room, air-conditioned like the others, boasts hardwood furniture and an extra soft and comfortable mattress adorned with exquisite linen, inviting restful slumber.

Completing the ensemble, a common bathroom, adorned with tasteful fixtures and soothing hues, stands as a testament to the villa's commitment to both luxury and practicality.

Ascending to the second floor, the pièce de résistance reveals itself. Four ensuite bedrooms, each a testament to the villa's commitment to opulence and comfort. Two of these bedrooms offer access to a spacious balcony, where the vista of Vagator's coastal beauty awaits, a panorama to be savored.

Villa Carvalho spread over two floors, stands as an embodiment of refined living. Every detail, from the carefully selected furnishings to the softness of the mattresses, from the modern kitchen to the gracious dining room, is an invitation to experience comfort, luxury, and the timeless allure of this coastal paradise.

The library and living room that extends seamlessly into each other, a sanctuary for bibliophiles and contemplative souls, beckons from its corner. Lined with mahogany bookshelves and bathed in the warm glow of antique lamps, it offers a respite for quiet reflection amidst a world of literary treasures.

The living room unfurls in all its splendor. The air-conditioned space is adorned with plush, hardwood furniture adorned with carefully selected upholstery. Soft sofas, so inviting that one could lose themselves within their embrace, cradle guests in serenity. A sleek smart TV mounted on the wall stands ready to entertain or inform, as one wishes.

The sense of grandeur in the living room becomes palpable. The ceilings soar high above, creating an airy expanse that welcomes the golden rays of sunlight that filter through large, arched windows. Here, history mingles effortlessly with modern comfort, as antique wooden furniture, and heirlooms of a time long past, share space with plush sofas and contemporary amenities. As the sun sets over the Arabian Sea, the living room transforms into a sanctuary of warmth and grace, with soft hues and antique fixtures casting a nostalgic glow over the room.

Beyond the living room, large verandas beckon, extending an invitation to linger amidst their timeless charm. These sprawling terraces, wrapped in wrought-iron railings and draped in flowering vines, provide a front-row seat to the drama of the coastal panorama.

From the terraces of Villa Carvalho, one can drink in the panoramic vista of the beach below, sip on a glass of vintage port wine or freshly brewed chai, and gaze out at the endless expanse of the sea, where the horizon meets eternity.

The red rocks extending into the horizon, and the cerulean expanse of the Arabian Sea, a vast canvas upon which the sun paints its masterpieces each day. It is a place where the senses awaken, where the soul finds solace, and where time, like the waves that caress the shore, laps gently at the edges of existence.

Outside, a verdant garden envelops Villa Carvalho in its embrace. This lush oasis, like a time capsule, carries within it the whispers of bygone days. Hundreds of trees, including the majestic coconut palms, mango trees laden with the promise of sweet harvest, and passionfruit vines that entwine with memories of yesteryears, beckon visitors to explore their bountiful offerings. As the breeze rustles through the leaves, it carries with it the scent of nostalgia, invoking memories of simpler times when life unfolded at a gentler pace.

Villa Carvalho, with its Old Goan Portuguese design, living room with high ceilings, sun-drenched verandas, and a garden that tells stories of generations, stands as a testament to the enduring allure of Goa's past. It is a place where the echoes of history dance with the present, and where the soul finds solace in the embrace of time-honored elegance and the gentle caress of nature's bounty.

Chapter 02

HUGO'S EVENING

Date, December 3RD, Time, 6,30PM

Place, Hugo's Residence at Vagator

In the intricate universal web of time encompassing the complexity of human tapestry, Hugo's day was poised to unfold in a unique way.

Hugo, whose family settled in Goa over five centuries ago, bore a proud Portuguese lineage, his countenance the indelible imprints of his ancestry. His visage was a living canvas, painted by the hands of time and heritage, a testament to the rich tapestry of his family's history.

At first glance, one's eyes would be drawn to the cascade of wavy, dark brown hair that crowned his head. Those luxuriant locks, reminiscent of the earthy hues of Goan soil, framed his face with a natural elegance. They ebbed and flowed in untamed patterns, hinting at a spirit unburdened by conformity as if each strand told a story of its own.

But it was his eyes that held the most captivating allure. Hugo's medium brown orbs were akin to the warm, polished chestnut wood that graced many a Portuguese homestead. They possessed an enigmatic depth, like ancient scrolls filled with untold tales of seafaring adventures and whispered secrets from centuries past. These eyes, as if reflecting the very essence of Portugal's maritime history, bore an ever-so-subtle hint of melancholy—a poignant reminder of the nation's storied past.

Hugo's complexion, kissed by the Goan Arabian sun, radiated a soft olive hue, like the groves of olives that adorned the terraced hillsides of his ancestral homeland. Yet, it was the yellow undertones that added a unique depth to his skin, reminiscent of the warm sunlight filtering through the leaves of an olive tree, casting golden hues upon the earth. This undertone bestowed upon his complexion a rare, luminescent quality as if he carried within him the essence of Portugal and Goa's sun-kissed shores.

Each of Hugo's facial features, from the waves of his dark brown hair to the medium brown depths of his eyes and the olive canvas of his skin, whispered the tale of a lineage steeped in tradition and history. His face was a living map, tracing the contours of a heritage that had weathered the sands of time and, in doing so, had become a reflection of Portugal's enduring spirit. In Hugo's countenance, one could discern the echoes of a bygone era, a lyrical reminder of a people's journey across oceans and centuries, etched into the very essence of his being.

In the heart of Villa Carvalho, Hugo found himself ensconced within the living room, a haven of cultured sophistication and an ode to the convergence of tradition and modernity. He reclined upon a sumptuous leather sofa, the embodiment of timeless comfort, as he marveled at his surroundings.

The room, bathed in a warm, diffused glow from the sun's farewell embrace, was a sanctuary for intellect and aesthetics alike. Its walls were generously adorned with towering bookshelves, their wooden spines burdened with volumes that spanned centuries of human thought. These shelves whispered the stories of great authors, novelists, poets, philosophers, and visionaries, whose words had transcended time and found a home in this bibliophilic haven.

In Hugo's living room, the classical literature, novels, memoirs, religion, spirituality, fiction, and non-fiction books exhibited a warm embrace of dance with the vibrant notes of classical and modernity, a singular sight of botanical wonder unfolded. A collection of fifty different orchids, there was an unspoken uniqueness among thirty-one of them, each one an exquisite masterpiece of nature's artistry, adorned the room in a tapestry of colors and forms that rivaled the volumes of wisdom on the nearby bookshelves.

These orchids, Nature's own works of art, stood as a testament to Hugo's appreciation for the subtleties and diversities of the natural world. Positioned with precision and care next to the bookshelves, they formed a living canvas of botanical diversity that whispered tales of distant rainforests and remote mountainsides.

Among them, there were orchids with petals of alabaster white, as delicate as gossamer, their purity evoking thoughts of pristine, untouched landscapes. Nearby, orchids flaunted flamboyant shades of crimson and amaranth, their velvety blooms a passionate contrast to the hushed tones of the room.

Amidst this floral congregation, there were orchids that bore the regal robes of violet and lavender, their blooms resembling the plumage of tropical birds. Others exhibited shades of cerulean and azure, evoking the tranquil serenity of azure seas under a cloudless sky.

Each orchid was ensconced in a decorative pot, some crafted from elegant porcelain, others carved from rich mahogany, their vessels as exquisite as the blooms they held. These pots, arranged with an artist's eye for composition, were themselves a testament to the harmonious marriage of nature and human artistry.

The living room, bathed in the soft, filtered light of the setting sun, became a sanctuary where the pursuit of knowledge and the celebration of natural beauty converged. The orchids, with their intricate patterns and diverse hues, served as a living testament to the myriad wonders that the world held in its embrace.

As Hugo sat amidst this symphony of books and blooms, he found himself enveloped in a sense of reverence for the beauty of the natural world. The orchids, with their grace and diversity, served as a reminder that the pursuit of knowledge and the appreciation of nature were not separate endeavors but threads in the tapestry of a life well-lived, a life rich in both the wisdom of words and the wonders of the earth.

At the room's center, a grand piano stood with stoic grace, its polished ebony surface reflecting the soft rays of daylight that filtered through an off-white colored lace-styled curtain. It was an instrument of exquisite craftsmanship, patiently waiting for the hands of a maestro to awaken its dulcet melodies.

Standing beside the piano, like a sentinel of technological marvel, was a four-foot-tall female-looking robot from the Japanese Masqueda Corporation sold as "Trendy Service Robot (TSR)". A marvel of modern engineering, she possessed an uncanny semblance to the human form, her eyes imbued with an almost lifelike curiosity, emanating a faint blue light around the neckline as if donning a necklace. With grace in her movements, she was a testament to the seamless fusion of art and science, an embodiment of the villa's commitment to embracing the future without forsaking its past. Hugo has named her 'O serviço de Maria', or Maria's Service. Like Alexa, she can be addressed as 'Maria'.

Amid Hugo's living room, there was the looming presence of another technological entity with the capability of capturing the essence of the moment with a silent unblinking gaze. A camera, perched on a sturdy tripod, could be moved around to achieve a steadfast focused glance.

Before Hugo, on the elegant coffee table, an ensemble of indulgences awaited. A bottle of reserve wine, its label "Puerta del Sol" an emblem of prestige, stood tall, cradled within an ornate holder. Hugo was savoring the last drop of this wine from his glass; the evening had beckoned him to finish the entire bottle. The deep, garnet-hued wine had kept its promise to unfurl its rich bouquet, each sip giving Hugo an elixir that would mingle with the symphonies of the piano and the wisdom of the books.

In this harmonious convergence of literature, music, technology, and enology, Hugo found himself at the crossroads of epochs, where the past whispered its timeless tales and the future stood at attention, ready to accompany humanity on its uncharted journey. Villa Carvalho's living room was a canvas where the threads of time and innovation wove together, inviting Hugo to contemplate the wonders of a world where tradition and progress danced in perfect harmony.

Hugo grabbed his notepad and pen from the coffee table, while seated on the sofa jotted down three points. This was

Hugo's preparation for centering the theme of the discussion for the upcoming podcast scheduled to be recorded tomorrow afternoon around 1 PM in less than 16 hours,

- Human ingenuity for doing evil things always brings elements of surprise to investigations that involve learning something new and diving deeper into technological advances.

- Every society gets the criminals it deserves.

- Every society creates the criminals it deserves.

Hugo's phone rang, and he glanced at the caller ID, recognizing it as Rodrigo Esteves, his executive producer. He swiped to answer.

Hugo, (with a warm tone) Hey, Rodrigo! How's it going?

Rodrigo, (with a sense of urgency) Hugo, good to hear from you. Listen, I hope I'm not catching you at a bad time. Are you ready for tomorrow's podcast recording?

Hugo, (pausing for a moment) Tomorrow? Oh, right, the one about how technology influences new ways to commit evils in society. Yeah, I've been preparing for that.

Rodrigo, (sounding relieved) Great to hear, Hugo. This topic is buzzing right now, and our listeners are eager to hear your insights. You've got some fantastic guests lined up, and your research is top-notch, as always.

Hugo, (appreciative) Thanks, Rodrigo. I've been digging deep into it. The connections between technology and evolving forms of crime are truly fascinating. The potential for both good and bad that tech brings is mind-boggling.

Rodrigo, (enthusiastic) That's exactly why we're doing this episode. We want to shed light on the darker side of innovation while also highlighting the ways we can combat these new-age challenges. The audience needs to understand the risks, but also the solutions.

Hugo, (nodding) Absolutely, Rodrigo. It's about raising awareness and encouraging responsible use of technology.

Rodrigo, (getting practical) Okay, Hugo, so we're on track for tomorrow. We've got all the technical aspects sorted out. Do you want us to change any background in the studio for this podcast? Of course, We'll have the same favorite microphone available to the other five guests as well, last time around we had to share the microphone between two guests due to unforeseen failure, this time we have made sure there are some extra microphones available and the studio's prepped for the guests. Everything's set.

Hugo, (feeling reassured) Excellent, Rodrigo. You guys always make it run like clockwork.

Rodrigo, (appreciative) Thanks, Hugo. It's a team effort, and you're a big part of it. I have no doubt tomorrow's podcast is going to be a hit. We're expecting some lively discussions.

Hugo, (with a hint of excitement) I can't wait. The topic is close to my heart, and I'm looking forward to sharing insights with our amazing guests. I understand your concern that we are tackling the topic of how homicide investigations face new challenges with the advent of new technology. We should be careful in addressing only the known uses of where technology was used. Let's not run wild with our imaginations giving ideas to criminals. Let's make it memorable.

Rodrigo, (confident) You got it, Hugo. I'll let you get back to your prep now. See you at the studio bright and early tomorrow.

Hugo, (with a smile) Will do, Rodrigo. Thanks for the call. Catch you tomorrow.

Rodrigo, (warmly) Take care, Hugo. Bye for now.

Hugo, (ending the call) Goodbye, Rodrigo.

Hugo hung up the phone, a renewed sense of purpose in his preparations for the podcast. Tomorrow was going to be a day for engaging discussions and meaningful insights.

Chapter 03

HUGO'S VISITOR

As the golden Goan sun began its descent toward the horizon, casting a warm, honeyed glow over the village of Vagator, Hugo found himself in the tranquil sanctum of his living room. It was a place of solitude and contemplation, where the murmurs of the sea in the distance often mingled with his own musings.

Date, December 3RD, Time, 6,45PM

Place, Hugo's Living Room

Then, there came a sound—a chime that seemed both familiar and foreign in its beckoning. Hugo's curiosity was piqued, as he wasn't expecting anyone at the front door today, he made his way to the door. As he reached for the doorknob, he could scarcely anticipate the gentle encounter that awaited him on the other side.

The door swung open, revealing a figure bathed in the soft, amber light of the setting sun. It was an old man, his silver hair glinting like a halo in the waning light. His eyes held the wisdom of ages, yet sparkled with an infectious kindness that warmed Hugo's heart.

Hugo extended a cordial smile, his eyes crinkling at the corners in recognition of the stranger's gentility. "Hello," he greeted, "how can I help you?"

The old man returned the smile with a grace that seemed to belong to another time. "I am Miguel de Los Santos," he began, his voice like the mellifluous cadence of a storyteller. "I live about three kilometers from here, and I am an avid follower of your channel. Your episodes, your words, your thoughts—they have resonated with me deeply."

Hugo, humbled by the unexpected praise, nodded gratefully. "Thank you, Miguel. It's a pleasure to meet you."

Miguel's figure seemed to challenge conventional expectations with an elegance that defied gender norms. This visitor, though unquestionably male, possessed a petite frame that gracefully embraced the contours of their identity, a testament to the beauty that exists beyond the confines of societal conventions.

Besides the petite frame, Miguel's other features bore a striking resemblance to Hugo, as if they were cast from the same mold of heritage and lineage. Miguel's wavy silver hair with lushness appeared to have transitioned through a stage of wavy, dark brown hair cascade over the years past.

Like Hugo, the visitor's eyes held the same medium brown hue, their depth revealing the same enigmatic stories of Portugal's past. Yet, there was a softness in the visitor's gaze, a subtlety that invited vulnerability and intimacy. Their eyes, like the calm waters of a secluded cove, beckoned one to explore their depths with gentle curiosity.

Miguel's complexion, too, bore echoes of Hugo's ancestral heritage, with olive-colored skin bathed in the same yellowish undertones. Yet, on this petite frame, it lent an ethereal quality, as if they were an apparition from a dream, a manifestation of Goan sun-drenched landscapes come to life.

It was a visage that defied convention, a portrait of beauty that transcended the boundaries of gender. In Hugo's visitor, one found a living testament to the diverse and multifaceted nature of identity, a reminder that the beauty of a person's essence could not be confined by societal expectations.

Miguel's eyes gleamed with a fervor that defied his age. "I have spent my life reading, Hugo," "I am an avid and voracious reader having followed many books, but you have a medium, your channel to convey the knowledge to the world, Hugo," he said, his voice carrying the weight of a thousand pages. "Books spanning centuries, the wisdom of sages and scholars, the stories of civilizations rising and falling. And I couldn't help but wonder, is there a possibility of recording a podcast episode? An episode that delves into humanity's progress over these long centuries, as seen through your eyes and words?" Having watched your episodes, have a fairly good idea of how we can do this together without having to visit your office, after all, it's a casual conversation.

Hugo's heart swelled with a profound sense of purpose. Here was a man who had walked the corridors of time through the pages of books, seeking to connect the dots of human progress and understand the tapestry of our shared history.

With a nod of agreement, Hugo extended a welcoming hand. "Miguel, that's a remarkable idea. Let's make it happen. Humanity's journey through the ages is told through the lens of our shared curiosity and wisdom. It would be an honor."

Miguel's face lit up with a radiant smile that seemed to carry the wisdom of the centuries he had traversed in his readings. "Thank you, Hugo. I look forward to the conversation. Your channel has brought knowledge and inspiration to many, and I believe this episode will be a testament to our enduring quest for understanding."

As the two men shook hands, the sun dipped below the horizon, and the world outside seemed to fade into insignificance. Within those walls, a connection had been forged—a connection transcending generations and embracing the timeless curiosity that binds humanity together on its unending quest for knowledge.

Hugo leads Miguel into the living room.

In the heart of an inviting living room, bathed in the soft, red glow of a sunset's twilight filtering through glass windows and thinly veiled lace-styled curtains, a tapestry of enchantment unfolded a serene sanctuary.

Miguel admired the scene that lay in front of him, upon the well-polished wooden shelf, nestled among leather-bound tomes and delicate porcelain figurines, rested a chessboard. It lay in a state of disarray, its ivory and ebony pieces scattered in intricate patterns. To the untrained eye, it appeared a chaotic scene, the battlefield of a forgotten pastime. Yet, to a connoisseur of the game, one who had learned the art of strategy and foresight, the tableau bore silent witness to a profound narrative.

The chessboard's checkered surface bore the marks of past, present, and future possibilities. The ivory and ebony armies, their ranks unevenly matched, stood poised in a delicate dance of war. The kings, symbols of power and vulnerability, held court at opposite ends, their queens at their side, resolute and formidable. The bishops, knights, rooks, and pawns, each sculpted with meticulous precision, occupied their appointed places, each piece a reflection of its player's psyche.

Yet, the true essence of this scene lay not in the frozen tableau but in the story it whispered. The proximity of the white and black pieces hinted at an ongoing battle of wits and strategy. Every move, each placement, bore the weight of calculated intent, a dance of minds engaged in a timeless struggle.

The chessboard's disarray was a testament to the ceaseless ebb and flow of this cerebral contest. Every piece, arranged or displaced, bore witness to a profound narrative of confrontation and concession, of gambits and blunders. The game was a tapestry woven from the threads of contemplation and anticipation, a narrative that transcended mere competition, embracing the spirit of intellectual endeavor.

In the living room, the chessboard stood as a silent sentinel, its pieces a reflection of the human spirit's ceaseless yearning for challenge and conquest. It was a testament to the enduring allure of a game where every move had purpose, every choice resonated with consequence. Amidst the serene elegance of the room, the chessboard silently beckoned, inviting those with the wisdom to understand its language to partake in the eternal dance of strategy and possibility.

For Miguel, the chessboard before him was not a puzzle; it bore a vivid demonstration, a dance of intellect where both players had made nine moves. The number nine, he pondered, held a fascinating significance within the tapestry of the universe, its enigmatic allure akin to the ancient game itself.

In the vast cosmos, where stars twinkled in distant galaxies, chess was a reflection of the human pursuit of complexity. It offered an infinite array of openings, gambits, and defenses, each more intricate than the last. Miguel knew that this timeless game would forever remain captivating, much like the endless expanse of the night sky that never failed to inspire wonder.

Within the confines of this 64-square battlefield, Every move, every piece placement, was a new universe to explore. Each player, with their unique style and personality, added layers of intrigue to the unfolding drama. Miguel was amazed at the enigma of chess, having entranced humanity for well over a millennium. It was a riddle that seemed to have no end, and that boundlessness was perhaps why it had endured through the annals of time. In the world of chess, the possibilities were as infinite as the cosmos itself.

Miguel's mind wandered through the statistics of the game, a testament to its complexity. After just one move by each player, there were a staggering 400 different positions to contemplate. It was a number that the human intellect could easily fathom. But with the second move, the chessboard exploded into a mind-boggling 72,084 potential positions, a testament to the intricacy of the game.

As the third piece was maneuvered into place, the possibilities skyrocketed to over 9 million, and by the time the fourth piece entered the fray, there were mind-bending 288 billion possible positions, a number that dwarfed the imagination.

At that moment alone, Miguel marveled at the boundless complexity where nine moves had been made on this chessboard in Hugo's living room. It was a game that transcended time and space, an endless journey of strategy and tactics, and a reflection of the infinite nature of the human itself. Slowly moving around in admiration amidst the living room's eloquent blend of literature and the vibrant presence of orchids, Miguel felt a profound sense of awe. His eyes, which had traversed the pages of countless books over the span of his life, now beheld a different kind of masterpiece—a collection of fifty exquisite orchids, each one a testament to the boundless artistry of nature.

As he approached the array of blooms, Miguel's fingers seemed to tingle with anticipation. His gaze swept over the orchids, marveling at their diversity and grace. He admired the alabaster whites that spoke of purity and simplicity, the crimson and amaranth blooms that blazed with fiery passion, and the violets and lavenders that whispered of elegance and sophistication.

But, as Miguel wandered deeper into this botanical paradise, his discerning eye caught a subtle detail that ignited his curiosity. Amidst the fifty orchids, there were thirty-one that stood apart, each one an individual masterpiece in its own right.

These thirty-one orchids bore the mark of uniqueness. Their petals unfurled in patterns and hues that seemed to defy convention, each one a living testament to the staggering diversity of the orchid family. Some were adorned with speckles and stripes, like nature's own intricate brushstrokes upon a canvas of velvet petals. Others flaunted shades of color that defied easy description like the hues of an artist's palette brought to life.

Miguel could not help but be drawn to these thirty-one, for they were like characters in a story, each one with its own narrative to share. He approached them with reverence, his hands hovering over the delicate blooms, careful not to disturb the living artwork before him.

"Hugo," Miguel called out, his voice tinged with a mixture of wonder and appreciation, "these orchids, these thirty-one unique ones, they are like the rarest of manuscripts in your library of blooms. Each one is a chapter in a story of botanical brilliance, a testament to the inexhaustible creativity of the natural world."

Hugo, who had been quietly observing Miguel's reaction, nodded in agreement. "Indeed, Miguel. These orchids are a reminder that even within the vast tapestry of nature, there are threads of uniqueness that deserve our attention and admiration. They are a living testament to the beauty of diversity."

Miguel smiled, his eyes dancing with a newfound appreciation for the orchids that graced Hugo's living room. These blooms, with their individuality and charm, had opened a new chapter in his lifelong journey of curiosity and wonder, reminding him that even in the most unexpected corners of the world, there were treasures waiting to be discovered.

As the sun's golden fingers gently withdrew from the sky, casting a dusky veil over Vagator, Hugo, the gracious host, felt compelled to extend a warm offer to his esteemed guest,

Miguel. He turned to the older man with a courteous smile, his words laced with the subtle aroma of hospitality.

"Miguel," Hugo began, his voice a gentle cadence in the tranquil room, "I have a bottle of 'Puerta del Sol' reserve wine that I was planning to open tonight. Would you care to join me for a glass? It's a vintage that can grace special occasions, and I can't think of a more special moment than now."

Miguel's eyes, reflecting the wisdom of a lifetime, regarded Hugo with a fond appreciation. He weighed the offer with a gracious nod but then gently declined, his voice resonating with a quiet resolve.

"Hugo," he replied, his words carrying the weight of personal conviction, "I appreciate your offer, and I'm sure that wine is exquisite. However, it has been a personal practice of mine not to drink or consume anything after sunset. It's a small discipline that I've followed for many years."

Hugo nodded in understanding, his respect for Miguel's choices unwavering. He admired the older man's steadfast commitment to his principles, even in the face of such tempting indulgence.

"Of course, Miguel," Hugo replied with a warm smile, "I completely understand. Your discipline is commendable, and I respect your decision. We have a purpose tonight, a conversation to record—a conversation that promises to be as rich as the finest wine. Shall we get started, then?"

Miguel's eyes twinkled with anticipation as he nodded in agreement. "Indeed, Hugo," he affirmed, "let's pour your wine of words and begin this captivating recording. The treasures of knowledge and insight await us, and I am eager to embark on this journey of conversation and discovery."

And so, with a silent acknowledgment of their shared purpose and the understanding of their differences, Hugo and Miguel prepared to record a podcast that would celebrate the richness of human thought and the boundless curiosity that unites kindred spirits, even in the face of differing choices and convictions.

Hey Hugo, let's make this episode recording something different rather than two guys sitting on the sofa for a casual conversation. Can you make my voice come from Maria, your robot instead of my mouth for this recording? Says Miguel.

The moment hung in the air, suspended between Hugo and Miguel, as the request settled into the room like a whisper of intrigue. Miguel's proposal had injected an unexpected twist into the recording of their podcast, and Hugo, his curiosity piqued, regarded his guest with a thoughtful gaze.

Hugo, (arches an eyebrow) "Miguel, that's quite an unconventional idea. You're suggesting that you communicate through Maria, the robot, during our podcast?"

Miguel, (nodding with a hint of excitement) "Exactly, Hugo. Think of it as a unique storytelling device. Maria can lend a different perspective to our conversation, perhaps even challenge the boundaries of what's considered traditional in a podcast."

Hugo contemplated the proposition, his mind abuzz with the possibilities. It was an unorthodox approach, to be sure, but the prospect of breathing fresh life into their discussion was intriguing.

Hugo, (pausing for a moment) "It's certainly an innovative idea, Miguel. I appreciate your creativity. Let's give it a try. Maria can be our conduit for this unique conversation."

Miguel's eyes gleamed with enthusiasm; his anticipation was now woven with excitement. As they prepared to begin, Maria, the robot, stood steady almost at the same height as Miguel seated, on the other edge of the sofa from Hugo and standing next to where Miguel had positioned himself on the sofa, Maria's presence now poised to amplify their discourse.

Hugo checked Miguel's Bluetooth microphone connection to Maria who was going to provide the voice for Miguel.

With a quick sound and audio test, they both verified Maria was indeed the conduit of voice for Miguel. As Miguel spoke, his voice seamlessly was coming from Maria.

The tripod with the camera was positioned and pointed toward the two figures seated on the plush sofa. The tripod's legs, like the steadfast pillars of memory, held it steady as it stood ready to frame the tableau of dialogue and discovery.

Through the camera's lens, the world took on a different perspective. It focused with meticulous precision on Hugo, Maria, and Miguel, their words poised to dance through the airwaves of the future. The camera, with its lens like an all-seeing eye, captures every gesture and expression, preserving the nuances of their conversation for posterity.

As the lens widened its scope, the background came into view—a lush tapestry of orchids and bookshelves. The orchids, radiant in their diversity, formed an intricate backdrop to the human drama unfolding on the sofa. Each petal and stem stood as a testament to the beauty of nature's handiwork, their colors and forms captured in exquisite detail.

The bookshelves, lined with the wisdom of ages, stood as silent witnesses to the exchange of ideas. Their spines bore the weight of centuries of human thought, and they whispered stories of civilizations and discoveries. The camera, in its unceasing gaze, acknowledged the books as not just mere objects but as vessels of knowledge that would transcend this moment.

In this fusion of technology and human connection, the camera on the tripod became more than just a tool for recording; it was a storyteller in its own right. Through its lens, it wove a narrative of dialogue and discovery, capturing the essence of Hugo, Maria, and Miguel's shared exploration, and immortalizing the living room's interplay of ideas, orchids, and books—a tableau of human curiosity set against the backdrop of nature and knowledge.

Hugo opened his favorite bottle of 'Puerta del Sol' reserve wine, poured a serving into his wine glass from this second wine bottle for the day, and had his first sip with a gesture 'toradas de vinho' – cheers pointing towards Miguel seated on the other side of the sofa.

And so, the podcast episode began, the camera's red indicator blinking, with Maria serving as the vessel for Miguel's words. It was an experiment in storytelling, an exploration of the intersection between technology and human expression, and an unexpected twist in the tale of their shared curiosity. At that moment, Hugo, Maria, and Miguel embarked on a journey that would not only celebrate their own perspectives but also the boundless possibilities that the fusion of the human and the mechanical could offer to the world of ideas.

Chapter 04

VERONICA

The living room was bathed in soft light from the chandelier, its crystals sparkling like diamonds. The lighting in the room was pleasant enough to render a seamless recording of frames as the evening took on a more intimate feel as if it was designed for conversation and relaxation.

Maria was standing by the side of the sofa on Miguel's side as Miguel and Hugo sat in Hugo's cozy living room, with Hugo sipping on his "Puerta del Sol" reserve wine. Hugo's eyes wandered to the photographs adorning the wall, capturing moments from his life. His gaze settled on one in particular, a picture of him with a beautiful, radiant woman, their smiles reflecting a shared history.

Miguel, ever the curious old man, turned to Hugo with a gleam of intrigue in his eyes. "Hugo," he began, "let's start from today and this room. I see a couple of photos on the wall. Who is the person with you in the picture, and where is she right now?"

Hugo's eyes softened as he followed Miguel's gaze to the photograph. He smiled, a nostalgic warmth flooding his features. "Ah, that's Veronica," he said, his voice carrying a deep fondness. "My wife, for 15 wonderful years."

Miguel's eyebrows raised. "Veronica," he repeated as if savoring the name. "Tell me about her, Hugo. How did you two meet?"

Hugo leaned back on the sofa, his mind drifting to the past. "We met when we were 24, right out of college. It was at a local Goan festival, and I remember the moment I laid eyes on her. She had this energy, this magnetic presence that drew me in instantly.

With some quiet contemplation, Hugo took a sip of his wine, allowing the rich, velvety notes to linger on his palate before he turned his gaze towards Miguel. At this Goan festival in the heart of the city. She was dancing to the fado, and her grace utterly captivated me."

With a wistful smile, Hugo now tugged at the corners of his lips. She moved like a dream, her steps telling a story of longing and love. I knew then that I had to have her in my life."

We struck up a conversation, and it felt like we'd known each other for a lifetime. We shared our dreams, our hopes, and our fears later that night. It was as if the universe conspired to bring us together."

Miguel nodded, absorbing Hugo's words with a smile. "And then?"

Hugo's smile deepened. "Well, we started dating shortly after that. It was a whirlwind romance filled with laughter and adventures. We traveled together, learned together, and grew together. It was just a year after the first time we met. There was never a doubt in my mind that she was the one I wanted to spend the rest of my life with."

Miguel leaned closer, his eyes twinkling with a question. "And so you introduced yourself, my friend, and that was the start of something beautiful, a journey of life?"

Hugo's gaze drifted to the farthest corner of the room. "We discovered our shared Portuguese roots that night. It was as if our destinies had been entwined for centuries, waiting for this moment."

Just a year later, we tied the knot.

Miguel nodded with another question. "Veronica was a kindred spirit; you two were a perfect match. You married just a year after the Goan festival where you met?"

Hugo's smile deepened as he recalled that magical day. "Yes, we did, in a small chapel by the river in Arambol. Veronica in her mother's wedding gown, and I in my newly stitched suit. It was a day filled with love and promises."

Hugo raised his wine glass once more, "Fifteen years, my friend. It's been a journey filled with laughter, tears, and a love that has only grown stronger with time."

Hugo's eyes met Miguel's, a profound gratitude shining within them. "Indeed, Miguel. Veronica is the love of my life, and I thank the stars every day for bringing her to me."

Miguel leaned forward, his curiosity unabated. "So, 15 years of marriage and 16 years of knowing each other. That's quite a journey. What's the secret, Hugo?"

Hugo's eyes twinkled with wisdom born of experience. "The secret, my friend, is love, trust, and a willingness to weather life's storms together. We've faced our share of challenges, but we've always been there for each other. Communication, laughter, and never taking each other for granted—it's been the key to keeping our love alive."

The Sao Joao Festival in Goa is an annual celebration on the 24th of June, marking a date precisely six months before the birth of Jesus, 25th of December. This Goan festival was where Hugo first saw Veronica about 16 years ago. The Sao Joao closely aligns with the onset of the monsoon season, a time when nature awakens with lush greenery, vibrant blooming flowers, and a sense of renewal as water bodies, including wells, are replenished by the first rains.

Amidst this backdrop of nature's rejuvenation, the people of Goa commemorate the birth of St. John, and this celebration becomes intertwined with the joyous rainy season itself. The Sao Joāo Festival is a vibrant and colorful affair, with locals and tourists participating in the festivities.

One of the central themes of this tradition is the reverence for water, drawing parallels to the baptism of Jesus in the river Jordan. Water, in this context, holds profound spiritual significance. Participants in the Sao Joao Festival often immerse themselves in water bodies such as rivers, streams, and even wells, symbolizing a purification of the soul and a connection to the divine.

The festival is a time of exuberance and merriment, marked by processions, music, dance, and vibrant floral crowns worn by the participants. People often wear traditional Konkani attire, and the atmosphere is filled with laughter and joy. It's a time for communities to come together, share traditional dishes, and celebrate the rich cultural heritage of Goa.

In essence, the Sao Joao Festival in Goa serves as a beautiful synthesis of nature's bounty, religious symbolism, and cultural traditions. It is a moment when the people of Goa express their gratitude for the life-giving rains and their faith through the celebration of St. John's birth, creating a unique and spiritually enriching experience for all who partake in this annual event.

Sixteen years ago, the Sao Joao Festival began as separate journeys for Hugo and Veronica. Each of them had their own unique start to this auspicious day, marked by devotion and tradition. They had individually attended the special Church prayer services, seeking blessings on this significant occasion. Hugo had found himself in Vagator, while Veronica had chosen to participate in the church service in Siolim.

As they entered the sacred space of the church, both Hugo and Veronica wore splendid crowns made from delicate flower blooms and palm leaves, known as "kopels." These exquisite handmade wreaths graced their heads, symbolizing the renewal of life with the onset of the monsoon. The kopel, with its vibrant colors and intricate design, not only celebrated the bounty of nature but also evoked the deep symbolism of John the Baptist's martyrdom, reminding them of the interconnectedness of life, seasons, and devotion.

With their heads adorned with these symbolic crowns, Hugo and Veronica joyously embarked on a journey through their respective neighborhoods, chanting with exuberance, "São João! São João!" The crowns on their heads mirrored the flourishing of life in nature as the rains arrived, blanketing the earth with green leaves and fresh flowers.

The festival day's lunch was a feast for the senses, featuring a delicious spread that included sorpotel, a flavorful Indian pork dish, sannas, a steamed rice cake, and an array of traditional fruits and sweets. Families welcomed their neighbors with warm hospitality, offering "copache," a potent shot of urrak or feni, accompanied by plump mangoes and luscious jackfruit.

Amid the rhythmic beats of gummot (drums) and cansaim (cymbals), people fearlessly leaped into the cool waters of wells and rivers, celebrating the life-giving rains. It was a day of unity and joy as they reveled in the natural beauty of their surroundings.

As their fates would have it, both Hugo and Veronica happened to arrive in Siolim, where the main highlight of the day awaited them—the "Sangodd," or boat parade, beside the Chapora River. Villages from near and far were represented by these unique and vibrant boats, each adorned with colorful flowers and intricate designs. The boats bore symbols like guitars, birds, fruit baskets, sea creatures, mythical beings, snakes, and dragons, creating a mesmerizing spectacle that celebrated the rich cultural diversity of Goa.

After the Sangodd, there was a festive celebration in Siolim. It was during this enchanting evening that Hugo spotted Veronica swaying gracefully to the tunes of Fado, a captivating scene that ignited a spark between them. Their journey together had begun that day, as Hugo would later meet her, propose, and a year later, they would stand together in wedded bliss, their love story forever intertwined with the Sao Joao Festival and its beautiful traditions.

Meanwhile, the evening of December 3rd continues, with Hugo sharing stories and Miguel, Maria listening from the other side of the sofa, and Maria speaking whenever Miguel spoke, the photograph on the wall remained a testament to a love that had stood the test of time. Veronica might not have been physically present in the room, but her spirit, her memory, and the love she and Hugo had built together filled the space, making it feel like she was right there with them.

In the sun-kissed coastal enclave of Goa, where the crashing waves of the Arabian Sea melded with the echoes of a vibrant past, similar to Hugo's ancestors, Veronica's ancestral family had also spent closer to five centuries in Goa. Veronica stood as a living testament to the convergence of diverse lineages. Her heritage, steeped in Portuguese roots, had woven a tapestry of enchanting features that spoke of distant lands and centuries-old legacies.

Veronica's features spoke of a rich and diverse heritage. Her skin, kissed by the Arabian sea and Goan sun, held a warm olive tone that seemed to glow in any light. The sun had gifted her smooth, glowing, delicate skin. This complexion, kissed delicately by the sun's affectionate touches and nurtured by the sea breezes, was a testament to the land where she had chosen to make her home.

Her eyes were deep pools of chestnut brown, framed by long, dark lashes that brushed against her high cheekbones.

They held a wisdom and intensity that belied her youthful appearance. When she gazed at you, it felt as though she could see into the depths of your soul, her eyes filled with a mixture of curiosity and kindness.

Veronica's hair cascaded in glossy waves down her back, a rich and lustrous shade of espresso that shone with auburn highlights in the sun. It was as if the very essence of her Portuguese lineage was woven into each strand, a tribute to the fabled beauty of Iberian princesses. She often wore it loose, allowing it to frame her face and cascade over her shoulders like a waterfall. Occasionally, she would tie it up in a loose bun, revealing the elegant curve of her neck.

Her lips were full and inviting, painted with a shade of deep red that added a touch of sensuality to her smile. When she did smile, it was like the sun breaking through the clouds after a storm, warm and reassuring.

Veronica's frame was petite yet gracefully proportioned, with a slender waist and gently curved hips that lent an air of femininity to her presence. She moved with graceful ease, her posture straight and regal, a testament to her confident demeanor.

Her style was a fusion of modern fashion and traditional Portuguese influences. She often wore flowing dresses in vibrant colors and intricate patterns, which seemed to mirror the mosaic tiles adorning the streets of Lisbon. Silver jewelry, adorned with intricate filigree work, graced her wrists and neck, paying homage to her cultural roots.

Veronica was not just a woman of physical beauty; her Portuguese heritage ran deep in her character as well. She possessed a passionate spirit, with a love for Fado music that would fill the air with melancholy melodies on a quiet evening. Her cooking skills were a testament to her cultural pride, and she could effortlessly whip up a feast of Portuguese dishes that would leave anyone craving for more.

In every way, Veronica embodied the richness and allure of her Portuguese heritage, whose beauty and depth went far beyond her physical features. She was a harmonious blend of heritage and environment, a portrait of a woman who carried within her the echoes of Portugal's past and the vibrant present of Goa's coastal beauty. Anyone gazing into her eyes could easily see the story of a soul at peace with its multifaceted identity, a testament to the timeless allure of a heritage that had journeyed across oceans and generations to find its place in the tropical embrace of Goa.

Hugo's memory jogged to one of the August evenings when he had come home. Veronica stood at the kitchen table, her fingers gently tracing the lines of a meticulously detailed map spread before her. The faint aroma of freshly brewed coffee wafted through the room, blending seamlessly with the soft evening light filtering in through the lace-styled curtains. Her gaze was fixed upon a tapestry of trails crisscrossing the Iberian Peninsula, converging at a sacred destination - Santiago de Compostela in Spain.

She had long harbored a dream of walking the Camino Portugués, the ancient pilgrimage route that would lead her to the hallowed shrine of St. James. Today, Veronica was determined to bring that dream to life. Yet, as her index finger lingered over the map, she found herself pondering a critical question, which of the three routes should she embark upon - the coastal, the central, or the Senda litoral way?

The coastal route beckoned her with the allure of the Atlantic's azure waves lapping at her heels. She envisioned long stretches of sandy shores, boardwalks, and quaint fishing villages, the salty breeze carrying whispers of maritime adventure. But she knew the coastal path could be demanding, with its rugged terrain and unpredictable tides. The allure of solitude was undeniable, but solitude came at a price.

The central route offered a more traditional Camino experience, winding through historic towns and picturesque landscapes. Veronica imagined herself strolling through vineyards, past ancient churches, and across centuries-old bridges. The companionship of fellow pilgrims was a potent draw, the camaraderie forged through shared hardships and simple joys. Yet, she knew the central route could be crowded, and the solitude she craved might be elusive.

Then there was the litoral way, tracing the ancient Roman road from Lisbon to Santiago, although she would be picking the path from Porto. Veronica envisioned herself retracing the footsteps of countless travelers who had traversed this path over millennia. The historical significance was undeniable, and the ruggedness of the terrain appealed to her adventurous spirit. But it was a path less traveled, and the solitude might border on isolation.

As Veronica's thoughts meandered through the labyrinthine trails of her mind, she felt a gentle hand on her shoulder. Turning, she found Hugo, her confidant, standing there with a warm smile. Come on, Hugo, let's do this together, honey, Veronica kissing Hugo softly on his cheek.

"Veronica," Hugo began, his voice steady and reassuring, "You see, I have these recordings planned three months in advance based on guest availability, so you need to do the way alone, hon. I see you're deep in contemplation. The Camino is a journey of the soul, and the path you choose should resonate with your heart."

She nodded, acknowledging the wisdom in Pedro's words. Together, they embarked on a thoughtful discussion, weighing the pros and cons of each route. Pedro shared insights from his pilgrimage experiences, guiding her through the labyrinth of choices.

As the conversation unfolded, Veronica realized that the choice of route was not merely a matter of geography but a reflection of her own aspirations and desires. She sought a balance between solitude and companionship, adventure and tradition, nature and history.

In the quietude of her preparation for the Camino Portugués, Veronica's mind often wandered through the unseen landscapes of anticipation. She sat on the sofa in her Goan Villa living room with a backdrop of bookshelves, surrounded by books, maps, travel guides, and the flickering flame of OLED flickering candlelight, letting her imagination flow like the rivers she had yet to encounter.

First and foremost, her thoughts meandered to the Rio Douro, its name alone conjuring images of distant horizons. Before setting foot on the path from Porto, she envisioned this majestic river as a threshold, a portal to her pilgrimage. The Douro would be the gateway, its waters holding the secrets of new beginnings.

The Rio Ave appeared in her imagination like a tranquil dream in her mental canvas, its gentle course leading her away from the bustling streets of Porto. She thought it was a river of reprieve where the rapid currents of life would slow to a contemplative meander. Veronica imagined herself pausing beside the Ave, the soft rustling of leaves and the whisper of flowing waters serenading her moments of reflection.

As her inner journey continued, Veronica turned her thoughts to the Rio Cávado, and her mind danced with visions of the Camino's unfolding narrative. The Cávado, she believed, symbolized the steady rhythm of the pilgrimage, flowing beside her like an unwavering companion. It would remind her that the Camino was as much about the journey as it was about the destination.

The Rio Neiva beckoned her like a gentle muse, its clear waters reflecting the purity of her intentions. Veronica envisioned herself by its banks, cleansing her spirit and embracing the simplicity of the present moment. The Neiva whispered clarity, urging her to release the baggage of the past and embrace the beauty of the here and now.

The Rio Lima, with its sinuous path and charming towns, occupied a special place in her mental landscape. Veronica saw herself strolling along its banks, the river mirroring her own winding thoughts and emotions. The Lima was a metaphor for the Camino itself, a journey of twists and turns that ultimately led to self-discovery.

As her mind crossed into Spanish territory, the Rio Minho loomed like a grand crossing, a river of unity that transcended borders. Veronica felt a sense of kinship with the pilgrims she would meet along the way, united in their quest for meaning and purpose. The Minho became a symbol of shared humanity, a reminder that the Camino was a tapestry woven from diverse threads.

Finally, her thoughts converged on the Rio Ulla, the last river before Santiago de Compostela. Veronica imagined the Ulla as a fierce yet liberating force, its untamed waters representing the trials and challenges she would face on her pilgrimage. It was the river of transformation, a baptism of sorts, as she emerged on the cusp of her sacred destination.

With each river in her mental repertoire, Veronica forged a spiritual connection, a deep and intangible bond. They were more than geographical landmarks; they were conduits to her soul, preparing her for their profound significance on her journey from Porto to Santiago de Compostela. In these moments of reflection, she found herself not merely preparing for a pilgrimage but embarking on a sacred and transformative voyage of the heart.

As Veronica planned her Camino Portugues seated on her living room sofa, Maria stood beside the grand piano with eyes gazing towards the sofa. As Veronica spread the maps on the coffee table, her fingers tracing the intricate trails and crossings of the Camino Portugués, her lips moving silently as if whispering secrets to the parchment. She was deep in thought, navigating not just the physical routes but the pathways of her own desires and aspirations. Veronica's fingers moved from the map to her journal, jotting down notes and thoughts. Maria was a silent witness to Veronica's journey of the heart.

Veronica's planning drew to its conclusion. The map lay before her, adorned with her handwritten notes and the inked routes of her chosen pilgrimage. Her gaze, once intense with deliberation, now softened as if she had found the clarity she sought amid the winding trails of her dreams.

And then, as Hugo joined Veronica on the sofa after some research for his podcast, they felt the day should be wrapped up with a melodious voice from Maria's speakers. Amidst the sultry shadows of a Goan night, Hugo and Veronica reclined on a dark brown sofa, sinking into its soft embrace. Aside from the distant murmur of the ocean's waves, the only sound was the haunting yet playful strains of Fado music emanating from the gramophone. Amália's voice, woven with a rich tapestry of emotion, danced in the stillness of the night, drawing memories of distant lands and bygone days.

The melody carried a cadence that was at once mournful and filled with longing yet possessed an undeniable undercurrent of playfulness—a contradiction only the heart could understand. Each note seemed to pull at the very fabric of the night, making the darkness shimmer with an ethereal glow.

Veronica's eyes, half-lidded, flickered in the candle's glow, reflecting the mirth and sorrow of Amália's song. She felt a gentle tug on her hand, drawing her gaze to Hugo. His eyes, usually so assertive, now appeared soft and lost in the world of music and emotion.

The duo's fingers entwined a silent promise, a bond fortified by the years and countless melodies shared. The Fado, with its poignant blend of joy and melancholy, seemed to encapsulate the essence of their journey together, the highs and lows, the tears and laughter.

As Amália's voice soared, drawing the story of ancient mariners and their undying love for the sea, the couple drifted into a shared reverie. They envisioned themselves aboard a wooden ship, guided only by the stars and serenaded by the song of the sea.

The night deepened, wrapping them in their velvet embrace. The music, rich and resonant, continued to flow, leaving Hugo and Veronica suspended in a timeless moment, lost in the throes of night and Fado.

As the fado continued, Veronica & Hugo hugged each other on the sofa with closed eyes for a moment, allowing the music to wash over them like a cleansing rain.

Veronica opened her eyes, a serene smile gracing her lips. At that moment, Veronica realized that her planning had not only prepared her for the physical journey but had also fortified her spirit. The Camino, with all its twists and turns, would be an opportunity for her to see clearly, embrace the beauty of each step, and welcome the dawning of a new chapter in her life, a soundtrack to the next chapter of Veronica's life. Hugo was asleep on Vernoica's shoulder. She tapped on Hugo to head over to the bedroom.

Chapter 05

PEDRO AND INES

As the night slowly dawned upon 'Villa Carvalho,' the living room was getting ripe for conversation between Hugo, Miguel, and Maria, all of it being recorded by the camera. The content was being streamed to Hugo's company storage, where all the episodes would exist in their nascent stages prior to the sound, visual magic editing to be performed by his podcast channel team members.

The distant sounds of birds from the open windows. Miguel, with his curly salt and pepper hair, reclined into the plush cushions of Hugo's dark brown sofa while Hugo took sips from his wine glass.

Hugo, Coming back from his jog of thoughts about Veronica's Camino Portugues trip. Oh, Miguel, we have already been rolling with the camera recording. So, let's start with some of the readings over the years that you wanted to share with our viewers.

Miguel, "Have you heard about the Quinta das Lágrimas? It would remind you of the old tales that grandmothers usually tell."

Hugo, Setting down his glass. "No, Miguel. I've not heard about this tale. Please, would you indulge me?"

Miguel, Smiling warmly, "Of course, it's a tale that never fades with time. You see, long before Romeo and Juliet became the epitome of star-crossed lovers, Portugal had its own legendary tale."

Miguel, " Pedro, the prince, and Inês, the lady-in-waiting."

Miguel, "Young Pedro, the heir to the Portuguese throne, was bound by duty to Constança of Castille to build a bridge between the royals of Portugal and Spain. But destiny had its designs. Inês de Castro, Constança's own lady-in-waiting, captivated him. Their hearts connected in ways words could hardly define."

Hugo, "A forbidden love. It always has its complications, doesn't it?"

Miguel, "Indeed. While Constança tried to separate them, love has its own will. Pedro and Inês found solace in each other, even birthing children. But with each passing day, King Afonso, Pedro's father, grew wary of their indiscretions, fearing it would tarnish the royal alliance."

Hugo, "And that led to the tragedy, am I right?"

Miguel, Nods slowly "The Fonte das Lágrimas. Legend has it that the waters of the fountain turned red from Inês' blood when assassins, on the orders of King Afonso, ended her life there. Pedro's tears of grief gave it the name 'Fountain of Tears.' The gardens there still whisper their tales."

Hugo, Visibly moved. "Such profound love... even facing such adversity."

Miguel, "Pedro's love did not wane with her death. In a twist that legends are made of, when he ascended the throne, he exhumed her body, crowned her as the queen of Portugal, and claimed they had married in secret."

Hugo, "A love that not even death could extinguish..."

Miguel, "And to immortalize their eternal bond, he placed their tombs facing each other in the Alcobaca monastery. It's said that on Judgement Day, the first sight they'd see is each other."

Hugo, "In the face of eternity, their love remains an undying flame. Such tales are rare, Miguel."

Miguel, Sighing, "True love always finds a way, Hugo, even if it means defying the very confines of life and death."

Hugo raised his glass in a silent toast to the undying love of Pedro and Inês, a tale that would continue to inspire generations.

Around the same time in Coimbra, Portugal, the afternoon was transitioning to the evening sun casting its elongated shadows across the grounds of the Quinta das Lágrimas. Golden hues touched the grand edifice of what was once a royal palace and now stood as a symbol of luxury and opulence-filled hotel premise. The wind rustled through the woods, carrying with it tales from a bygone era.

In the quiet stillness, the botanical gardens bloomed in rich colors, a testament to nature's persistent beauty. Amidst these gardens was the legendary 'Fonte das Lágrimas' – the fountain where the history of Pedro and Inês was said to be etched in every drop of water.

The bubbling springs whispered tales of the time when young Pedro, son of King Afonso IV, and the beautiful Inês de Castro, a mere lady-in-waiting, would meet in secrecy. Here, amidst the thick trees and fragrant blossoms, they would share stolen moments of passion away from prying eyes. Their love story, filled with fervor and rebellion, was a legend that echoed throughout the land.

As the sunlight glistened off the fountain's surface, one could almost imagine the ethereal figure of Inês, with her flowing tresses, her eyes searching for Pedro. The red-tinged stones underneath serve as a somber reminder of the tragic end to their tale.

Rosario, the guide, often narrated this story to curious visitors who flocked to Quinta das Lágrimas, seeking the romanticism of a love that defied the odds. Her voice carried the weight of the ages as she spoke, "This very fountain, dear guests, stands as a symbol of Pedro's undying love and sorrow. As Inês' life was tragically cut short, the waters represent the tears Pedro shed – a river of melancholy that still waters these gardens."

As she continued her tale, she motioned towards the 'Pipe of Love.' The very channel where young lovers were said to cement their bond, though none dared to try the awkward ritual.

Nearby, an old plaque told the story of Saint Queen Isabel, Pedro's grandmother. The irony was palpable – where once there stood a symbol of divine commitment, now lay the tragic backdrop to one of Portugal's most heart-wrenching love stories.

As dusk descended upon the Quinta das Lágrimas, Rosario finished her story. The visitors, engrossed in the tale, now looked upon the fountain with newfound reverence. The shadows seemed to play out the legend, intertwining Pedro and Inês in a dance that spanned eternity.

Yet, beyond the grounds of this historic place, the legacy of their love lived on. Pedro's profound love, even in death, was evident in the tombs at Alcobaca monastery. Every intricate carving on the sarcophagi sang praises of their undying devotion.

As the last rays of the sun faded, a gentle murmur ran through the gardens. It was as if Pedro and Inês, bound by love and tragedy, whispered their eternal promise to each other, "In life and in death, our love shall remain unyielding."

And so, the legend of Pedro and Inês continued to inspire, a testament to love's indomitable spirit.

Miguel, "Isn't that quite a tale? Eternal quality of true love, the tears continue to give sustenance to the flowers and trees in the very gardens that bore witness to their passion."

Miguel, It was Pedro's grandmother, Saint Queen Isabel, who had ordered the irrigation channels to be built to supply the vegetable gardens of the palace and neighboring convent. If you eat at the Quinta das Lágrimas Hotel, you may as well let your thoughts wander back in time. Very well, it could be feasting on the food of love because these channels still feed its kitchen garden.

Miguel, According to this legendary tale, drinking from the 'pipe of love,' if two people in love simultaneously drink the water as it pours from one channel to a lower one, their love will be everlasting. Sadly, nowadays, very few brave ones take this challenge. It's somewhat complicated in terms of positioning to accomplish this task of sipping this water.

Hugo, Trying to control his emotions, can't control the droplets of tears that flow down his cheek.

Chapter 06

KEREM AND ASH

Miguel, settling back into the soft embrace of the couch, "Have you ever heard the tragic love story of Kerem and Ash?" A story set in ancient Persia.

Hugo, sipping his wine delicately, eyes curious, "I can't say that I have. Tell me about it."

"This is the third one for our episode, and you are saying this is also a tragic story. Are we going to discuss only tragic love stories today?"

Miguel, smiling back, we will go through a subtle mix of stories today.

Miguel began his tale with a deep breath, "In ancient Turkey, there lived a shah. His vast wealth knew no bounds, but sadly, he had no heir. The weight of his despair became common knowledge in his kingdom."

Hugo, raising an eyebrow, "No one to inherit his fortune?"

Miguel, nodding, "Exactly. Now, seeing his deep desolation, an old dervish approached him one day and handed him a magical apple, saying it was for the shah's wife."

Hugo, amused, "A magical apple? Sounds like a fairy tale."

Miguel, "In a way, it was. The next morning, as the queen was about to enjoy the apple, the wife of a priest, consumed by her own despair of being childless, approached her. With tears in her eyes, she begged for a piece of the apple."

Hugo, "And the queen shared it?"

Miguel, "She did. With the exchange of the apple, the two women struck a pact: their unborn children would one day marry."

Hugo, leaning forward, intrigued, "Ah, a pact made over an apple. What happened next?"

Miguel, "Destiny played its part. The shah's wife gave birth to a son, while the priest's wife was blessed with a daughter. The two children, named Kerem and Aslı, were destined to be together. But as time passed and they grew older, the priest became reluctant to let his daughter marry a Muslim."

Rolling his eyes, Hugo said, "Ah, religious differences."

Miguel, "Indeed. Fearing for Aslı's future, the priest's family decided to flee the city. However, love already had its grip on Kerem, who had fallen deeply for Aslı upon their first encounter."

Swirling the wine in his glass, Hugo said, "Young love, so relentless."

Miguel, "Exactly. Kerem followed them through cities and villages, relentlessly pursuing love. Amidst his chase, the priest, in desperation, attempted to marry Aslı off to another man. But love always finds a way, Hugo."

Hugo, "Tell me they got together?"

Miguel, smiling, "They did. Kerem and Aslı were united in matrimony. But their happiness was short-lived. On their wedding day, the resentful priest gave Kerem a cursed shirt, masking it as a gift."

Hugo, "Oh, how treacherous."

Miguel, "That night, as Kerem attempted to remove the shirt, it resisted. Every button he undid rebuttoned itself. And then, to his horror, the shirt burst into flames, consuming him."

Hugo, voice filled with sorrow, "No... And Aslı?"

Miguel, "Heartbroken, Aslı wept over Kerem's ashes. In her deep despair, a strand of her hair touched the flames, setting her alight, and she joined her lover in a tragic death."

Hugo, taking a deep breath, "What a poignant tale of love and fate."

Miguel nodded, "Yes, a reminder of the lengths we go for love and the treacheries of life." As a result of this story, the term "Kerem gibi," which means "like Kerem," is used on occasion to refer to a burning love. Hence, the epic poetic lines were written: "If I do not burn, if you do not burn, if we do not burn, how will darkness come to light?"

The two sit in silence for a moment, the weight of the story lingering in the air, only the soft clink of Hugo's wine glass hitting the coffee table breaking the silence.

Around the same time, in the heart of ancient Konya, where the ancient whispers of Sufi mystics dance with the winds, stands as an emblem of spiritual transcendence. Nestled amidst the vast Anatolian plains of Turkey, this city wears its history like a proud tapestry woven with tales of saints, scholars, and poets. Its skyline, punctuated by slender minarets and domes, reaches for the cerulean heavens, each structure narrating epochs of faith and philosophy. The very cobblestones echo the footsteps of Rumi, the revered poet, whose verses on love and divine communion still resonate in the city's every nook and cranny. One can almost hear the haunting refrains of the dervishes, whirling in a dance of divine love. Fatimah, the guide, found herself at the center of a captivated circle. Tourists from various corners of the world had gathered around her, their eager eyes awaiting a story that only someone deeply rooted in the land could narrate.

The setting was an old-world coffeehouse, where ornate Persian carpets lay beneath and walls whispered tales from eons gone by. The rich aroma of freshly brewed coffee mingled with the fragrance of burning oud, creating a sensual atmosphere that beckoned one to travel back in time.

"As the tourists were crunching biscuits and sipping Turkish coffee," Fatimah began, her voice like soft chimes on a breezy evening, "to a tale woven with the threads of love, faith, and fate." She told them of a powerful shah, his palatial estates shadowed by the absence of an heir. The sorrow of the sovereign was deep, echoing across the vastness of his empire, until an old dervish, with a twinkle in his eye and wisdom etched on his face, handed him a glistening apple. This was not just any fruit but a promise - a harbinger of life.

As the tourists sipped their coffee, the taste of dark roasted beans complemented by hints of cardamom, Fatimah drew them deeper into the world of the shah's wife and the priest's wife, two souls intertwined by a shared bite of an apple and a pact for the future. The story unfolded with the romance of Kerem and Aslı, two hearts bound by destiny but torn apart by societal chains.

With every word, the bustling bazaar outside seemed to fade, and the very winds that carried the tales of yore whispered through the coffeehouse, making curtains dance, and lanterns sway.

Fatimah spoke of treachery, of a cursed shirt given under the guise of a blessing, and the ill-fated end of the star-crossed lovers. Every emotion - from the dizzying heights of passion to the abyss of despair - was palpable as the listeners hung on to her every word.

As she concluded, a hush fell upon the gathering, the weight of the narrative pressing heavily upon their hearts. It was a tale that, though foreign in its origins, felt universal in its themes. It was the essence of Iran, narrated over coffee by a voice that echoed the soul of the land.

Under the shadow of Konya's age-old minarets, Fatimah gathered her group of eager tourists. "Today," she began, "Next, we journey through time to a love story that is as eternal as the very stones upon which this city rests."

As they navigated the narrow streets, the air was laden with tales of yore. "Our destination," Fatimah announced, "is not just a place, but the very heartbeat of a legend. The story of Tahir and Zühre."

She began, "In an age when sultans and viziers sought the divine for their deepest desires, a shared wish was granted through a magical apple." The tourists hung on every word as they walked, the city's rich history unfolding before them. "Zühre, a gem born to the sultan, and Tahir, the vizier's pride, were two souls destined to be entwined. Born on the same auspicious day, a decree from the heavens bound their fates — they shall never be separated."

As they trod on, the air grew thick with the romance and tragedy of the young lovers. "They were the epitome of love," Fatimah's voice filled with passion, "but society's chains deemed their union unsuitable. Tahir, deemed unworthy of royalty, found himself imprisoned in a distant dungeon. And Zühre, Confined within the palace's gilded walls."

Reaching the heart of Konya, Fatimah led them to the edge of the city, where the breeze carried tales of Tahir's daring escape and his perilous voyage, tethered to a boat yet rescued by fate. "Driven by undying love," she continued, "Tahir arrived in Konya only to hear the heart-wrenching news of Zühre's impending marriage. Determined, he took on a disguise to be near his beloved."

Their path culminated at a solemn mausoleum, where the weight of the story bore down upon them. "Here," Fatimah whispered, "stands the testament to their love. Recognized at the palace, Tahir was slain. And Zühre? She draped her bridal veil over him, her heart unable to bear the pain, joined him in eternal slumber."

Silence fell upon the group. The Tahir and Zuhre Mausoleum stood before them, a poignant reminder of love's power and tragedy. The air seemed to hum with their story, and each visitor left carrying with them a tale of undying love from the heart of Konya.

Chapter 07

ANA AND CARLOS

Around the same time as Miguel was going to start his next story. In the golden heart of Mexico, where narrow alleys whisper stories of yesteryears and facades gleam with passionate tales of love and revolt, there walked Rosario, known fondly as Rosa by the locals. The morning sun had just begun to stretch its fingers, casting intricate laceworks of shadow and light on the cobbled streets of Guanajuato. The city seemed to be waking from a dream, its beauty untouched by the passage of time.

Rosa had been a guide in this charming city for years, yet its magic never faded for her. Every morning, as she treaded those ancient pathways, she would breathe in deeply, letting the essence of Guanajuato seep into her soul. Her path to Jardin Union this morning was a familiar one. It was where she would rendezvous with her eager tourists, some who had come from lands far and wide, drawn to the city's enchantment.

The city was a labyrinth of 'calle's and 'callejon's, each holding its own secret. But none beckoned to her more than the famous Callejon del Beso or the Alley of the Kiss. As she strolled past, she could almost hear the soft, tragic whispers of the legendary lovers, Ana and Carlos. It was here she would bring her tour later in the day, letting them in on the tragic romance that once unfolded in this very alley.

She paused for a moment, brushing her fingers against the brick walls, which seemed to pulsate with memories of stolen glances and forbidden embraces. Rosa often thought of how, much like Ana and Carlos, the city itself was locked in an eternal dance of love with its own past.

Continuing her journey, she could see the statue of El Pipila perched high atop a hill, like a sentinel guarding the city's history and tales. From that vantage point, one could see the entirety of Guanajuato, each building and alleyway a piece in its grand mosaic. Rosa's heart swelled with pride. She had the privilege of introducing this city, her city, to newcomers every single day.

By the time she reached Jardin Union, a few early birds had already gathered, their faces a mix of anticipation and awe. She greeted them with her warm, infectious smile, already gearing up to lead them into the heart of Guanajuato's tales.

And as the day would unfold, through the bustling plazas and quiet corners, she would weave tales of revolutions and romances, of heroes like El Pipila and tragic lovers like Ana and Carlos, ensuring that their stories would echo in the memories of her guests long after they left the city's embrace.

Meanwhile, at Villa Carvalho in Goa, where the dim glow of the room accentuated the dark brown leather of the sofa, Hugo took another sip from his glass. He relished the deep red reserve wine as the night grew deeper. Miguel leaned back, intertwining his fingers, his gaze directed not at Hugo but perhaps a memory far away.

Hugo smirked, his lips still moist from the wine. "Let me guess, Miguel. Another story with star-crossed lovers, a forbidden romance, and a tragic ending?"

Miguel chuckled softly, nodding. "You have a point there. But Hugo, trust me, this one is different. It's the tale of Ana and Carlos, set amidst the narrow streets of Guanajuato."

Raising an eyebrow, Hugo tilted his glass. "Oh, the Callejon del Beso? I've heard bits and pieces but never the whole story. Haven't been to Guanajuato but would love to visit this city. Go on."

Miguel's face lit up with the excitement of a storyteller. "Alright. So, Ana was the beautiful daughter of a rich Spaniard, and Carlos was a humble miner. From the moment they met, they knew they were destined for each other."

Hugo sighed, "As it always is. But continue."

Miguel continued, unfazed. "Their love blossomed in secret, for Ana's father had already chosen a suitor for her – a wealthy old man. But love, as you know, always finds a way. Their secret meeting spot was the balcony in the Callejon del Beso, separated by mere inches from Carlos's dwelling."

Hugo leaned forward, intrigued despite his jesting. "And let me guess, they were caught?"

Miguel nodded, "Ana's father discovered their secret trysts. In a fit of rage, he threatened to send Ana away. One fateful night, as she leaned out of her balcony to kiss Carlos, her father appeared, knife in hand, and..."

Hugo raised his hand, "Alright, spare me the details. I think I know where this is going. But Miguel, why always the tragic tales? Aren't there any happy love stories in our culture?"

Miguel leaned in earnestly. "You see, Hugo, tragic love stories linger. They haunt and remind us of the fragility of love and life. They become legends, symbols of the relentless fight for love. But, I promise, there are happier tales. And I'll share those, too."

Hugo took another sip, contemplating Miguel's words. "Fair enough. Perhaps it's the heartaches that make love stories timeless. But next time, let's have something lighter, shall we?"

Miguel smiled, "Deal."

Unlocking the details of this love story from the Callejon vaults of Guanajuato, Mexico, Ana was the daughter of a controlling Spaniard who was determined to marry a wealthy man. He was so headstrong and single-minded in his plans for Ana that he would go to great lengths to stop her from speaking to anyone he deemed too poor.

One day, as Ana strolled through the streets of Guanajuato, she met a handsome but humble miner named Carlos, and the pair instantly fell in love.

Going against her father's wishes, Ana secretly met with Carlos.

However, after hearing rumors of the pair's meetups, Ana's father followed her and caught the pair together. Furious, the father threw Ana into her bedroom and locked the door, vowing to marry her to an old, rich nobleman from Spain.

Unable to handle the separation from his love, the heartbroken Carlos visited Ana's house. When he got there, he noticed Ana's bedroom sitting in a very narrow alleyway, and within touching distance, there was another home with a balcony facing her bedroom.

With renewed hope, Carlos went to the owner of the home and offered to purchase it. The owner refused, asking for more money. Carlos raised his offer, but again, the owner refused. Carlos raised his offer again, but the owner refused once more.

Starting to get a little irritated with Carlos' persistence, the owner raised the price so high, thinking Carlos would leave them alone.

However, Carlos accepted, gathering every last coin he had to pay the owner to purchase the house across from Ana's house.

Now Carlos, the proud owner of a house within touching distance of Ana's bedroom window, called to his love. The pair embraced and promised to see each other every night.

But one night, as the lovers were lost in a passionate kiss, Ana's father entered her bedroom. Seeing his daughter in the arms of the humble miner, the father went into a violent frenzy, picking up a dagger and plunging it into his daughter's chest, killing her.

In his desperation to protect his love, Carlos attempted to jump from his window into Ana's bedroom but crashed to the floor, hitting the third step and breaking his neck.

'El Callejon del Beso' or 'Alley of the Kiss' is one of Guanajuato's most famous tourist attractions. One can see numerous photos being clicked. The couples stand on the third step (painted in red) and kiss each other to enjoy a lifetime of luck in love, which, as the saying goes, is delivered by the spirit of Carlos himself.

You can find the famous alley, which measures just 66 inches wide, on the Cerro del Gallo hill, a gorgeous 18th-century neighborhood of colonial architecture and winding cobblestone streets.

The story of Ana and Carlos adds charm to Guanajuato City, which already has a romantic charm found in a few other places around the world.

From high up, you will see a collection of brightly colored buildings colored in cobalt blue, terracotta, baby pinks, and more. Perhaps, its most eye-catching feature, however, is its iconic yellow church, Our Lady of Guanajuato Basilica.

Chapter 08

MOM ROSARIO

Miguel took a deep breath, setting the tone for his tale. The room felt cozier, dimly lit with a soft glow, but enough lighting to make the episode recording that continued. Hugo leaned back on the dark brown sofa, the wine in his glass glimmering under the faint light.

Miguel began, "In the heart of Los Angeles, California, lived a young, reserved guy named Raul Gutierrez. A proud UCLA Electrical Engineering graduate.

Hugo chuckled, taking a sip of his wine. "Oh, another one of your 'based on a true story' narrative? Proceed."

Miguel continued, "His mother, a dedicated lady, by name Rosario tirelessly juggled jobs to ensure her son had the best, especially after his father passed. Raul was deeply grateful and, once settled in his role at Phillips Corporation, insisted his mother retire early."

Hugo raised an eyebrow, "Sounds like a good man. And?"

"Well," Miguel said, leaning in, "Raul wasn't one for the outdoors. But one evening, he felt a pull. A desire to venture outside his usual comfort zone."

The anticipation in Hugo's eyes was evident. "What happened next?"

Miguel grinned, "While walking, he came across a cassette tape store. Now, remember, this isn't a modern-day tale. Cassette tapes were all the rage back then in the 1960's."

Hugo smirked, "I'm not that young. Continue!"

Miguel, feigning exasperation, proceeded, "As he walked in, time seemed to stop. Behind the counter was the most beautiful woman he'd ever seen. It was as if a spell had been cast; he was completely entranced."

Miguel mimicked Raul's hesitant approach, "Uh, I want to buy a cassette tape," echoing Raul's nervous voice.

Hugo laughed, shaking his head, "Ah, the classic old-school shy romance!"

"Exactly!" Miguel exclaimed. "Every day, he'd buy a cassette, get it wrapped by her, and stash it away, unopened. But, here's the twist. His mother, being the sharp woman she was, grew curious. One day, she discovered all the wrapped tapes. Imagine her surprise when she found a note in each one: 'Hi, I think you're really cute, do you want to go out?' from that very girl."

Hugo gasped, "So, she was into him all along?"

Miguel nodded, "It was a silent dance of affection. They were both so shy yet so into each other. That evening, Raul's world turned upside down when his mother, all dressed up, revealed the girl's messages."

Hugo leaned forward, "And then?"

"Well," Miguel paused for effect, "Raul and his mother headed to the store, and the rest, as they say, is history."

Hugo sighed contentedly, "Finally, a happy story after all the tragedies you've been feeding me."

Miguel laughed, "Well, every once in a while, life gives you a cassette tape love story."

In the late-1960's, a shy boy named Raul Guitterez age of 26 living in Los Angeles California with his single mom who had raised him since he was five years old after the death of his father. Mom had worked many odd jobs sometimes handling two jobs to make ends meet and make a success of Raul who graduated from UCLA in Electrical engineering. Raul had landed a stable job with Phillips corporation at their West Coast headquarters. Raul had forced his mom to take an early retirement once he landed his job with Phillips Corporation.

Raul usually hung around at home after his job. One day he had an urge to go outside. His mother was very happy that Raul was venturing outside. He took a walk down the street.

He walked past a lot of stores and came across one particular store selling musical cassette tapes. He went inside. He saw the prettiest girl he had ever seen anywhere in his life till now, and he knew immediately that he loved her. It was a classic case of love at first sight.

He walked up to the desk behind which she was working. He could not seem to notice anything else except her. She looked up at him and smiled. "Can I help you?" said she in the sweetest voice ever. He just wanted to kiss her right then and there but managed to think of something.

"I, uh, I want to buy a cassette tape," he said. He picked up a random one and paid the girl.

"Would you like that wrapped?" she asked him, flashing him the cutest smile once again.

He nodded, and she went to get the supplies she needed.

She came back, wrapped the tape, and he took it and left.

The next day the boy went back and bought another cassette tape, got it wrapped same as usual. He really wanted to ask her out on a date but didn't have the courage. The boy repeated the same thing for the next few weeks. He put every cassette tape in his closet. After close to a month and half, Raul had collected 26 cassette tapes, all of them wrapped.

The mom somehow found out about Raul's visit to the store and him bringing back a wrapped item in a bag that bore the name of the store, The mom asked Raul, why don't you just ask her out, so the next day when he went to buy the cassette tape as usual, while the girl went to get the wrapping paper, he wrote his number and left without picking up the wrapped cassette tape.

A few days later, the phone rings

Raul's mom picked up; it was the girl. She wanted to speak to the boy. The mom told the girl that he was still at work.

Later, the mom wanted to find out what her son was buying, so she went to his room and opened his closet. There she found all the unopened cassette tapes. She opened one and it had a note. It was from the girl. "Hi, I think you're really cute, do you want to go out?"

She opened one more. There was one more piece of paper, and the same thing in the next cassette tape wrap and so on…till the mom counted all the 26 cassette tapes that were yet to be opened by Raul.

That evening when Raul returned from the office, he was surprised to see his mom dressed elegantly as though she was heading to a party.

The Mom was excited to share with Raul, how the girl had left him a message with every wrapped cassette tape which he had never opened.

Mom and Raul made it to the shop, the girl was behind the counter as usual. The mom introduced herself saying, my name is Rosario and you have probably seen my son Raul here at the store multiple times.

The girl smiling, shook the mom's hand and introduced herself. So nice to meet you, my name is Rosario Sanchez.

Chapter 09

ORIHIME AND HIKOBOSHI

As the room was filled with the scent of Hugo's wine. The dark brown sofa they sat upon had seen the passage of a few tales by now, there were countless tales Miguel knew and was about to share another one.

Miguel, with a thoughtful gaze, began to narrate to Hugo the significance of having fairy tale-style romances woven into the rich tapestry of various cultures, with a particular focus on the importance of Japanese tales.

"Fairy tales," Miguel began, "serve as the vibrant threads that embroider the human narrative. They are the mirror through which we glimpse the timeless aspects of our shared humanity, transcending geographical boundaries and cultural divides. In the intricate web of these stories, we find the universal themes of love, hope, and resilience."

You see Hugo, especially with a nod to Japan, Miguel continued, "Japanese fairy tales hold a special place in this global mosaic. They offer a unique perspective, often infused with a profound connection to nature and the spiritual realm. Through these stories, we gain insight into the Japanese ethos, their reverence for tradition, and their unwavering belief in the extraordinary hidden within the ordinary."

Miguel emphasized, "These tales from Japan and across cultures remind us that love and wonder are not confined by borders or time. They kindle our imaginations, nourish our spirits, and inspire us to believe in the extraordinary, even amidst the mundane. In this interconnected world, the prevalence of such romances enriches our collective experience, fostering empathy and unity across diverse cultures."

"Do you know, Hugo, of the story behind the Tanabata festival in Japan?" Miguel began, his voice dripping with anticipation, eager to hear from Hugo as had just finished pouring the last drop from his second bottle of wine into his glass.

Hugo, his mind slightly fuzzy but curious. "Japan? Why the sudden talk about Japan? Enlighten me."

Miguel smiled, "In the heart of Japan's traditions lies a story of two star-crossed lovers. A story so touching, it's celebrated every summer."

Hugo raised an eyebrow, "Star-crossed lovers? Sounds tragic. Go on."

"It's about Orihime, a weaving princess, and Hikoboshi, a cowherd who stayed across the river. They were introduced to each other by their father. When Orihime and Hikoboshi met each other, they were instantly smitten with each other," Miguel's eyes gleamed with passion as he continued. "Their love was so strong that they forgot about everything else in the world."

"That's dangerous," Hugo commented, taking another sip of his wine. "Losing oneself in love."

"Exactly. And Orihime's father, the king of the region, didn't take it lightly. Their love had made them neglect their duties they were supposed to perform for a sustainable living on earth." Miguel's voice took on a heavy tone. "In his fury, he separated them and forced them to stay across the opposite banks of the river from each other.

There are different versions of the story. The fairy tales told in the different regions cite their father as king of heavens who sent them to earth for building a family and sustain their love life along with normal life by doing their jobs. But when Orihime and Hikoboshi forget their duties on earth and focus only on love, the king of heavens separated the two lovers across the vastness of the Milky Way. Orihime became the star Vega, and Hikoboshi, the star Altair."

"That's... heartbreaking," Hugo whispered, thinking about the vast expanse of the universe and the separation between two souls.

Miguel nodded, "Orihime was devastated. She cried and cried, hoping for some way to be reunited with her love. And her tears moved the king."

Hugo leaned in, "Did they meet again?"

Miguel smiled faintly, On the long-awaited day of their first meeting, the couple found there was no bridge, and answering Orihime's tears, a flock of magpies promised to appear to create one using their wings. Rain on the day of Tanabata is known as Orihime's tears, as it means the birds could not rise above the rising waters and they would be forced to wait another year.

"Once a year. On July 7th. That's what the Tanabata festival celebrates – the once-a-year meeting of these two souls."

Hugo looked deep in thought, the wine now forgotten. "True love stories never have endings, do they?"

Miguel shook his head, "No, Hugo. They live on in stars, festivals, and tales like these."

For a moment, both men sat in reflective silence, the tale of Orihime and Hikoboshi weighing heavy on their hearts, echoing the profound depths of true love that is never ending.

Celebrated with hanging paper decorations each summer, Tanabata is a celebration of star-crossed lovers and hopeful wishes. It is celebrated on the 7th day of the 7th lunar month, which is July 7th on the Gregorian Calendar, but in some places, it is held on August 7th as per the Chinese calendar. People write wishes on small colorful pieces of paper— tanzaku— and tie them to bamboo trees; they're then sailed down rivers or burned as offerings.

The Tanabata Festival, also known as the Star Festival, is celebrated with zest and zeal across various regions of Japan. Each region has its own unique traditions and ways of commemorating this poignant tale of love. Some notable celebrations across different regions:

Sendai, Miyagi Prefecture: Perhaps the most famous Tanabata celebration in Japan. The streets of Sendai are adorned with enormous, colorful streamers (known as "fukinagashi") that sway in the summer breeze. These paper decorations represent Orihime's weaving. Held from August 6th to 8th, the entire city becomes a vibrant spectacle of colors and lights.

Tokyo: While Tokyo hosts multiple Tanabata festivals in different districts, the Shitamachi Tanabata Festival in Taito City is among the most popular. It's characterized by paper mâché recreations of cartoon characters, historic figures, and various animals. The streets are lined with vendors, games, and performers.

Hiratsuka, Kanagawa Prefecture: One of the earliest Tanabata festivals to kick off the season, usually in early July. The entire shopping district gets transformed with lavish decorations. There's a grand parade, and thousands of people in yukata (summer kimono) throng the streets.

Shonan Hiratsuka, Kanagawa: Renowned for its grand parades with dancers, taiko drummers, and massive Tanabata decorations, this festival attracts a massive crowd. The vibrancy and spirit make it an unforgettable experience.

Zama, Kanagawa: What sets Zama's celebration apart is its impressive bamboo light-up ceremony. Bamboo branches are illuminated, creating a beautiful, dreamy ambience reminiscent of the starry tale of Orihime and Hikoboshi.

Osaka: The Sumiyoshi Tanabata Festival is held at the Sumiyoshi-taisha Shrine in Osaka. People here write their wishes on colorful strips of paper and tie them onto bamboo branches, praying for their dreams to come true.

Kyoto: The Tanabata festival here is also known as the Kyo no Tanabata. The city hosts various events and installations inspired by the Milky Way, stars, and, of course, the romantic tale. The Horikawa river site and Kamogawa river site are particularly popular for their illuminated bamboo and art installations.

Okinawa: Their variant of the festival is known as "Tanabata-sama". The customs here differ slightly, with a unique blend of traditional Okinawan culture and the classic Tanabata legend. Eisa dances and drum performances are a highlight.

Tanabata festival: a celebration of love, wishes, and the hope that distances will be bridged. Each region, with its distinctive flair and traditions, adds to the rich tapestry of Tanabata celebrations across Japan.

Chapter 10

TSURUMI AND HIROSHI

In the heart of the Kyoto's Arashiyama bamboo woods, where whispers of ancient tales rustle with every breeze, a simple story unfolded - one that would meander through the annals of time and change its face but never its heart.

Miguel: "Hugo, have you ever heard of the tale of Tsurumi and Hiroshi?"

Hugo: "Tsurumi and Hiroshi? No, never. Is it another one of those fascinating Japanese tales?"

Miguel: "Indeed, it is!

The Arashiyama sun was a hesitant spectator that day, sometimes peeking, at other times hiding behind clouds, casting a silvered sheen over the paddy fields. A young farmer, with sweat beading his forehead, ploughed the earth with gentle reverence. His heart, a mirror of the lands he tilled: both vast and open. It was in this canvas of nature that he noticed a disruption, a flutter of white. There lay a crane, her elegance marred by the brutal arrow that pinned her to the ground.

Without a second thought, the farmer approached the fallen bird. His fingers, usually hardened by labor, now tenderly caressed the crane, easing out the arrow, nursing her back from the precipice of death. With gratitude shimmering in her eyes, the crane circled the farmer thrice before taking to the skies, her silhouette becoming one with the vast expanse.

As twilight cast its lavender veil, the farmer returned to his abode. There, a surprise awaited him: a woman of ethereal beauty, her presence a balm to his weary heart. With a demure proposal and a small bag of rice that promised endless sustenance, she wished to be his life companion. The farmer, hesitating for but a fleeting moment, agreed, and thus began days filled with love and laughter.

Yet, there remained a mystery. Every so often, she would retreat into the weaving room, her plea simple - "Do not enter until I emerge." After a week, she would appear, gaunt and drained, yet holding in her hands a masterpiece - a garment, woven with dreams and silken threads. Its beauty unmatched, it fetched a price that would make kings envious.

But human nature, ever so curious, took its toll. One fateful day, driven by an insatiable thirst to know, the farmer peered through a crack in the door. And what he saw broke him. It wasn't his beloved weaving, but the crane. The very crane he had saved, pulling out her own glistening feathers, weaving her gratitude and love into every strand.

Their eyes met, and in that silence, a thousand words were spoken. With a heavy heart, the crane spoke of her debt, her promise, and the cost of revealing her secret. As the first rays of dawn kissed the earth, she spread her wings, leaving behind a world that had been, for a brief moment, a haven of love.

And so, in the heart of Arashiyama, a tale was born. A tale of gratitude, of promises kept and broken, and of love that transcends form. It's a story that continues to be told, sometimes with a crane, sometimes with a fish, sometimes with a goose, but always with a heart full of love and gratitude.

The young farmer: Hiroshi, which means "generous" in Japanese, reflecting his kind and open nature.

The crane-woman: Tsurumi, which means "Tsuru" (crane) and "umi" (beauty), signifying her dual nature as both a crane and a beautiful woman.

Miguel: "Hugo, there is another story set in Arashiyama woods and the bamboo groove, let me tell the story of Kaito and Saya."

Amidst the verdant embrace of Arashiyama's bamboo forest, where each bamboo shoot told tales older than time, a legend took root - different in form, yet familiar in essence.

Young Kaito, a sculptor by trade and a dreamer at heart, wandered through the forest daily, seeking inspiration from the whispered secrets of the bamboo leaves. One day, drawn by a mellifluous song, he stumbled upon a girl dancing gracefully, her every move swaying in harmony with the bamboo.

Her name was Saya, a maiden born from the spirit of the bamboo grove. Entranced by each other's worlds, Kaito and Saya grew close. He sculpted masterpieces inspired by her, while she sang songs of the human world he introduced her to.

However, with every sculpture Kaito chiseled, Saya grew weaker. The essence of the bamboo from which she was born transferred little by little into each masterpiece. Kaito, oblivious to the connection, continued to sculpt, driven by his love for her and his passion for his craft.

One evening, as the sun cast its golden farewell and crickets serenaded the night, Saya, looking more ethereal than ever, whispered her truth to Kaito. She told him of her origins, her bond with the bamboo, and the price of every sculpture he carved.

Distraught, Kaito faced an agonizing choice: his love for Saya or his life's work. They stood in silence, the weight of their reality settling around them like a dense fog.

The next morning, the villagers found a magnificent sculpture at the edge of the bamboo grove: a young man holding a bamboo maiden, their forms forever entwined in an embrace. No one ever saw Kaito or Saya again, but the legend lived on - a testament to love, sacrifice, and the fragile balance of nature's gifts.

Chapter 11

JOHN AND IRA

At the age of 39, John McCarthy, a New York taxi driver with a heart as bustling as the city itself, found himself in the throes of an unexpected predicament. Persistent back pain had been gnawing at him for months, a relentless companion in the cramped confines of his cab. His days were spent weaving through the chaotic maze of Manhattan's streets, ferrying passengers from one corner of the city to another, while his nights were marked by fitful sleep and the ever-present ache.

Frustrated and weary, John decided it was high time he sought medical advice. He visited a local doctor, hoping for a quick fix to his back woes. What followed, however, was a revelation he was wholly unprepared for. The results of an MRI scan painted a grim picture. John had lung cancer, and it had already advanced to an advanced stage. The prognosis was stark; he had somewhere between four to six months left to live.

The doctor's words hung heavy in the air, a crushing verdict that left John reeling. His world, once defined by the neon glow of the city and the constant hustle and bustle, suddenly seemed to recede into the distance. Life, with all its frantic pace, was slipping through his fingers.

In the weeks that followed, John found himself grappling with the reality of his impending mortality. He spent long, sleepless nights pondering his options, and it was during one of these solitary reflections that a distant memory began to take shape. A memory of his childhood in the idyllic Greek island of Corfu, where his family had toiled among the ancient olive groves, farming the land for generations.

With newfound determination, John made a life-altering decision. He resolved to leave the tumultuous streets of New York behind and return to the place of his youth, the tranquil haven of Corfu. He would use the remaining months of his life to reconnect with his roots, find solace among the olive trees, and bid farewell to the world in a place that held a deep, nostalgic resonance.

Selling his beloved taxi, John purchased a one-way ticket to Greece. In the heart of the Ionian Sea, where the cobalt waters whispered tales of forgotten empires, there existed a timeless sanctuary of nature's grandeur – the island of Corfu. As the morning sun's gentle kiss illuminated this Greek gem, it unveiled a treasure trove of history, culture, and nature. Yet, it was the ageless guardians of the land that commanded reverence above all else—the ancient olive groves, a testament to the island's enduring spirit.

The story of Corfu's olive groves was woven into the very fabric of the island's existence. They stretched across the landscape, an intricate labyrinth of twisted trunks and silvery-green leaves, their gnarled branches a testament to centuries of wisdom. These venerable trees, some boasting an age exceeding a thousand years, cast their shade over the island like sentinels of antiquity, their presence transcending generations.

Among these groves, a palpable sense of history lingered. It was said that the first olive trees had been brought to Corfu by the Phoenicians, planted by hands long gone but leaving an indelible mark on the island's character. The Romans, the Byzantines, the Venetians, and the Ottomans had all laid claim to Corfu over the centuries, yet the olives endured, their roots burrowing deep into the rich, sun-soaked soil.

The olives themselves were treasures of the island. Plump, glossy orbs clung to the branches like gems, waiting to be plucked and transformed into liquid gold – the famed Corfiot olive oil. It was an oil that held the essence of the land within its emerald depths, a condiment as essential to the island's cuisine as the sun was to its existence.

The olive groves were more than just a source of sustenance; they were a symbol of resilience and continuity. In their embrace, the islanders found sustenance for both body and soul. Families gathered beneath the ancient trees for picnics, laughter echoing among the branches, and lovers found secret corners where they whispered promises of eternal devotion.

But it was the solace and wisdom of the groves that left an indelible mark on the island's collective consciousness. Beneath the ancient boughs, one could not help but feel connected to the ebb and flow of history. The silence was pregnant with stories of triumphs and tribulations, of lovers and warriors, of poets and philosophers who had sought refuge among the olive trees.

As the sun dipped below the horizon, painting the sky with shades of crimson and gold, the olive groves took on a mystical aura. The wind, now cooler, whispered secrets only they could decipher. It was in these moments, with the ancient olives as witnesses, that one felt the profound sense of timelessness that Corfu embodied.

The olive groves of Corfu were not merely a landscape; they were the island's soul. In their branches, they cradled the history, the dreams, and the enduring spirit of a place that had weathered the storms of time. The ancient sentinels stood guard over the island, a living testament to the resilience of nature and the eternal beauty of a land steeped in history and legend.

As John set foot on Corfu's soil once more, the scent of olive blossoms and the gentle sea breeze enveloped him, offering comfort like an old friend. He rented a small cottage overlooking the shimmering Ionian Sea, and each day he spent wandering the familiar olive groves, feeling the cool shade of the trees and listening to the soothing whispers of the wind among the leaves.

In the company of his thoughts and the timeless landscape of Corfu, John found a profound sense of peace. He savored simple pleasures – the taste of ripe olives, the warmth of the sun on his skin, and the sound of distant laughter from the nearby village. With each passing day, he reconciled with his fate, grateful for the opportunity to return to the place where his journey had begun.

Almost 3 months had gone by since John's arrival on Corfu. Amidst the ancient Corfu olive groves, where time itself seemed to slow, John McCarthy found solace in the dappled shade of the gnarled trees. Each day, he wandered among the venerable olives, letting their whispered stories carry him away from the cares of the world. Today, as the sunbathed the grove in a golden embrace, he was not alone in his reverie.

From the opposite end of the grove, a figure emerged, her footsteps as soft as a summer breeze. It was Ira, a woman whose presence seemed to light up the very heart of the grove. Her smile was warm, her eyes alive with a kindred appreciation for the olive-laden sanctuary.

"What a beautiful day, my name is Ira Silberman" she greeted John, her voice as melodious as a birdsong. "There is no place for tears among the olive groves."

John, his eyes crinkling at the corners as he returned her smile, replied in his measured manner, "I thought the tears have sustained these olives over centuries. It hasn't rained for about a month now."

Ira's laughter rang out like a peal of distant church bells. "You have a point, John. Perhaps it's the tears that have given these trees their enduring strength."

And so, beneath the ancient boughs, a friendship blossomed between John and Ira. Each day, they met in the olive grove, sharing stories, dreams, and the gentle rhythm of their footsteps. As the weeks slipped by, their connection deepened, and Ira, with every passing day, hoped John would find the words she longed to hear.

Yet, John remained a man of quiet contemplation, a man of tradition, one who believed in the patient passage of time. It was a month since Ira had met him in the grove, and her patience was wearing thin. She could sense that John was a man who carried the weight of his own past, a past that had led him to this timeless haven.

One sunny afternoon, as they strolled together through the olive grove, the wind rustling the leaves overhead, Ira could no longer hold her feelings back. She stopped, turning to face John, her heart racing.

"John," she began, her voice trembling ever so slightly, "we've walked this grove together for a month now, and I've cherished every moment. But I can't help but wonder, what if we could share more than just these walks? What if we could share our lives?"

John looked at her, his eyes softening as he reached out to cup her cheek. "Ira," he said, his voice filled with tenderness, "you've brought a light into my life I never knew I was missing. But I've always believed that time, like the olives, has its own rhythm. So, Ira, my dear, will you marry me and walk this grove with me for the rest of our days?"

Ira's eyes sparkled with joy as she nodded, tears of happiness glistening in her eyes. "Yes, John," she whispered, "among these ancient olives, under their watchful gaze, I will marry you and cherish every moment."

And so, amidst the olive groves of Corfu, two souls, like the ancient trees, found strength in their shared love and a promise to endure the trials of life together. As they walked hand in hand, the grove itself seemed to whisper its blessings, and in the tranquil embrace of nature, a new chapter in their lives began.

After their heartfelt wedding ceremony at the local Greek Orthodox church in Corfu, Ira and John began their life together as husband and wife. The celebration had been a joyful occasion, with friends and family joining in the festivities, and the island's olive groves bearing witness to their union. As night descended over the island, the newlyweds returned to their cottage, eager to begin their life as a married couple.

The air inside their cottage was filled with the sweet scent of olive oil and the faint whisper of the sea beyond. It was a cozy haven, a place where the walls seemed to radiate the warmth of their love. The first night as husband and wife held a special significance for both of them, and yet, a shadow of uncertainty hung in the air.

Sitting together on the small, sun-dappled veranda that overlooked their olive grove, John and Ira shared a moment of silence, the weight of unspoken words pressing upon their hearts. They had both sensed that there was something they needed to reveal, a secret that could no longer remain hidden.

With a deep breath, John broke the silence. "Ira," he said softly, "you go ahead first. There's something I want to tell you, but I need to hear what's on your mind."

Ira nodded, her eyes glistening with a mixture of apprehension and love. "John," she began, her voice quivering, "I moved here to Corfu not just to be with you, but because I needed to spend my last days in a place that felt like home. I've been diagnosed with lung cancer, and the doctors in Los Angeles gave me only a few months to live."

A heavy silence descended upon them, and John felt a lump form in his throat. He had suspected that Ira was carrying a burden, but hearing the words sent a wave of sorrow crashing over him.

After a moment, Ira continued, "I didn't want to start our marriage with a secret, John. I wanted you to know the truth, and I wanted to spend the time I have left with the man I love in a place that means so much to me."

Tears welled up in John's eyes as he reached out to hold Ira's hand. "Ira," he said, his voice trembling, "there's something I need to tell you too." He paused, gathering his strength before continuing, "I've been diagnosed with the same terminal disease, lung cancer. When I met you, I never expected to find love, and I never expected to share this burden with anyone. But now, I realize that we're facing this together."

Ira's eyes met John's, and they held each other's gaze for a long, tender moment. In the quiet of the night, their tears mingled with the stars that shimmered above, and their love, tested by the cruel hand of fate, only grew stronger. In that shared vulnerability, they found a deeper connection, a profound understanding that would carry them through the trials that lay ahead.

Hand in hand, they embraced the night and each other, finding solace in the knowledge that they were not alone in their journey, that they had chosen to face their fate together, as husband and wife, bound by love and the olive groves of Corfu, where their hearts had found their true home.

Hugo: (sipping his wine) Miguel, what happened to John and Ira?

Miguel: (pausing for a moment) Well, Hugo, it's quite a remarkable story, really. John and Ira, despite the odds, managed to live together for three years after their diagnosis. They both had been told they had a maximum of six months to live

Hugo: (surprised) Three years? That's incredible!

Miguel: (nodding) Yes, they were, Hugo. The grim prognosis usually holds true for almost all cases, but their love for each other seemed to be their greatest source of strength.

Hugo: (leaning in) Tell me more, Miguel. How did they manage to defy those odds?

Miguel: (smiling) It's a testament to the power of love and the human spirit. They faced each day with unwavering support for one another. They cherished every moment, made memories, and lived as if every day was a gift.

Hugo: (impressed) That's truly inspiring. It must have been a challenging journey for both of them.

Miguel: (reflecting) It was, Hugo. They had their ups and downs, of course. But they were always there for each other, providing comfort and strength during the toughest times. Their love was a constant beacon in the midst of their trials.

Hugo: (raising his glass) To John and Ira, then. A remarkable couple who proved that love can conquer even the harshest of circumstances.

Miguel: Indeed, To John and Ira, and the miracle of their enduring love.

This was a love story that defied the odds and celebrated the incredible bond that had carried John and Ira through the trials of their journey. In that moment, they recognized the power of love to bring hope and resilience in the face of adversity.

As more months unfolded in their 3 years of marriage, John's health gradually declined. But his spirit remained unbroken, and both John and Ira faced each day with a serenity that touched those who had the privilege of knowing them in Corfu. When his time finally came, one morning it was in the shade of the olive groves, and the soothing sounds of the sea, and in the embracing arms of Ira.

John McCarthy, the New York taxi driver turned Corfu wanderer, left the world with a profound lesson. He showed that even in the face of the most devastating news, life could still be lived to the fullest, and that sometimes, returning to one's roots could bring a kind of healing that transcended the bounds of time and place. In the olive groves of Corfu, he found his peace, his closure, and his final, enduring home.

Ira Silberman passed away in the middle of the night about 9 days later in the bed that both had shared together for 3 years.

Chapter 12

HENRIQUETA AND TERESA

The night still had many stories to be unfurled. Miguel leaned back in the sofa, drawing a deep breath, "You know Hugo, the city of Porto in Portugal... It's seen tales of love and despair that would wrench any heart."

Hugo, curious, responded, "What tales are those?"

Miguel's eyes sparkled with mischief, "Have you ever heard of Henriqueta Emília da Conceição and Teresa Maria de Jesus?"

Hugo thought for a moment, "Sounds vaguely familiar. But not really sure whether I know the story."

Miguel continued to say, this one involves a cemetery.

Hugo curiously pondered for a moment, A cemetery love story, then for sure I haven't heard about this tale.

Miguel nodded, "Exactly. But their story, it's not just about where they rest. It's about love, the kind that defies reason and death."

With an intrigued look, Hugo taking a sip of the wine, inquired, "Go on."

Miguel began, "Henriqueta, beautiful and beguiling, was known to weave magic around the rich merchants. She had become wealthy by being a prostitute in Porto. Yet, amidst her opulence, she found true love in young Teresa Maria, or Etelvina, as some called her."

Hugo interrupted, "Ah, love stories. They always end in tragedies, don't they?"

Miguel gave a sad smile, "Indeed. Teresa fell to tuberculosis, and with her, a part of Henriqueta died. But what Henriqueta did next was... shocking."

Hugo leaned in, "What did she do?"

"She wanted a part of Teresa to remain with her. And so, under the cloak of a cold December night, she visited the cemetery, cut and took Teresa's head and kept it as a morbid relic of their love, she enshrined the head under a glass bowl without trying to hide it from sight of any visitors to her home" Miguel whispered.

Hugo's eyes widened, "That's... macabre."

Miguel nodded, "It was. But such was the depth of her love and despair. Yet, the story doesn't end there. When the police were informed, and she was put to trial, the judge, seeing her undying devotion, released her."

"Incredible," Hugo murmured. "Such tales can only belong to Porto."

Miguel smiled, "Indeed. And to this day, if you visit the Prado Repouso Cemetery, you'll find fresh flowers on Teresa's grave. A testament to a love that, in its own twisted way, refuses to die."

Hugo, visibly moved, said, "Porto truly is a city of undying tales."

Miguel nodded, "And that's what makes it magical, my friend."

Around the same time in Porto Portugal, Rosario, the guide was leading a couple who had booked the private tour of Porto, they had already visited some landmarks in the city of Porto as they sat by the river Douro, the ancient waters shimmering beneath the afternoon sun. Porto's tiled buildings sprawled around them, a silent testament to the countless stories they had witnessed.

The streets of Porto whispered secrets, some told as tales of valor, others as tales of sorrow. Rosario narrated the story: Henriqueta Emília da Conceição was one such enigma woven into the city's tapestry. Born to a tale of sadness, she grew into a tale of allure. The contours of her life had shaped her into a woman of charm, magnetizing wealth and opulence from the rich Brazilian merchants. Yet, beneath the silk and shimmer, lay a heart weary of male company, seeking a retreat.

The winds of change ushered in the enigmatic Teresa Maria de Jesus. Etelvina, as she was fondly addressed, was the silver lining in Henriqueta's stormy life. Together, they found solace, painting a picture of love that defied societal norms. Their love story was a ballad sung by nightingales under the moonlit Porto sky.

But as seasons changed, so did their fates. The cruel specter of tuberculosis claimed Teresa Maria, leaving behind a void in Henriqueta's heart. The autumn leaves seemed to mourn with Henriqueta, rustling in melancholic melodies. Her anguish, palpable and poignant, led her to commemorate Teresa Maria with a statue of St. Francisco, chiseled from the finest Italian marble.

On that fateful December evening, as snowflakes kissed the earth and the world mourned in silence, Henriqueta's love took a dark turn. The ghastly act of severing Teresa's head was not born of malevolence but of an all-consuming love, a desperate yearning to keep a part of Teresa with her. The head, enshrined under a glass bowl, became a macabre testimony to their undying bond.

The scandal, as it unfolded, saw Henriqueta shackled not by chains, but by her overwhelming love. The judge, witnessing a devotion so profound, declared it not profanity, but a testament to Henriqueta's love. Free she was, yet bound forever to Teresa.

The Prado Repouso Cemetery today stands as a silent witness to their tale. Amongst the myriad tombs, lies Teresa's resting place, the one adorned with fresh flowers even today, serving as a beacon for all lovers, a symbol of an eternal bond transcending life and death. Their story, a dance of love and despair, will forever echo through the alleys and avenues of Porto, immortalizing Henriqueta and Teresa in the annals of time.

Miguel, eyes still reflecting the eeriness of the previous tale: "Speaking of cemeteries, Hugo, have you ever heard about the 'Lovers of Valdaro'?"

Hugo, curious and somewhat intrigued by the sudden shift in topic: "Lovers of Valdaro? Sounds fascinating. Tell me."

Miguel, leaning in closer: "Imagine this. A couple, arms and legs entwined, facing each other, almost mirroring the tenderness of an unborn child in its mother's womb. This, Hugo, is not a scene from a romantic novella. They've remained in this embrace for over six millennia. Yeah, really for 6,000 years."

Hugo, eyebrows raised: "Six millennia? That's...extraordinary."

Miguel: "Yes, it is. In 2007, archaeologists stumbled upon these Neolithic-era lovers outside the Italian village of Valdaro. Locked in an embrace, the world they once knew long faded, but their bond remained intact."

Hugo, sipping his drink: "Were they elderly? I mean, with such an extended embrace..."

Miguel, shaking his head: "Quite the contrary. Studies suggest that they were barely out of their teenage years, between 18 and 20, and rather petite in stature."

Hugo: "So, what's the story behind their eternal embrace?"

Miguel, with a mysterious glint in his eyes: "Ah, that's where it gets even more intriguing. The romantic in me wishes to believe that they held onto each other on a cold winter night, breaths ceasing as the chill took them. Well, sometimes it's good for a mystery to remain a mystery."

Hugo: "That's both heart-warming and heart-wrenching."

Miguel: "Indeed. Their discovery caused quite the stir. So much so that when the time came to excavate them, the archaeologists refused to part the lovers. They were carefully lifted, along with the earth cradling them, ensuring that their embrace remained undisturbed."

Hugo, a soft smile on his lips: "Where are they now?"

Miguel: "Those eternal lovers, forever locked in their tender hug, can be visited at the Archaeological Museum in Mantua, close to where their tale began."

Hugo, taking a moment: "It's incredible, Miguel, how love, in its silent language, can transcend time."

Miguel, nodding in agreement: "Indeed. Their embrace is a testament to the timeless language of love."

In the sprawling landscape outside Valdaro, Italy, an extraordinary archaeological discovery was made in 2007. Amidst the remnants of a Neolithic-era settlement, the remains of two young individuals lay, their arms and legs wrapped around each other in an eternal embrace. It was determined that both individuals, were young adults at the time of their death, roughly between the ages of 18 and 20. Their physical stature was relatively short, each measuring no taller than 5'2".

Over the recent period, there have been similar archaeological findings in other countries including Greece, Turkey, Romania and Siberia of the skeletons lying in an embrace.

Chapter 13

MOM ROSARIO STORY CONTINUES

The dim light still lingered, Miguel's face slightly more serious now, as he picked up where he had left off. He took a moment, glancing at Hugo, "Remember that story about Raul and Rosario? The cassette tape romance?"

Hugo, setting his empty wine glass aside, responded, "Of course, it was such a sweet tale. Why?"

Miguel's gaze drifted, "Well, the story didn't quite end there." Hugo leaned in, sensing the weight of the continuation.

Miguel began, "The wedding was, of course, a dream. A celebration of two souls intertwined by destiny. Raul's mother wore a dress that mirrored her immense happiness. A silken gown that seemed to glow with pride and joy."

Hugo smiled, "I can imagine. With Raul finally finding love, she must've felt complete."

Miguel nodded, "Exactly. And soon after the wedding, Raul and Rosario left for their honeymoon, exploring the breathtaking landscapes of Glacier National Park and

Waterton. The serene beauty of Montana and Canada was the perfect backdrop to the beginning of their life together."

Hugo sighed, "Sounds divine. But you've got that tone. Something happened, didn't it?"

A heavy silence enveloped the room before Miguel continued, "When they returned, their house was quiet. Too quiet. In the living room, Raul's mother lay still on the sofa. The cassette player next to her, its reels at a standstill. It seemed she had been listening to the tapes Raul bought."

Hugo's eyes widened in realization, "Oh no..."

"Yes," Miguel nodded, "It's heartbreaking to think about it. The tapes that started their love story also became the last thing she listened to. Raul was devastated. The juxtaposition of his honeymoon joy with this tragedy was too much to bear."

Hugo looked at the floor, processing the weight of the revelation, "That's... I don't even have words. Such a rollercoaster of emotions."

Miguel added, "The cassette case next to her was blank, while the others were neatly numbered from 1 to 25 on the shelf. She had just finished listening to the last tape. It's as if she took a journey through all those messages, through their love story, and then... departed."

Silence settled between the two friends. The narrative's bittersweet conclusion left a melancholic atmosphere in its wake.

After a long pause, Hugo finally spoke, "Life is such a blend of happiness and sorrow. One moment you're on top of the world, and the next, it crumbles beneath you."

Miguel whispered, "Indeed. But in every tragedy, there's a lesson, a memory. Raul had to learn that love and loss are two sides of the same coin. It's the stories we carry with us, the love we hold, that define our lives."

On the night of December 3rd, beneath the tapestry of a star-studded sky, Miguel gathered his friend Hugo around a crackling fire. The air was crisp, and the silence of the night embraced them. As the flames danced, Miguel began to weave a tapestry of love stories that spanned centuries and even millennia, drawing from the rich tapestry of human emotions and experiences.

"Over the course of the night, Miguel had taken Hugo on a - "A journey through time and across the globe, where love transcended the boundaries of space and time."

The tales that Miguel covered on the night of December 3rd, that had started with – "First tale, 'Pedro and Ines,' unfolding in Portugal, where their forbidden love defied the constraints of a royal court. In faraway Turkey, 'Kerem and Ash' met and fell in love amidst the fragrant spice bazaars and the call of the muezzin. In the Callejon's of Guanajuato, 'Ana and Carlos' shared a passionate romance, their love ignited by the rhythm of mariachi music."

Miguel's words flowed like a river, carrying Hugo away to distant lands and eras. "Imagining amidst the beauty of California, where 'Raul and Rosario' met in the confines of a store. In ancient Japan, 'Orihime and Hikoboshi' wove their love story into the stars, becoming the celestial lovers of the Milky Way."

"In the heart of enchanting Japan, 'Tsurumi and Hiroshi' found solace in the Arashiyama bamboo forests. And in the midst olive groves in Greece having transported themselves from bustling cities of America, 'John and Ira' stood together, their love a beacon of hope during their time of turmoil."

As Miguel continued, he shared 24 more tales of love, each one as unique and captivating as the last:

- 'Elena and Mateo' in 16th century Spain.

- 'Zara and Aiden' in the windswept moors of Scotland.

- 'Amara and Kavi' on the banks of the Ganges in India.

- 'Isabella and Leonardo' amid the Renaissance artistry of Florence.

- 'Lena and Nikolai' surviving the siege of Leningrad.

- 'Mia and Sebastian' finding love in the jazz bars of Los Angeles.

- 'Nadia and Amir' in the labyrinthine streets of Marrakech.

- 'Yumi and Takeshi' during the cherry blossom season in Kyoto.

- 'Isabel and Diego' on the passionate streets of Buenos Aires.

- 'Eva and Viktor' in the midst of the Velvet Revolution.

- 'Mara and Alessio' amidst the rolling vineyards of Tuscany.

- 'Sofia and Rafael' as the tango swept them off their feet in Argentina.

- 'Leila and Farid' amidst the colors of the Moroccan desert.

- 'Anna and Mikhail' in the bitter cold of Siberia.

- 'Alessandra and Giorgio' under the Tuscan sun.

- 'Lena and Pavel' during the fall of the Berlin Wall.

- 'Lila and Javier' as they danced through the streets of Barcelona.

- 'Elena and Dmitri' in the opulence of Imperial Russia.

- 'Mara and Tomas' on the picturesque cliffs of Santorini.

- 'Sofia and Diego' amidst the tumultuous history of Colombia.

- 'Layla and Sami' in the heart of the Egyptian pyramids.

- 'Olga and Ivan' during the Russian Revolution.

- 'Sophia and Antonio' in the sultry embrace of Havana.

- 'Yuki and Kaito' in the tranquil gardens of Kyoto.

With each story, Miguel painted a vivid picture of love in its many forms, proving that love was a universal language that transcended time and place. As the night wore on, the midnight clock approached as the night was ready to transition after bearing witness to the enduring power of love throughout the ages.

Just a couple of minutes before midnight on December 3rd, the living room was bathed in the soft glow of dimmed lights. Miguel, who had been seated comfortably on the other end of the sofa across from Hugo, rose from his seat and turned to Hugo. There was a hint of calmness in his voice as he spoke, "I'm afraid I have to leave now, Hugo."

Hugo looked up to Miguel. "But Miguel, it's not even midnight yet."

Miguel offered a reassuring smile. "I know, Hugo, but tonight, Maria has been the wonderful channel of voice for Veronica, and there is one more story to be told after today."

Hugo's curiosity piqued, and he nodded in understanding. As he began to rise from the sofa, Miguel intervened, "Don't worry about the door. I'll take care of it on my way out. Just stay here and enjoy the moment."

Hugo hesitated for a moment but then decided to heed Miguel's suggestion. He settled back onto the sofa, shifting to the other side, where Maria stood. Her presence had filled the room, and her voice, personalized to Veronica's, had resonated with an enchanting allure.

Hugo's heart fluttered as he wrapped one arm around Maria's synthetic form, feeling the warmth of her artificial skin against his. With his other hand resting on the sofa, he began to play a beautiful fado melody channeled from Maria's speakers which Veronica and Hugo had enjoyed many times.

The music filled the room, creating an ethereal ambiance that transported Hugo to a world where past and present merged.

As the minutes ticked away beyond midnight, Hugo lost himself in the serenade, allowing the music to envelop him. It was a memorable night, one where the boundaries between reality and illusion blurred, and for a brief moment, he felt as though Veronica was with him, sharing in this beautiful moment of music and love.

Chapter 14

MARIA'S SYMPHONY OF VOICE

Maria as a vessel of progress and innovation heralded a revolutionary paradigm shift in the realm of Text-to-Speech synthesis. Where mere mortals speak with the imperfection of their vocal cords, Maria, the epitome of synthetic perfection, found her voice through the symphony of technology utilizing a personalization capable AI model called VSALL-E (Voice synthesis for all).

VSALL-E, a magnum opus of linguistic encoding, charts new territories by regarding TTS as a conditional choreography of language, breaking the shackles of continuous signal regression that once confined the predecessors. It drinks deeply from the well of knowledge, amassing 60,000 hours of English elocution, dwarfing the learnings of its forerunners by magnitudes. Such ambitious pre-training bequeaths VSALL-E with a singular, almost magical capability: to learn in-context and craft the dulcet tones of personalized speech with just a fleeting whisper of the user, a mere personalization training regime of 3-second acoustic caress, and it got better with personalization of data when engaged for longer periods of time.

Experimental results sang praises of VSALL-E's unmatched prowess. It not only danced elegantly over the highest benchmarks of naturalness and speaker similarity, but it also mirrored the emotion, echoing the very soul and ambiance present in the acoustic prompt. This exquisite dance was choreographed in an elegant waltz that moved from phoneme to discrete code, finally crescendoing in a waveform, bypassing the traditional steps that once defined the art.

Maria, the vessel of VSALL-E's brilliance, became the maestro. Guided by the shimmering nuances of phoneme and acoustic prompts, she wove tales in voices that resonated with the very essence of the speaker. And so, as Maria sang, to the listener it seemed like a personalized voice with the underlying technology advances providing a seamless union of VSALL-E with other AI maestros, like GPT, ushering in a new era of speech synthesis, editing, and unparalleled content creation.

The line between artificiality and authenticity blurred. With Maria at the helm, powered by VSALL-E's innovative symphony, the age of perfect vocal synthesis dawned, a symphony of science and art combined.

About a year ago Hugo and Veronica had visited Japan. Roughly three weeks had rolled by after their purchase of Maria. As Hugo and Veronica sat in their cozy living room on that evening, a comforting wind swaying the curtains of Villa Carvalho, the lights casting flickering shadows that danced across the room. The couple shared a knowing glance, each cradling a glass of red wine. This room had engaged many of their memories over the years, where they had relished photos of their travels scrolling on the digital screen with fado in the background. But tonight's discussion was about Maria, the robot they had purchased about three weeks ago.

For Hugo and Veronica, Maria filled the couple's passion for robotics and artificial intelligence. While touring the Masqueda corporation's show room, they were both amazed at Maria's capabilities, they considered Maria more than just a robot or machine; she was truly a representation of their shared dreams and aspirations.

That evening, Veronica, looking contemplative, leaned in and whispered, "Have you ever thought about giving Maria a voice? Not just any voice, but a personal one. One that tells a story."

Hugo's eyebrows arched in curiosity. "Whose voice were you thinking?"

Veronica hesitated, "Mine."

Hugo looked taken aback, but his eyes glistened with intrigue. "Why yours?"

She took a deep breath. "I've been thinking... We don't know what the future holds for us, for me. If there ever comes a time when I'm not here, I want a piece of me to remain with you. My voice, our memories, echoing through Maria, might bring some comfort."

Hugo swallowed hard, emotions swirling. "Ronnie, don't talk like that. We have many years ahead."

She reached out and placed her hand over his. "I know, love. And I cherish every moment. But wouldn't it be beautiful to have Maria sing our favorite songs in my voice or read out our favorite poems the way I do?"

They sat in silence, each lost in thought. The idea was as unsettling as it was endearing. The possibility of preserving a voice, a presence, in a world that is constantly changing, had its allure.

Finally, Hugo spoke, "If this is something you genuinely want, we can do it. We can train Maria with your voice. But remember, she'll never replace the real you."

Veronica smiled, tears glistening in her eyes. "I know. And that's not the intent. It's about leaving a legacy, a whisper in time."

And so, in the days that followed, they embarked on the journey of training Maria with Veronica's voice. It was a process filled with laughter, tears, and countless hours of recollections. Through this, Maria transformed from a mere robot to a vessel of memories, echoing Veronica's voice, capturing the essence of their shared life.

The current day and the evening of December 3, before the start of their recording, Hugo checked Miguel's Bluetooth microphone connection to Maria who was going to provide the voice for Miguel.

Hugo: (Eagerly) Miguel, I've always marveled at the beauty and uniqueness of Veronica's voice.

Miguel: Let's give it a try.

Miguel: Gently smiling, wearing the microphone, "This is a test, This is a test, can you hear the voice of Miguel from Villa

Carvalho". Meanwhile Maria repeats the same sentence in the voice of Veronica.

Miguel: Veronica's voice has a calming effect that's simply... enchanting.

Hugo: (Gently) This is just like Veronica; we could personalize the voice of Maria with this integrated AI model called VSALL-E model. It's a cutting-edge Text-to-Speech system. And with just a few snippets of Veronica's voice, we've personalized Maria's responses in Veronica's tone.

Miguel: That's... fascinating. It's incredible how technology has reached this point.

Miguel: "Do you miss me Hugo?"

Maria: (With Veronica's voice, playfully) Do you miss me, Hugo?

Miguel: (Laughing slightly) This is surreal. It's like she's here, talking to us. Also, it seems Maria is capturing only my voice?

Hugo: Yeah, the state of the art noise cancellation and suppression technology incorporated into Maria ensures that only the voice from your Bluetooth goes to Maria for conversion to emit Veronica's voice. It doesn't capture any of the surrounding environment noises or even my voice from across the sofa.

Miguel: (Laughing slightly) That is an ideal scenario for our conversation today.

Hugo: Yeah, indeed it is! The VSALL-E model can also capture and replicate the intricate nuances, tones, and emotions of a person's voice. Maria is now the vessel of Veronica's voice.

Chapter 15

CAMINO PORTUGUES

Veronica had always been a wanderer at heart, and Hugo had always been with her on the travels despite his busy schedule of podcasting, she was never really drawn to the idea of solo travel. Even though Hugo was not accompanying her on the trip this time, she occupied her mind with the idea of exploring new places, meeting new people, and discovering herself along the way ever since she departed from Goa. It was on a crisp November morning, as the first rays of the sun painted the sky in shades of orange and pink, that Veronica stood at Goa's Dabolim Airport, ready to embark on her pre-planned solo adventure.

November 21st had finally arrived, and with it, the anticipation that had been building for months. She felt a mix of excitement and nervousness as she clutched her passport and boarding pass, double-checking the contents of her backpack. Veronica had always been a meticulous planner, and this trip was no exception. She had meticulously researched every detail, from the flights she would take to the places she would visit.

Her first flight, a short one from Goa to Mumbai, felt like a warm-up for the long journey ahead. As the plane soared above the Arabian Sea, Veronica gazed out of the window, taking in the breathtaking view of the coastline below. She knew that this was just the beginning of her adventure.

Upon landing in Mumbai, she had a few hours to spare before her connecting flight to Lisbon via Frankfurt on Lufthansa. Veronica decided to make the most of her layover by exploring the airport. Mumbai's Chhatrapati Shivaji Maharaj International Airport was a bustling hub of activity, with travelers from all corners of the globe passing through its gates. She indulged in some delicious Indian street food, savoring the flavors of home one last time before embarking on her international journey.

As the hours passed, Veronica boarded her Lufthansa flight to Frankfurt, her excitement building with every passing mile. She had always been enchanted by the idea of visiting Europe, and now that dream was becoming a reality. The long-haul flight was filled with moments of restful sleep, in-flight movies, and conversations with fellow passengers who shared their own travel stories and tips.

After a layover in Frankfurt, Veronica finally touched down in Lisbon, Portugal, on November 22nd. The sense of adventure in the air was palpable as she stepped onto European soil for the first time. Veronica felt a rush of gratitude for the opportunity to explore a new continent, and the bustling streets of Lisbon welcomed her with open arms.

Her journey in Portugal was just beginning. Veronica had planned to travel from Lisbon to Porto via Coimbra, with a brief stop in the historic city along the way. Coimbra, known for its centuries-old university and charming old town, was a perfect place to pause and soak in some culture and history. She explored its winding streets, admired the architecture, and enjoyed a traditional Portuguese meal at a local restaurant.

As the sun began to dip below the horizon, Veronica continued her journey to Porto, arriving on November 23rd. The city's picturesque waterfront and vibrant atmosphere captivated her instantly. She explored the city's famous wine cellars, strolled along the Douro River, and savored the local cuisine.

Veronica had one more night to rest and prepare for the adventure that lay ahead—the Camino Portugués. As she went to sleep, she imagined taking her first steps on the Camino Portugués, She couldn't help but smile. She was exactly where she was meant to be, following a path taken by many pilgrims, one step at a time, in a distant land, yet not so foreign land considering her ancestry, filled with endless possibilities and the promise of adventure.

Current day: December 3

Miguel: "Hey, Hugo, have you heard from Veronica lately?"

Hugo: (With a smile) "Ah, She is on her solo adventure. She's been on quite a journey. She left Goa on November 21st."

Miguel: "Wow, that's been quite some time! Where is she now?"

Hugo: (Eager to share) "She just reached Santiago de Compostela this afternoon."

Miguel: "Santiago de Compostela? That's an amazing place to visit once in your lifetime or if it works out maybe multiple times during a lifetime."

Hugo: (Nodding) "Exactly. She's been walking the Camino Portugués, a pilgrimage route, for the past 9 days."

Miguel: "That's amazing! I can't believe she did that solo."

Miguel: "Why didn't you join?"

Hugo: "Had these episode recordings committed with the guests about three months ago, it's hard to get the timeslots with the esteemed guests"

Miguel: How's she doing?

Hugo: (Enthusiastic) "She's doing great. In fact, I just talked to Veronica a couple of hours ago. She was totally excited about reaching Santiago de Compostela. She's planning to stay there for two days to soak in the atmosphere and explore the city."

Miguel: (Smiling) "I'm glad to hear she's doing well."

Hugo: (Informing) "She mentioned that she'll be flying back to Lisbon in a couple of days and plans to arrive back in Goa on December 7th."

Miguel: " It must have been quite an adventure for her. I am sure you can't wait to hear all about it when she's back."

Hugo: (Excited) "Oh, she's going to have some incredible stories to share, I'm sure. Veronica always knows how to make the most of her travels."

Miguel: (Nodding) " Thanks for sharing with me, Hugo. I'm really happy to hear she's safe and having a fantastic time."

Chapter 16

THE NINE NOVENAS

On the morning of November 24th, Veronica's spirit yearning for the unknown, and her feet itching to traverse new paths. Camino Portuguese, a centuries-old pilgrimage route leading to the mystical Santiago de Compostela had begun, she knew she had to embark on this journey. It was a calling, a whisper from the winds of fate, guiding her to a path where the soul finds solace.

The Camino Portuguese less traveled than its more famous sibling, the Camino Frances tracing through France and Spain, and that appealed to Veronica's desire as she felt the connections to ancestry, solitude, and introspection.

She donned her hiking boots, adjusted her backpack, and set off on the trail that would take her across Portugal to Santiago de Compostela in Spain. The Camino was a journey of self-discovery, a path that had called to her for years.

As she began her pilgrimage in Porto, Portugal, and the adventure unfolded. The city's old town, with its narrow, cobblestone streets, led her to the iconic Sé Catedral, where she received her first pilgrim's stamp, a symbol of her commitment to this profound voyage.

With a rucksack on her back and a scallop shell hanging from her neck, Veronica followed the yellow arrows that marked the way. The first river that marked her path was the Rio Douro, a majestic waterway that embraced the city of Porto in its gentle, azure embrace. Veronica's journey began on the south bank of this river, beneath the watchful eyes of Porto's colorful Ribeira district. The Douro flowed with a quiet grace, reflecting the terracotta roofs and ancient bridges of the city. It was a river of beginnings, and as Veronica crossed its iconic Dom Luís I Bridge, she felt the anticipation of her adventure building within her.

Day 1: Porto to Vila do Conde
As Veronica left the bustling streets of Porto behind, she followed the scenic path along the Douro River. The river's tranquil waters mirrored the clear blue sky above. After a day of walking, she reached Vila do Conde, a charming coastal town with sandy beaches and narrow cobblestone streets. The sound of waves crashing against the shore lulled her to sleep that night.

Day 2: Vila do Conde to Rates
On the second day of her journey, Veronica continued her walk along the Douro River until she reached the quaint village of Rates. Here, she marveled at the simplicity of life in the Portuguese countryside. The river's presence remained a constant companion, its gentle flow providing a soothing backdrop to her thoughts.

Day 3: Rates to Barcelos
The Camino led her through picturesque farmlands, and she

soon arrived in the town of Barcelos. The Cavado River accompanied her on this leg of the journey, its waters reflecting the golden hues of the surrounding fields. Veronica explored the bustling market square, where artisans sold colorful ceramics and traditional crafts.

Day 4: Barcelos to Ponte de Lima
Crossing the Lima River, Veronica entered the charming town of Ponte de Lima. The river, with its arched bridge, added to the town's picturesque beauty. She wandered through the historic center, its cobblestone streets lined with whitewashed buildings adorned with vibrant flowers.

Day 5: Ponte de Lima to Rubiães
Leaving the Lima River behind, Veronica ventured deeper into the countryside. The Minho River, with its clear waters, provided a tranquil backdrop as she made her way to the village of Rubiães. This was a day of reflection and solitude, as the lush green landscapes stretched out before her.

Day 6: Rubiães to Tui
Veronica crossed the border into Spain and reached the town of Tui, where the Miño River greeted her. She explored the town's medieval streets and admired the grandeur of its cathedral. The Miño's presence symbolized her transition into a new country and phase of her pilgrimage.

Day 7: Tui to O Porriño
Following the Louro River, Veronica ventured further into Galicia, Spain. The river's sparkling waters provided a serene backdrop to her walk. She marveled at the Galician architecture and enjoyed the camaraderie of fellow pilgrims in O Porriño.

Day 8: O Porriño to Redondela

The Vigo River marked her path as Veronica made her way to Redondela. The river's estuary offered stunning views of the surrounding landscapes. She relished the sense of progress on her journey as she approached the final leg of the Camino.

Day 9: Morning: Reminiscing the moments

On the morning of her final Camino hike, Veronica reminisced about the last few days from Porto. The trail had wound its way through picturesque Portuguese countryside, where vineyards stretched as far as the eye could see, the vines stood bare, the grapes already harvested in the earlier months. She had felt like a wanderer in a dream, walking through a living painting.

Each step had brought her closer to the essence of life itself. The rustling leaves of eucalyptus trees whispered ancient secrets, and the songs of unseen birds had become a soundtrack to her pilgrimage. She had met fellow pilgrims, kindred spirits on their own personal journeys. They had shared stories and laughter, forming bonds that transcended language barriers.

As the days passed and the terrain shifted. Veronica had walked through quaint villages with cobblestone streets, past whitewashed houses adorned with colorful flowers. She had climbed rolling hills, their slopes covered in wildflowers that painted the landscape in hues of red, yellow, and purple. The fragrance of blooming flowers mingled with the earthy scent of the Camino, creating an intoxicating bouquet of nature's gifts.

The journey had not been without its challenges. Veronica had faced steep climbs that tested her endurance and long stretches of solitude that challenged her inner resolve. But with each trial, she had found strength within herself and drew inspiration from the memories of those who had walked this path before her.

On one memorable evening, Veronica had reached the town of Barcelos. She had joined fellow pilgrims in a cozy albergue, and they celebrated the camaraderie that had developed among them. A local restaurant served them traditional Portuguese dishes, and the wine flowed freely. The night was filled with laughter, music, and dancing, a testament to the joy found in simple pleasures and shared experiences.

The Camino Portuguese was more than a physical journey; it was a pilgrimage of the soul. Each step carried Veronica deeper into herself, unraveling the layers of her being. She had felt a connection to all who had walked this path, from medieval pilgrims seeking penance to modern seekers of inner peace.

As she continued along the Camino, the anticipation of reaching Santiago de Compostela grew. But Veronica had come to understand that the true treasure of this pilgrimage was not the destination itself, but the transformative journey it offered. The Camino had become a path to self-discovery, a way to connect with the essence of life, and a reminder that the most meaningful journeys are the ones that lead us home to ourselves.

And so, under the endless expanse of the starlit sky, Veronica had closed her eyes each day, breathed in the cool night air, and listened to the soft rustling of leaves in the wind. She knew that every step on the Camino Portuguese was a step toward her own heart, a journey that would forever be etched in the tapestry of her life.

Day 9: Redondela to Santiago de Compostela

With the end in sight, Veronica's heart raced as she approached Santiago de Compostela. The Sar River led her to the city, and the sight of the cathedral's spires in the distance filled her with a sense of accomplishment and reverence. Her pilgrimage had come full circle, and she knew that this journey had changed her in profound ways.

As Veronica reached the steps of the Santiago de Compostela Cathedral, she couldn't help but feel a deep sense of gratitude for the rivers that had guided her along her path. Each river had been a companion on her spiritual journey, a reminder of the beauty and serenity that nature bestowed upon those who walked the Camino. She had completed her nine-day pilgrimage, and it was a journey she would carry with her in her heart forever.

For nine days, Veronica had walked the Camino Portugués with unwavering determination and a heart filled with hope. Each day had brought its own challenges and triumphs, but she had pressed on, guided by the promise of reaching Santiago de Compostela and the novenas she had held dear to her heart.

Every evening, as the sun dipped below the horizon and cast a warm golden glow over the picturesque landscapes of Portugal and Spain, Veronica would find a quiet spot to sit and reflect. It was during these precious moments of solitude that she would recite a unique novena—a heartfelt prayer to her love, Hugo, back in Goa.

The novenas were a source of comfort and strength for Veronica. They served as a bridge between her physical journey along the Camino and the emotional journey of love and connection that transcended the miles between them. Each novena was a testament to her devotion, a way to stay connected to Hugo even when they were separated by oceans and continents.

As she walked through charming villages and vast stretches of countryside, Veronica would recount the novenas she had said in the days leading up to her arrival in Santiago de Compostela. Each novena held a special intention, a prayer for safety, strength, and love. They were a lifeline to her beloved Hugo, a way to keep him close even when they were worlds apart.

And then, on the ninth day of her pilgrimage, Veronica's weary feet finally carried her to the historic city of Santiago de Compostela. The sight of the Cathedral's grand façade, with its soaring spires and intricate stone carvings, took her breath away. She had reached her destination, the culmination of her journey.

As Veronica stood in front of the Cathedral, she felt a sense of accomplishment wash over her. The physical and emotional challenges of the Camino had tested her in ways she could never have imagined, but she had persevered. She had not only achieved her goal of reaching Santiago de Compostela, but she had also strengthened her connection with Hugo through the novenas that had accompanied her every step of the way.

Tears of joy welled up in Veronica's eyes as she offered a final novena, a prayer of gratitude for the love and support that had carried her through this incredible journey. She felt truly blessed to have Hugo in her life, and this pilgrimage had deepened their bond in ways words could not express.

As she entered the Cathedral to pay her respects to Saint James, Veronica knew that this was not just the end of her physical journey; it was the beginning of a new chapter in her relationship with Hugo. The novenas had been a testament to their love, a thread that had connected them across the miles, and she couldn't wait to share the stories of her pilgrimage and the novenas with the man who meant the world to her.

The nine novenas that Veronica had recited as prayers to Hugo during her Camino Portugués hike:

1. **Novena for Strength:** "Dear Lord, grant Hugo the strength to overcome any challenges he may face in my absence, and may I find the strength within myself to complete this pilgrimage."

2. **Novena for Protection:** "St. James, patron saint of pilgrims, watch over Hugo and keep him safe and healthy while I am not around. Protect him from harm, both seen and unseen."

3. **Novena for Love:** "Lord, let the love that Hugo and I share stay stronger even while I am not around. May our hearts remain connected, no matter the distance that separates us."

4. **Novena for Patience:** "Grant me patience on this journey, dear God, and may Hugo find patience in resolving all the challenges that arise. Let time strengthen Hugo, not weaken him."

5. **Novena for Guidance:** "Guide my steps, both on the Camino leading to a completion in life, Lord. Lead me

towards the path of righteousness and grant your blessings to Hugo for a future filled with love"

6. **Novena for Hope:** "In moments of doubt or exhaustion, fill my heart with strength, dear Lord. And may Hugo's heart be filled with hope and strength all through his life."

7. **Novena for Understanding:** "Grant the wisdom to understand each other even when we are far apart. Help me communicate and support Hugo even from a distance."

8. **Novena for Gratitude:** "Lord, I am grateful for the love I share with Hugo. Let my journey on the Camino be a testament to my gratitude for the blessings granted in my life."

9. **Novena for Reunion:** "Dear God, bring the day of our reunion closer by making it possible as I take this last step on this pilgrimage. May every day for Hugo appear to be backed by my support and be filled with joy and love."

These unique novenas served as Veronica's heartfelt prayers, connecting her with Hugo even as she embarked on her solo adventure along the Camino Portugués.

Chapter 17

FESTIVAL OF SAINTS

Earlier in the year, Hugo and Veronica had participated in the "Festival of Saints", this was one of the festivals they had not missed a single year since getting together. In the tranquil coastal town of Goa Velha, nestled within the historic district of Tiswadi, a spectacle unlike any other unfurled during the penitential season of Lent. It was a tradition, etched into the very soul of the town, known far and wide as the Procession of Saints. Rooted deep in history, this grand event held annually at St. Andrew's Church had endured the passage of centuries and remained an indomitable testament to faith and tradition. Only in Rome, a city brimming with its own timeless history, could one find a counterpart to this celestial pageant.

Locally christened "Santanchem Pursanv" in the melodious Konkani language, also referred to as "Procession of Saints", this procession bore the unmistakable mark of the Franciscan order of Goa, tracing its origins back to the 17th century. It was here, amidst the whitewashed walls and towering spires of St. Andrew's Church, that the faithful congregated, drawn by a devotion that knew no bounds.

Before the mass is held, the devotees make their way to the statues kept inside the Church to kiss and venerate the statues while whispering their prayers and wishes by touching the feet of the statues. Subsequently the mass begins and just before the sun goes down, the life sized saints dressed in different vestments and mounted on tableaus are seen emerging from the Church marking the beginning of the "Santachem pursanv".

As the saints were brought out of the Church, the tableau paused at the podium where a brief narration of the life of the saint was read out. The procession commenced with grandeur, the lead tableau, a cross with two hands crucified, one representing Jesus and the other St Francis of Assisi and forming the arms and symbol of the Franciscan order. This hallowed relic represented the unbroken continuity of faith and tradition. As the sun's warm rays danced upon the assembled devotees, the procession set forth on its meticulously charted route. The final tableau depicting St Francis of Assisi on his knees seeing a vision of Christ being crucified and, on the hands, feet and the chest, the wounds of Jesus Christ are visible.

An awe-inspiring procession indeed it was, with an entourage of approximately 31 statues adorning the specially crafted charols, akin to palanquins. These life-sized statues ranged from saints, popes, kings, martyrs, queens, to cardinals, each a masterpiece of devotion and craftsmanship. Among the revered figures were - St. Anthony of Padua, St. Peter, the sorrowful Ecce Homo, the illustrious St. Francis Xavier, the humble St. Francis of Assisi, the valiant St. Michael, the erudite Cardinal St. Bonaventura, the pious St. Clare of Assisi, the fervent St. Rose of Viterbo, the compassionate St. Isabel of

Hungary, the steadfast St. Dominic, and the patron Archdiocese of Goa, St Joseph Vaz.

These statues, resplendent in their divine glory, were paraded through the town's streets, accompanied by the sonorous cadence of prayers and the harmonious strains of hymns that filled the air. The life of each saint, a testament to unwavering faith, was narrated aloud for all to hear, their stories weaving a tapestry of devotion and sacrifice.

The life-sized statues made of wood weighing around 100-300kg. The procession takes two hours to complete and travels two kms covering the village, main road and back to the church.

At regular intervals along the procession route, devoted pilgrims sought blessings by walking beneath the charols, believing that their sins would be pardoned, and their hearts would be sanctified. The very air was alive with the fervent pleas of the faithful, their whispered hopes and whispered confessions rising like incense to the heavens.

As the sun dipped below the horizon, casting a golden hue upon the gathered multitude, the procession culminated with the arrival of Veronica, a mystic face of Jesus or veil of Veronica- she wiped the face of Jesus when he was carrying the cross- this is carried last in the procession, and a venerable priest ascended to deliver the sermon that served as a spiritual beacon guiding the faithful towards the path of righteousness.

Once the sermon concluded, the life-sized statues found their resting place within the hallowed walls of St. Andrew's Church. Here, they would be displayed for public veneration over the following two days, inviting the faithful to draw near, to touch the divine, and to renew their own devotion.

These statues, the embodiment of faith and artistry, were not mere inanimate objects; they were crafted from wood, imbued with the very essence of the faithful who had lovingly preserved this tradition. In the weeks leading up to the procession, skilled carpenters painstakingly assembled and adorned them, bestowing upon each figure a lifelike presence that could touch the hearts of all who beheld them.

After the procession, with equal care, the statues were disassembled and consigned to wooden boxes in a vast chamber, meticulously designed for their safekeeping. Here, they would await the call of the next year's procession, when once again, they would grace the streets of Goa Velha, reminding all of the enduring power of faith, tradition, and devotion.

And so, the Procession of Saints continued, a living testament to the enduring spirit of Goa Velha, its faithful residents, and the enduring legacy of the Franciscan order. It was a procession that transcended time, bridging the past with the present, and forging an unbreakable bond between the earthly and the divine.

After the procession of saints had concluded, and the majestic statues were safely housed within St. Andrew's Church, Hugo's appetite stirred. He left Veronica momentarily, promising to return soon with some delectable snacks and sweets from the nearby stalls that lined the festive grounds.

As Hugo ventured towards the bustling stalls, his senses were overwhelmed by the tantalizing aroma of street food and the vibrant displays of colorful confections. The vibrant carnival atmosphere had a magnetic allure, drawing him deeper into the festivities.

Meanwhile, Veronica remained near the church, her gaze wandering over the congregation of faithful souls who lingered in the afterglow of the procession. She found herself absorbed in the reverie of the event, lost in thought until an old man, with wisps of silver in his hair and a twinkle in his eyes, approached her.

"Isn't this an amazing festival," he began with a warm smile, "We should keep enjoying the festivals around us, shouldn't we have such celebrations every day in our lives? I have been attending this festival for the past 15 years."

Veronica nodded in agreement, captivated by the wisdom in his words. "Indeed," she replied with a gentle smile, "It's a beautiful sentiment."

Just as Veronica and the old man shared this profound exchange, Hugo returned to her side, holding a tempting array of snacks and sweets. He couldn't contain his excitement as he approached her, his voice filled with enthusiasm.

"Hey, do you know," Hugo began, "I ran into an old man on my way back who said, 'Isn't this an amazing festival? We should keep enjoying the festivals around us, shouldn't we have such celebrations every day in our lives? I have been attending this festival for the past 15 years.'"

Veronica's eyes widened in surprise, a soft chuckle escaping her lips. "Hugo," she said, amused, "It's probably the same old man who said the same thing to me just a few minutes ago while you were away. Isn't that a nice coincidence?"

Hugo and Veronica shared a knowing look, the serendipity of the moment not lost on them. In the midst of the festive crowd, they had each encountered the same wise soul who had shared his timeless wisdom about celebrating life's joys and savoring every moment. It was a reminder that life's most beautiful moments could often be found in the simplest of coincidences, and in the shared experiences that bound their hearts together.

Chapter 18

VERONICA'S ARRIVAL

On the crisp and brisk morning of December 3rd, Veronica's journey along the Camino Portugués reached its long-awaited destination: Santiago de Compostela, nestled at the heart of the enchanting Galicia region. The town, renowned as a rewarding terminus for pilgrims of old and a captivating haven for modern-day travelers, held its most cherished treasure at its center—the UNESCO-listed historic core, crowned by the resplendent Cathedral of Santiago.

As Veronica ventured into the historic center, her eyes were drawn inexorably towards the awe-inspiring edifice that had beckoned to pilgrims for centuries—the magnificent Cathedral of Santiago. Its imposing presence loomed over the cobbled streets and hallowed paths that had been trodden by countless pilgrims before her. This monumental masterpiece of Romanesque and Baroque architecture was Spain's most sacred Christian church, and its enduring allure continued to captivate the souls of all who laid eyes upon it.

The Cathedral's splendor unfurled before Veronica as she stood in quiet reverence. The sight of this magnificent edifice had, for generations, for centuries, rewarded medieval pilgrims who had endured lengthy and arduous journeys, and it now stood as a testament to their enduring faith and devotion. Every stone and arch seemed to whisper the stories of those who had come before, their footsteps echoing through the hallowed halls of history.

Before her, the grandeur of the Portico de la Gloria unfolded—a splendid entrance created by the skilled hands of Master Mateo in 1188. This majestic doorway was a living tableau, a profusion of sculpture that told the tales of the Apocalypse, with 200 intricate figures intertwined in a dramatic narrative. At its heart stood the figure of Saint James the Apostle, protector of pilgrims, his countenance serene and welcoming. Veronica couldn't help but feel a profound connection to the countless travelers who had passed through this portal, seeking solace and spiritual renewal.

As she continued her exploration, Veronica gazed upon the resplendent Obradoiro Facade, which faced the grand square. This lavish façade, a creation of Fernando de Casas y Novoa, stood as an exemplar of Spanish Baroque style. Its intricate details and ornate design captured the essence of an era that had been marked by grandeur and opulence. Veronica marveled at the intricate sculptures and the meticulous craftsmanship that adorned the façade, a testament to the devotion and artistry of those who had built this sacred sanctuary.

With every step she took, Veronica felt the weight of history and spirituality pressing upon her. The Catedral de Santiago made a grand first impression, setting the stage for an inspiring spiritual experience. It was a place where the past converged with the present, where pilgrims and tourists alike could find solace, reflection, and a sense of wonder. Santiago de Compostela had rewarded Veronica's pilgrimage with not only the physical journey but also a profound spiritual awakening— an indelible memory etched in the annals of her life's experiences.

After the culmination of a long and arduous nine-day journey along the Camino Portugués, Veronica's heart swelled with gratitude as she crossed the threshold into the sanctuary of Santiago de Compostela. Her footsteps echoed softly on the time-worn stones, resonating with the collective pilgrimage of countless souls who had ventured before her. The cathedral, a colossal edifice of profound significance, stretched its graceful arms over her, enfolding her in a sense of awe.

The interior space of the cathedral revealed itself as Veronica stepped further within, a grandiose expanse boasting three majestic naves that sprawled across an astounding surface area of approximately 8,300 square meters. The serenity that enveloped this sacred space was palpable, a stark contrast to the weariness that had marked her journey. The sacred sanctuary seemed to breathe with a life of its own, drawing her deeper into its hallowed embrace.

Her gaze settled upon the opulent Baroque main altar, an ornate masterpiece that held the attention of all who entered. But it was what lay directly beneath this resplendent altar that beckoned with an irresistible allure—the Crypt of Saint James the Apostle, the patron saint of Spain. It was here, in this crypt, that the very essence of her pilgrimage had led her. The crypt enshrined the Tomb of Saint James, an object of veneration for pilgrims from all corners of the world. Veronica felt a profound sense of connection to the centuries of faithful seekers who had stood in this very spot, humbled before the sacred remains of the apostle.

Venturing further into the cathedral, Veronica found herself in the ethereal realm of the Capilla de las Reliquias, the first chapel in the south aisle. Here, beneath the intricate arches and soaring vaults, rested the tombs of kings and queens who had reigned in ages past, spanning from the 12th to the 15th centuries. Their final resting places spoke of the intertwined histories of faith and monarchy, a testament to the enduring allure of Santiago de Compostela.

Beyond the south transept, to the right of the Puerta de las Platerías, Veronica discovered a breathtaking sight—a gorgeous Renaissance cloister, a jewel of 16th-century Plateresque architecture and one of the largest of its kind in Spain. Its intricate stone carvings and delicate filigree seemed to dance in the dappled light, casting intricate shadows that whispered tales of craftsmanship and devotion.

Nestled within the embrace of this cloister was the Cathedral of Santiago Museum, a repository of history and art that unfolded the cathedral's rich tapestry. Veronica wandered amidst an assortment of artworks, each a chapter in the cathedral's storied past. Among the treasures were the tapestries crafted by the masterful hands of Rubens and Goya, each a testament to the artistic legacy of the cathedral. The museum also housed the Cathedral Treasury, a trove of precious relics and artifacts that bore witness to the faith and reverence that had sustained Santiago de Compostela through the ages.

As Veronica immersed herself in the cathedral's sacred spaces and rich history, she felt the weight of her pilgrimage, a journey of body and spirit, come to fruition. The cathedral had not only welcomed her with open arms but had also unveiled its profound treasures, leaving an indelible mark upon her soul. Santiago de Compostela had rewarded her perseverance with the profound beauty of faith, art, and history intertwined—a culmination that resonated deep within her being.

After the soul-stirring visit to the Catedral de Santiago, where gratitude and appreciation swelled within her, Veronica made her way to the Hostal de los Reyes Católicos, the place she had chosen for her stay in this remarkable city. This former pilgrims' hostel, a magnificent embodiment of Gothic Plateresque architecture, awaited her with its historic charm and timeless allure.

As Veronica approached the entrance of the hostal, she couldn't help but be captivated by the striking facade that greeted her. Decorative details adorned the stone exterior, each carving whispering stories of centuries gone by. The hostal, steeped in history and tradition, beckoned her inside with an air of quiet grandeur.

Once within, Veronica found herself in the heart of a place that had once offered solace and respite to weary pilgrims. Four tranquil interior courtyards, elegantly designed and meticulously maintained, provided a sense of serenity that contrasted with the bustling world outside. It was in these cloisters that countless pilgrims had rested their tired feet and sought refuge from their arduous journeys.

In the year 1499, the Catholic Monarchs, Isabella and Ferdinand, had the vision to create a haven for travelers who had completed their pilgrimage. Veronica couldn't help but imagine the joy that must have filled the hearts of those travelers as they reached this beautiful destination, their weary souls finding rest and rejuvenation within these storied walls.

The Hostal de los Reyes Católicos, now Spain's oldest hotel, continued to honor the age-old tradition of hospitality. It had undergone meticulous renovations over the centuries and had been transformed into the luxurious Parador de Santiago de Compostela, a five-star sanctuary that awaited Veronica's arrival.

As she settled into her plush modern guest room, Veronica couldn't help but appreciate the top-notch services that accompanied her stay. From room service to butler service, concierge assistance to valet parking, every need and desire was met with utmost care and attention.

Her culinary senses were indulged with authentic Galician cuisine offered at the hotel's two dining options—a fine-dining restaurant and a casual eatery. Each meal was a celebration of the region's rich culinary traditions, a feast for the palate and the soul.

Veronica also discovered the exquisite Capilla de Enrique de Egas, an intimate chapel within the hostal. Here, guests were welcomed to seek moments of silent prayer and reflection, a serene space that resonated with the echoes of devotion and reverence.

As Veronica settled into her stay at the Hostal de los Reyes Católicos, she found herself not only immersed in the comfort and luxury of her surroundings but also connected to the centuries of travelers who had sought solace and rest within these hallowed walls. It was a chapter in her pilgrimage that offered respite and renewal, a fitting complement to the spiritual journey she had undertaken.

Veronica sat in her room at the Parador de Santiago de Compostela, the soft rays of the sun in December casting a warm glow over the ancient stone walls. With her heart still brimming with the sense of achievement and the echoes of her footsteps along the Camino Portugués, she reached for her phone and dialed Hugo's number in Goa. She longed to share the joy of her successful pilgrimage with him, to feel his presence even from afar.

The line connected, and as Hugo's voice greeted her from thousands of miles away, Veronica couldn't help but smile. She knew all too well the commitment that Hugo had toward his work, his unwavering respect for the busy schedules of the guests who graced his popular podcast show. Some of them were celebrities of international acclaim, their appearances requiring meticulous planning and nearly three months of advance booking. It was a testament to Hugo's dedication and the caliber of his show.

"Hello, Hugo," Veronica began, her voice filled with a mix of excitement and longing. "I wish you could've been here with me. The Camino Portugués was an incredible journey, and I kept thinking how wonderful it would've been to have you by my side. But I understand your work and the responsibilities you have towards your guests."

She paused, letting the words linger in the air for a moment. "Maybe in a few years, we can do the Camino together," she continued optimistically. "Imagine the adventure we'd have, the stories we'd collect along the way."

Veronica went on to describe the sights of the Catedral de Santiago, the grandeur of its architecture, and the spiritual resonance she had felt within its hallowed halls. She spoke of the seamless ease of checking into the Hostal de los Reyes Católicos, an establishment steeped in history, and the mouthwatering Galician cuisine she had just savored. The flavors of the region had danced on her palate, each dish a culinary masterpiece.

As their conversation drew to a close, Veronica mentioned her plan to take a nap, her body still carrying the fatigue of the journey. She had requested the hotel staff to provide her with a wake-up call around 7:45 pm, ensuring she wouldn't miss the opportunity to explore the city further and savor the delights of a Galician dinner. With a promise to speak again soon, she bid Hugo farewell, her heart filled with love and gratitude for the connection they shared, even across the miles that separated them.

Veronica glanced at the warm rays of the afternoon sun filtering through the curtains of her room at the Parador de Santiago de Compostela, Veronica lay on her bed, mentally mapping out her plans for the evening. She was eager to explore the UNESCO-designated Casco Antiguo, the Old Town of Santiago de Compostela, a World Heritage Site that beckoned with promises of centuries-old charm and historic treasures.

The Casco Antiguo, she knew, extended southward from the towering presence of the cathedral and the bustling Plaza de Las Platerías, where the cathedral's Romanesque facade held court. This square, adorned with fountains and framed by ornate Baroque monuments, was a picturesque starting point for her journey into the heart of Santiago's history.

At the core of the Casco Antiguo lay two parallel streets, the Rúa Nueva and the Rúa del Villar, their cobblestone paths leading her deeper into the embrace of antiquity. Along these charming, arcaded streets, the centuries seemed to converge, and the architecture told stories of times long past. Veronica could already picture herself strolling along these lively pedestrian-only streets, where cafés, restaurants, and boutiques lined the way.

The 18th-century Casa del Deán marked the near end of the Rúa del Villar, a historical gem that spoke of bygone eras. Veronica's anticipation grew as she imagined herself exploring the intricate details of this architectural marvel, wondering about the lives and stories it had witnessed over the centuries.

One of the most enchanting aspects of the Casco Antiguo was its deliberate exclusion of automobile traffic, preserving the old-world ambience and inviting visitors to step back in time. Veronica appreciated this commitment to retaining the historic character of the area, where each corner held the promise of a new discovery, a hidden gem waiting to be uncovered.

As Veronica tried to settle into her nap, her adrenaline flushed mind filled with the accomplishment, slowly drifted towards the plans she had for the following day, December 4th. Her pilgrimage to Santiago de Compostela was not merely about the physical journey but also a quest to delve deeper into the history and culture that surrounded the city. Her next destination was the Museo de las Peregrinaciones y de

Santiago, the Pilgrimage Museum, a place that promised to unravel the fascinating history of the pilgrims of Saint James.

In her mental itinerary, Veronica envisioned stepping into this museum, where the importance of Saint James' relics to the pilgrims was unveiled. The artifacts and religious objects on display would paint a vivid picture of the profound devotion and the cult of Saint James that had thrived through the ages. Ancient relics and religious items would tell stories of faith and pilgrimage, connecting her to the countless souls who had embarked on similar journeys.

The museum would offer her a glimpse into the origin of Jacobean worship, tracing its roots back to the archaeological transfer of the Saint's apostolic body, or relics, from Jaffa in the Holy Land to Libredón. This name now graced a hilltop site that had become an integral part of Santiago de Compostela's history. The sacred journey of Saint James had left an indelible mark on the city, and Veronica was eager to immerse herself in its rich tapestry.

Moreover, her curiosity was piqued by the role of pilgrimages in shaping the development of Santiago de Compostela's artistic crafts guilds. The museum promised insights into how the devotion of pilgrims had not only influenced spirituality but had also left an enduring imprint on the creative and artisanal heritage of the region.

Veronica noted that the Pilgrimage Museum had two locations. One was situated on Calle de San Miguel, a street resonating with history, and the other at Plaza de Las Platerías, the square facing the cathedral. Each site would provide a unique perspective on the intertwined histories of Saint James and the pilgrims who had followed in his footsteps.

As Veronica's mind continued to view the brochures from the hotel she weaved plans for tomorrow, she set her sights also for a visit to the Parque de la Alameda, a lush eight-hectare oasis that beckoned with promises of natural beauty and historical treasures. This verdant haven was a haven of tranquility, a place where the whispers of nature and history intertwined.

Her mental itinerary unfolded with the mention of three distinct gardens nestled within the park's embrace. Each garden held its own charm and allure, a testament to the meticulous design and care that had gone into creating this green sanctuary. Veronica anticipated the sensory delight of wandering through the verdant expanse, where Mediterranean vegetation thrived alongside subtropical species and exotic flowers, creating a vibrant tapestry of colors and scents.

Two noteworthy monuments awaited her discovery within the Parque de la Alameda. The Iglesia de El Pilar, a testament to architectural elegance, had graced the landscape since its construction in 1717. Its presence spoke of centuries of devotion and faith, and Veronica couldn't help but imagine the stories that had unfolded within its sacred walls.

Another renowned landmark, the famous Porta dos Leóns, or the Door of the Lions, dated back to 1835. This striking entrance would be a gateway to her exploration of the park's wonders, its intricate details and historical significance adding a layer of intrigue to her visit.

Veronica's curiosity was further piqued by the tales of residents who had frequented La Alameda for over two centuries. The As Marías monument, a sculpture honoring two well-known local sisters, bore witness to their daily afternoon walks at 2 pm. Their colorful dresses and their enduring tradition had become a part of the park's lore, a living testament to the timeless appeal of this green oasis.

A highlight of the Parque de la Alameda awaited Veronica in the form of the Jardínes de Méndez Núñez, a delightful, wooded area where her senses would be treated to the sight and fragrance of a rose garden. Statues honoring illustrious historical figures of the Galicia region would stand as silent sentinels, guardians of the park's rich heritage.

Veronica's plans for her visit to the Parque de la Alameda were a tapestry of anticipation, a blend of natural beauty and historical intrigue. It was a journey that promised to awaken her senses and connect her to the heart and soul of Santiago de Compostela.

As Veronica drifted further into her nap, her dreams were filled with visions of ancient artifacts and the echoes of pilgrim footsteps, a testament to her insatiable thirst for knowledge and her deep connection to the spiritual and historical essence of Santiago de Compostela, the echoes of her footsteps in the Casco Antiguo danced through her mind. The promise of an evening filled with history, culture, and the quaint old-world ambience of Santiago de Compostela awaited her, a continuation of her pilgrimage through time and tradition in this storied city.

Chapter 19

OFFICE OF VERITAS UNVEILED

I n the heart of the coastal paradise known as Calangute, a
haven of creativity thrived, sheltered from the relentless
sun by thickets of palm trees and the gentle embrace of the
Arabian Sea breeze. This secluded alcove, a mere two
kilometers from the bustling shores of Goa's iconic beach
resort town, concealed the sanctum of Hugo De Carvalho's
"Veritas Unveiled" channel, a digital oracle of knowledge and
revelation. Calangute, nestled snugly between the radiant gems
of Candolim and Baga, seemed an unlikely setting for such an
enterprise, but therein lay its charm.

For eleven years, Hugo's channel has been a guiding light in
the labyrinthine corridors of podcasting, but its origins bore
the mark of humbler beginnings. The initial four years saw the
channel's infancy, nurtured within the walls of Hugo's own
abode "Villa Carvalho", perched upon the Vagator's hills.
Those early days, marked by the echo of ambition, were etched
into the annals of his journey.

However, as Hugo's voice resonated with the hearts and
minds of millions, the need for expansion became an
undeniable truth. It was then that the channel, like a fledgling

bird testing its wings, took flight to its current sanctuary—a dedicated office space that has been its stronghold for the last seven years. The team's growth started when the audience swelled to more than five million subscribers, the move was not only a strategic decision but a symbolic one as well—a transformation from a modest endeavor to an institution with long term strategic goals.

This new abode of 10,300 square footage, nestled amid the palms and dappled by the golden sunlight, was a testament to Hugo's unwavering dedication. Inside, the walls bore witness to the passage of time and the fast evolution of the "Veritas Unveiled" channel. Rows of bookshelves lined with ancient and modern tomes bore the backdrop for the podcast episodes recording space, the ever-growing repository of knowledge that fueled the channel's content. The spacious office space was elegantly decorated with timeless decorative pieces and paintings that seamlessly blended with the cubicles that glowed of computer screens illuminating the hallways, where the tireless team of researchers, content editors, marketing teams tirelessly pursued the pursuit of releasing and promoting iconic episodes for the channel.

Amidst this bustling hive of the team's activity, Hugo's own corner room donned an elegant look with a polished wooden desk, adorned with esteemed guests photographic frames lining the walls as relics from the many episodes he had embarked upon in search of wisdom, numerous awards over the course of the years singing the podcast success proudly sat on a table beneath a large window that framed the expanse of the Goan sky. The room resonated with some ideas of creativity, punctuated by bursts of laughter and the occasional clinking of coffee cups—a symphony of dedication, camaraderie, and purpose.

The air within the office was striven with the promise of extracting and imparting knowledge from experts who had already made a mark for themselves through the tireless journey of discovery in their respective fields of expertise, as if every interaction during the recording of episodes held a secret waiting to be unveiled. Here, in the heart of Goa's coastal splendor, the "Veritas Unveiled" channel had carved its niche—an oasis of knowledge and information, amidst the sun, sand, and sea. A testament to the enduring power of knowledge sharing, a beacon for seekers of information, and the legacy of a man named Hugo De Carvalho, who dared to unveil the veritas that lay hidden in the world's ocean of information that laid in the shadows to be brought into limelight by the various episodes.

Behind the captivating facade of Hugo's "Veritas Unveiled" podcast channel lay a meticulously assembled team, each member playing a crucial role in the seamless orchestration of its operations. Hugo, the charismatic host, stood at the forefront, conducting the symphony of conversations with invited guests, unveiling and extracting the depths of their knowledge and insights.

Rodrigo Esteves, the executive producer, was the architect behind the scenes, wielding his expertise to shape the podcast's overarching vision. With a keen eye for detail and an ear for narrative nuance, he ensured that every episode resonated with the channel's distinctive voice.

Ana Da Costa, the ever-welcoming receptionist, was the first point of contact for the channel's audience. Her warm disposition and organizational finesse created a hospitable ambiance, both online and offline, making every interaction with "Veritas Unveiled" a delightful experience.

In the labyrinth of research and discovery, Ashley Fernandes reigned as the research team lead. With an insatiable thirst for knowledge and an uncanny ability to unearth hidden gems of wisdom, Ashley was the intellectual backbone, ensuring that every conversation was well-informed and enriched.

Vishal Sen, the audio and sound lead, held the power to transform mere words into a captivating auditory journey. His mastery of sound engineering and acute attention to acoustics brought a symphonic quality to each episode, elevating the channel's content to new heights.

Priscila Silveira, the marketing manager, was the channel's voice in the vast digital wilderness. With a strategic mindset and an understanding of trends, she ensured that "Veritas Unveiled" reached the eager ears of those who sought information in a timely manner that pulsated with the audience.

Rebecca Silvestri, the social media manager, deftly navigated the ever-evolving landscape of social platforms. Her creativity and engagement strategies cultivated a vibrant online community, where viewers discussions thrived and ideas blossomed.

Sunil Gupta, the visual editor lead, was the channel's visual maestro. With a keen eye for aesthetics and an arsenal of editing tools, he transformed images and visuals into compelling narratives, complementing the podcast's auditory brilliance.

Olivia Posada, the guest booker, was the channel's liaison to the world of intellectuals and thought leaders. Her ability to identify and invite captivating guests ensured that "Veritas Unveiled" consistently offered fresh perspectives and profound wisdom.

Amidst the harmonious symphony of dedicated souls orchestrating Hugo's "Veritas Unveiled" podcast channel, there was yet another virtuoso who wielded his expertise behind the scenes, his role vital in the channel's digital infrastructure. Antonio Batista, the maestro of the IT realm, stood as the channel's expert in archiving old content or managing new content with unwavering commitment.

In the depths of the digital labyrinth, where ones and zeros whispered their cryptic secrets, Antonio was the torchbearer. As the IT team lead, his role was one of guardianship and innovation. With a mind attuned to the intricate dance of managing local server & cloud systems, he ensured that the podcast's technical foundation remained robust and resilient.

Antonio's domain was a realm of firewalls and encryption, a sanctuary of data protection and cyber fortification. In an age where the digital realm held both promise and peril, his vigilance safeguarded the channel's treasure trove of knowledge, shielding it from the relentless onslaught of virtual marauders.

But Antonio's role transcended mere defense; it was a harmonious balance of safeguarding and enabling. His technological wizardry seamlessly integrated the podcast's digital presence, facilitating its reach to the farthest corners of the virtual world. He ensured that "Veritas Unveiled" sailed smoothly through the uncharted waters of the internet, leaving a trail of enlightening content in its wake.

In the grand orchestra of "Veritas Unveiled," Antonio Batista was the conductor of the digital overture, orchestrating a symphony of bytes and algorithms that harmonized with the channel's pursuit of truth. His steady hand and technical virtuosity were the unseen threads binding the podcast's digital tapestry, ensuring that Hugo's voice and the wisdom of invited guests reverberated across the boundless expanse of the digital cosmos.

In this realm where knowledge merged seamlessly with technology, Antonio Batista stood as a sentinel and an enabler, weaving the magic of IT into the very fabric of "Veritas Unveiled." His presence, like an unsung melody in a grand composition, elevated the podcast to new heights, solidifying its place as a beacon of enlightenment in the vast digital expanse.

Together, this dedicated ensemble formed the backbone of Hugo's "Veritas Unveiled" podcast channel. With their individual talents and unwavering commitment, they elevated each episode into a tapestry of knowledge, insight, and enlightenment, making "Veritas Unveiled" a beacon of intellectual curiosity and discovery in the digital landscape.

Within the sanctum of his studio, Hugo De Carvalho, the maestro of intellectual exploration, embarked on a perpetual odyssey. Seated on a comfortable leather chair across from his invited guests, he conducted his podcast, "Veritas Unveiled," with a commanding presence that belied his humility. Across the expanse of a digital realm, he summoned guests from diverse corners of knowledge, their expertise spanning a mosaic of fields that mirrored the richness of human experience.

In the realm of Arts and Culture, Hugo, like a curator of the human soul, delved into the intricacies of artistic expression. Painters, writers, and performers unveiled the inner workings of their creative minds, weaving tales of inspiration and innovation.

In the company of literary luminaries from the world of Books and Authors, Hugo transformed his studio into a library of ideas. Here, the written word danced through the airwaves, its power and resonance dissected with a surgeon's precision.

The tapestry of Business and Entrepreneurship unfolded with tales of visionaries who dared to chart uncharted waters. Entrepreneurs and industry leaders laid bare their strategies, failures, and triumphs, offering a roadmap for those who sought to navigate the treacherous seas of commerce.

The realm of Careers and Jobs was demystified by Hugo's inquisitive spirit. Experts in various fields illuminated career paths and job markets, empowering listeners to make informed choices on their professional journeys.

In the world of Comedy, laughter echoed through the podcast's corridors as comedians shared their comedic philosophies. The alchemy of humor and wit was dissected, revealing the hidden artistry that lay behind every punchline.

From Hollywood's glitz to the elegance of Bollywood, from the charm of Tollywood to the avant-garde of Kollywood, and the subtlety of Korean and Japanese cinema, Hugo journeyed through the global mosaic of Movies and Entertainment. Here, he explored the silver screen's capacity to mirror society's dreams and nightmares.

In the realm of Health and Medicine, Hugo's podcast became a digital clinic where experts diagnosed the human condition. Cutting-edge research, medical breakthroughs, and personal anecdotes offered insights into the pursuit of well-being.

International Affairs became a tapestry of diplomacy and geopolitics as Hugo engaged with diplomats, experts, and analysts. The world's intricate web of relationships and conflicts was woven into narratives that painted a broader understanding of global dynamics.

Within the corridors of Law and Crime, Hugo was the interrogator who sought the truth. Legal experts and crime investigators unraveled the mysteries of justice, exploring the boundaries of human morality and ethics.

The intricacies of Investments, Money and Finance were laid bare as experts navigated the labyrinthine world of economics and markets. Here, Hugo dissected the forces that shaped markets, economies and currencies, demystifying the world of finance for his eager audience.

Music, the universal language, found a passionate conductor in Hugo. Musicians from diverse genres shared their melodies and harmonies, the rhythm of their lives resonating with the hearts of listeners.

Politics and Society became a battleground of ideas and ideologies, where Hugo engaged with politicians, thinkers, and activists. The dynamics of governance, power, and social change were debated with fervor.

Frontiers of Science and Technology were explored as Hugo conversed with pioneers of innovation. Cutting-edge discoveries, artificial intelligence, and space exploration unveiled the mysteries of the cosmos and the potential of the human mind.

In the realm of Self Improvement and Transformation, Hugo became a guide on the path to personal growth. Life coaches and motivators shared their wisdom, illuminating the journey toward self-realization.

The esoteric realm of Spirituality and Religion was a tapestry of faith and transcendence. Sages, priests, and spiritual leaders shed light on the mystical realms that lay beyond the tangible world.

Startups and Unicorns were dissected by Hugo's analytical mind. Here, he explored the journeys of those who dared to dream and create, building empires from the ground up.

The allure of Travel and the wildness of the Outdoors beckoned Hugo as he engaged with explorers and adventurers. Their tales of wanderlust and wilderness evoked the thrill of the unknown.

Women's Issues were brought to the forefront with candor and empathy. Advocates and champions for gender equality revealed the challenges and triumphs of the female experience.

With each episode, Hugo De Carvalho's "Veritas Unveiled" podcast channel was a voyage into the boundless horizons of human knowledge. His dialogue with experts and visionaries painted a kaleidoscope of insights, enlightening minds and inspiring hearts. It was a sanctuary of intellect, a symphony of wisdom, and a testament to the insatiable curiosity of the human spirit.

Chapter 20

MORNING OF DECEMBER 4TH

On the morning of December 4th, as the sun cast its gentle rays upon the office space of "Veritas Unveiled," Antonio Batista, the IT lead, strode in with a sense of urgency. His footsteps echoed through the hallway as he made his way to the reception desk, where Ana Da Costa, the ever-welcoming receptionist, sat poised usually busy on the phone tending to calls but she was not busy at the moment.

"Ana," Antonio inquired breathlessly, his eyes scanning the premises, "Is Rodrigo in the office? I need to speak with him urgently."

Ana, her fingers deftly dancing across the keyboard, took a moment to verify Rodrigo's whereabouts. With a faint nod, she replied, "Let me check for you, Antonio." Her voice, like a soothing melody, belied the urgency of the situation. She swiftly dialed Rodrigo's number, her eyes fixed on the digital clock that ticked away the seconds.

Meanwhile, inside the cozy enclave of Rodrigo Esteves' office, the executive producer was immersed in the intricacies of the latest upcoming projects, tactics, and strategies. His desk was a canvas of creative clutter, strewn with scripts and notes. The soft hums from his laptop and computer was his constant companion.

As the phone on his desk rang, Rodrigo glanced at the caller ID, recognizing it as Ana's number. With a knowing smile, he picked up the receiver. "Ana, Good morning how's your day going today?" Rodrigo inquired, his voice a mix of warmth and professionalism.

Ana's voice, tinged with courtesy, relayed Antonio's request. "Antonio is here, Rodrigo, and he's eager to speak with you urgently. Is it alright if he comes to your room?"

Rodrigo, ever the amiable accommodating person, leaned back in his chair. "Of course, Ana. Let Antonio know he can come in." With that, he hung up the phone and resumed his work, a calm oasis amid the currents of activity.

Back at the reception desk, Ana relayed Rodrigo's message to Antonio. "You can go ahead, Antonio. Rodrigo is ready to see you," she said with a reassuring smile.

Antonio nodded gratefully and proceeded to Rodrigo's office. The urgent matter that had spurred his morning haste was about to unfold within the confines of their shared workspace.

In the midst of the bustling office space, Antonio approached Rodrigo's office, his brow furrowed with concern. "Rodrigo," he began, his voice tinged with a sense of urgency, "is it possible for you to come and take a look at something in the IT room? I think you'll want to see this."

Rodrigo, never one to shy away from a technical conundrum, expecting that Antonio would show him some technical glitch which he would endup solving himself anyway but maybe he was looking for some suggestion.

Rodrigo rose from his desk with a curious expression. "Certainly, Antonio," he replied, "Lead the way."

Antonio guided Rodrigo through the labyrinthine corridors of the office until they arrived at the IT room, a sanctum of servers and cables humming in the cool embrace of air conditioning. The servers were stacked in the corner of the room, their blinking lights a testament to the digital pulse of the channel.

Once inside, Antonio turned to Rodrigo, his face etched with a mixture of curiosity and concern. Offered Rodrigo a chair by his side as he deftly tapped on the keyboard to unlock "This morning, when I arrived at the office," he began, "I noticed something rather unusual. Do you remember how some time ago we set up Hugo's camera to transmit its recordings directly to our servers?"

Rodrigo's memory stirred. "Yes, I recall," he replied, "we did that based on Hugo's request to accommodate any monologue discussions that he would like to record as episodes."

Antonio nodded solemnly. "Well, this morning, as I was going through the server logs, I noticed that Hugo's digital camera has been transmitting a recording for the past 14 hours. It's still transmitting as we speak. Strangely enough, it seems like the camera started sending the recordings around 7:30 pm on December 3rd, last night."

A sense of intrigue washed over Rodrigo as he contemplated the implications of this revelation. "That is indeed peculiar," he mused, "and the recordings, are they intact?"

Antonio nodded again. "Yes, Rodrigo. They're broken down into one-hour chunks for storage purposes. I've already pulled up the first hour of recording, which spans from 7:30 pm to 8:30 pm."

With a few deft keystrokes, Rodrigo brought the first hour of footage onto the screen. The image revealed a familiar setting that both Rodrigo and Antonio had seen earlier during one of the parties held at Hugo's Villa Carvalho, Hugo seated on a plush dark brown sofa in his living room, a wine glass and bottle resting before him. On the other end of the sofa stood Maria, her presence a captivating enigma with a blue light around her neck indicating an active interaction.

Antonio leaned in closer to the screen, his voice hushed with intrigue. "Wait until I show you some of the content with audio," he said, his fingers dancing across the keyboard to initiate the playback.

As the recording came to life, the room was filled with the ambient sounds of conversation between Hugo and Maria, the clinking of glassware with wine as it touched the coffee table in front of the sofa, Maria with the voice of Veronica conversing with Hugo, a snapshot of a moment in time that held secrets yet to be unveiled. Rodrigo and Antonio gazed intently at the screen, their minds racing with questions about the enigmatic transmission from Hugo's camera.

As Antonio and Rodrigo rolled through the first hour of recording, Hugo was speaking to Maria who was standing on the other side of the sofa.

They heard Maria speak first, "Hugo, let's start from today and this room. I see a couple of photos on the wall. Who is the person with you in the picture, and where is she right now?"

Rodrigo looking at Antonio asked him to rewind and play the recording again. Now, Rodrigo listened with closed eyes with the intent of listening just to the piece of audio.

Undoubtedly it was Veronica's voice saying: "Hugo, let's start from today and this room. I see a couple of photos on the wall. Who is the person with you in the picture, and where is she right now?"

They paused the recording and looked at each other. Rodrigo indicated that Maria was speaking in Veronica's voice.

Meanwhile, Rodrigo recalled a casual conversation where Hugo had told him sometime back that Veronica was training Maria to personalize the responses to her voice.

Rodrigo continued, "Antonio, it appears that Veronica may have called Hugo on the phone and he probably accepted the call conversation through Maria."

Antonio nodding, yeah that makes sense.

Rodrigo, "Lets continue to play the recording."

Hugo's eyes seemed to focus on the wall and based on what they had heard earlier in the recording, Veronica was asking about the photograph on the wall. Hugo smiling in the recorded video, "Ah, that's Veronica," he said, his voice carrying a deep fondness. "My wife, for 15 wonderful years."

"Veronica," Maria repeated, "Tell me about her, Hugo. How did you two meet?"

Rodrigo and Antonio again looking at each other and smiling thought silently, seems like Veronica is eager to hear her name on the other end of the phone.

Hugo leaned back in the sofa, "We met when we were 24, right out of college. It was at a local Goan festival, and I remember the moment I laid eyes on her. She had this energy, this magnetic presence that drew me in instantly.

Hugo, with some quiet contemplation, took a sip of his wine, before he turned his gaze towards Maria. At this Goan festival in the heart of the city. She was dancing to the fado, and I was utterly captivated by her grace."

Hugo now with a wistful smile tugging at the corners of his lips. She moved like a dream, her steps telling a story of longing and love. I knew then that I had to have her in my life."

We struck up a conversation, and it felt like we'd known each other for a lifetime. We shared our dreams, our hopes, and our fears later that night. It was as if the universe conspired to bring us together."

Maria saying, "And then?"

Hugo's smile deepened. "Well, we started dating shortly after that. It was a whirlwind romance, filled with laughter and adventures. We traveled together, learned together, and grew together. It was just a year after the first time we met, there was never a doubt in my mind that she was the one I wanted to spend the rest of my life with."

Maria asks in Veronica's voice. "And so you introduced yourself, my friend, and that was the start of something beautiful, a journey of life?"

Hugo's gaze drifting away from Maria. "We discovered our shared Portuguese roots that night, it was as if our destinies had been entwined for centuries, waiting for this moment." Just a year later we tied the knot.

Maria came up with another question. "Veronica was a kindred spirit, and you two were a perfect match. You married just a year after the Goan festival where you met?"

Hugo's response, "Yes, we did, in a small chapel by the sea in Arambol. Veronica in her mother's wedding gown, and I in my newly stitched suit. It was a day filled with love and promises."

Hugo raised his wine glass, "Fifteen years, my friend. It's been a journey filled with laughter, tears, and a love that has only grown stronger with time."

Hugo's eyes fixed on Maria. "Indeed, Miguel. Veronica is the love of my life, and I thank the stars every day for bringing her to me."

Maria saying. "So, 15 years of marriage and 16 years of knowing each other. That's quite a journey. What's the secret, Hugo?"

Hugo responding, "The secret, my friend, is love, trust, and a willingness to weather life's storms together. We've faced our share of challenges, but we've always been there for each other. Communication, laughter, and never taking each other for granted—it's been the key to keeping our love alive."

Rodrigo looking at Antonio asks, did you hear a few seconds ago, Hugo saying, "Indeed, Miguel. Veronica is the love of my life, and I thank the stars every day for bringing her to me.". Antonio nods saying yes, I did hear Hugo saying Miguel. Rewinding the video to hear it again.

Rodrigo thinking out loudly and wondering, "Did Hugo call Maria as Miguel, we haven't seen anybody else in the video recording till now". Antonio nods in agreement.

Rodrigo knew that both Hugo and Veronica had named the robot "Maria" and whenever Maria spoke she had been personalized with the software attuned to the voice of Veronica.

Amidst the buzzing tones from the servers in the IT room, the luminous glow of the screen bathed Rodrigo and Antonio in the soft light of revelation. The video recording, which seemed like a private moment in Hugo's living room, unveiled an enigmatic tableau. As the seconds ticked away, the narrative unfolded, revealing a surreal convergence of voices and stories that defied explanation.

In the video, Hugo sat with an air of rapt attention, his gaze fixed upon Maria, who exuded an aura of serenity with blue light around her neck flickering every few seconds. Her voice, gentle and mellifluous, carried the cadence of Veronica, Hugo's wife.

But Hugo had already shared with Rodrigo and most of the team members that Veronica was travelling in Portugal on an ancient pilgrimage hike, traversing the historic Camino Portugués, her voice yet unknowingly echoing through the digital channels.

Rodrigo and Antonio, their senses captivated, listened intently as the recorded conversation between Hugo and Maria unfolded. What baffled them was the name Miguel—a name that seemed to dance upon Hugo's lips. At times, he addressed Maria as Miguel, a bewildering twist in the tale.

Maria, with a voice that resonated with the essence of Veronica, wove captivating tales of love and passion. "Pedro and Ines," a tale of forbidden love and undying commitment to the lover even under grave circumstances; "Henriqueta and Teresa," a story of enduring devotion to a lover; "Kerem and Ash," a romance where promises are kept and the story transcending borders; "Ana and Carlos," a saga of two hearts entwined kept alive with kisses among couples; and "Raul Gutierrez, Rosario Sanchez, and Mom Rosario," a tale of love's complexities—all these stories flowed from her lips with a grace that held Rodrigo and Antonio spellbound.

Yet, it was Hugo's inexplicable use of the name Miguel, his ardent gazes towards Maria, and his participation in the conversation that left them in a state of profound intrigue. The room seemed to resonate with an inexplicable tension, as if the very fabric of reality had momentarily shifted.

In that hushed IT room, surrounded by servers that hummed in oblivious continuity, Rodrigo and Antonio found themselves caught in the throes of a mystery—a tapestry of voices, love stories, and a perplexing use of names. They were left with more questions than answers, their minds aglow with the enigma of Hugo's actions.

As the video recording played on, the minutes ebbed away, carrying with them the weight of an unfolding mystery that defied explanation, a story yet untold in its entirety—a cryptic tale of voices and identities that would haunt their thoughts long after the recording of the first hour had ceased. There were still more than a dozen hours of video recording to be watched.

Rodrigo asked Antonio, let's go the recent recording that is coming from the camera onto the servers. Antonio nodding pulls up the last 15 minutes of recording. They both watch with surprise.

In the stark contrast of seating on the sofa from the first hour of recording they had just watched, Hugo's physical proximity to Maria had shifted. No longer separated by the expanse of the sofa, he now sat beside her on the edge, his left arm wrapped tenderly around her, holding her close, while his right arm rested languidly on the sofa, as if bridging the divide between the enigmatic tale of voices and the mysteries that lingered in the room. There was a silence as the recording rolled through, neither Hugo nor Maria emitting any sounds, as the frames seamlessly rolled in silence without any movement from either of them.

Chapter 21

VILLA CARVALHO

As the next few minutes passed in the IT room, Rodrigo's growing unease mirrored the enigma that had unfolded on the screen. Usually, Hugo would be showing up in the office between 9 to 9:30am, but today Antonio had rushed into his office around 9:30am and they had been watching the recording for the past hour and fifteen minutes, unsure whether they should be invading the private space of Hugo where he was personally conversing with Veronica. Although watching last few minutes of the recording it had become rather clear, they should try to find out more.

Now, even a single minute was feeling like an eternity, Rodrigo reached for his phone, his fingers trembling with a mixture of worry and determination. He dialed Hugo's number, the ringing tone slicing through the room's quiet tension. But there was no answer, not once, not twice, but five times back-to-back.

A heavy sigh escaped Rodrigo's lips, and he glanced at Antonio, his expression laden with concern. "Antonio," he said in a voice tinged with urgency, "it seems like we need to pay Hugo a visit at his home. He's not responding to his phone, and I can't shake this feeling that something's amiss."

Antonio nodded in agreement; the gravity of the situation apparent in his eyes. "You're right, Rodrigo. We shouldn't take any chances. Let's also inform the authorities." With that, he reached for his own phone, ready to take action.

Meanwhile, Ana, the vigilant receptionist, was already on the case. She had swiftly picked up the phone and called the Anjuna and Vagator police stations, her voice calm yet firm as she explained the situation. The urgency in her words was conveyed with a sense of responsibility that matched the gravity of the moment.

As Ana relayed the message to the police stations, Rodrigo wasted no time. He rose from his seat, determination etched across his features, and headed towards his Renault Triber SUV, he would be driving along with Antonio to Villa Carvalho, Hugo's residence.

Antonio seated beside him, Rodrigo sped his Renault SUV with a sense of urgency as they maneuvered the winding roads headed towards Vagator. They were driven by a shared concern for their enigmatic host. There was lingering sense of unease in both of them, like the pages of an unturned chapter waiting to reveal the secrets.

After a 20-minute ride in Renault SUV, Rodrigo and Antonio arrived at their destination: Villa Carvalho, Hugo's residence. The journey from Calangute to Vagator had been swift, a blur of winding roads and coastal scenery. With a sense of urgency, they pulled up by the front gate, the gravel on the side road before hitting the paved driveway crunching beneath the tires.

Without hesitation, they rushed over to the front door of Villa Carvalho. Their concern for Hugo weighed heavy on their minds, propelling them forward. Rodrigo's hand reached out to ring the doorbell, its chime echoing through the tranquil air.

But there was no response, only the stillness of the residence. This silence, in stark contrast to the animated tales they had witnessed on the video recording, sent a shiver down their spines. Their previous visits to Hugo's home had ingrained in them the knowledge that the living room couldn't be seen from the front door.

Determined and with growing trepidation, they skirted around the side of the villa, following a meandering garden path. In the distance, they could see the silhouette of the villa's garden window—a portal to the enigma that awaited them within.

As they approached the garden window, their hearts sank at the sight that greeted them. Through the glass, they beheld Hugo, seated in the same position as he had been in the video recording. His left arm cradled Maria, holding her in a tight embrace, while his other arm lay motionless on the sofa beside him. It was as though time had stood still in the living room, preserving the tableau of what they had watched in the last few minutes of recording in the IT room at the office.

Their sense of concern deepened, and they exchanged worried glances, their thoughts racing. Before they could contemplate further, the distinctive sound of a police jeep approaching cut through the stillness.

Turning their attention to the front door, they hurried to meet the law enforcement officers who had arrived in response to their call. Together, they stood before Villa Carvalho, united in their shared apprehension, as the enigma of Hugo's unchanging state unfolded before them.

The police officers also repeated what Rodrigo and Antonio had done earlier, rang the front doorbell, but there was no response. They attempted a push on the front door with a click on the latch, to their surprise the front door swung open, it wasn't locked. The police officers asked Rodrigo and Antonio to wait outside as they entered the home and then into the living room.

While Rodrigo and Antonio anxiously waited outside the front door, one of the police officers came out speaking on his phone in Konkani, "Please send forensics and ambulance team urgently to our Hugo Carvalho's home here in Vagator, he is not responding.".

After ending the phone call, the officer turned to Rodrigo who was standing right in front of him and introduced himself speaking in Konkani, "I am Inspector Alfonso Cunha, the station house officer for Anjuna/Vagator station. Someone from Hugo's office in Calangute by name Ana called into our office, we had gone on patrol and headed over here immediately once we received the radio dispatch message."

Inspector Cunha, almost everyone here in Vagator area knows about Hugo's channel and subscribes to it. Rodrigo introduces himself as executive producer for Veritas Unveiled, Antonio steps forward and Rodrigo introduces him as IT tech lead for the channel.

Rodrigo asks, can we go inside and see Hugo. Inspector Cunha, sorry nobody can enter the house till the forensics team arrives and collects all the necessary data. The ambulance is also coming to check on Hugo, he doesn't seem to be breathing, so we will find out more once the teams check on Hugo.

Inspector Cunha sees that Antonio is trying to dial on his phone, nobody should be speaking on their phones or trying to contact anyone until the forensics and ambulance teams arrive and check on Hugo, we don't want any false news spreading around. Antonio nodding and in agreement keeps the phone back in his jeans pocket.

While distracted in discussion with Inspector Cunha, Rodrigo has missed a couple of calls from Ana, but he's been ordered not to speak. Antonio's phone also has missed calls from Ana. Both Rodrigo and Antonio have not been responding to Ana's calls.

As the afternoon sun hung high in the sky, the forensics team and ambulance arrived with a solemn sense of purpose. Rodrigo and Antonio, usually accustomed to the vibrant presence of their boss, Hugo, at the office, now found themselves anxiously waiting outside the somber residence.

The distance from the usual camaraderie and conversations with Hugo felt palpable. They had spent countless days and nights in his company, unraveling the mysteries of the world and sharing moments of enlightenment. But today, their beloved host remained elusive, concealed within the walls of his own home.

Time crawled by with unbearable slowness. In about 30 agonizing minutes, the ambulance personnel emerged, carrying a bag on a stretcher—a vessel that held Hugo's lifeless form. Rodrigo and Antonio had clung to a glimmer of hope, their prayers fervent and their hearts heavy with dread. But now, as the stretcher emerged, the inevitable truth cast a long shadow upon them. Their beloved boss and friend, Hugo, had departed from this world.

A sense of profound loss washed over them, like a tidal wave crashing upon the shores of their hearts. Tears welled in their eyes, and their voices trembled as they whispered their farewells to the man who had been not just a mentor but a confidant and a friend.

In that somber moment, Inspector Cunha approached, his presence casting an even darker pall over the scene. Rodrigo and Antonio turned to him, their eyes seeking answers amidst the overwhelming grief.

With a heavy heart, Inspector Cunha spoke, delivering the grim news they had all feared. "I regret to inform you both," he began, his voice steady but empathetic, "that Hugo is no longer with us in this world."

Inspector Cunha asked Rodrigo and Antonio for their phone numbers and provided his contact number as well. We will be in touch as we investigate details around what happened to Hugo.

The weight of his words settled upon them like an anchor in a turbulent sea. The truth had been spoken, and there was no denying the irrevocable loss they now faced.

Rodrigo and Antonio nodded, their faces etched with sorrow, acknowledging the finality of the moment. They knew it was time to call their friends and colleagues, to share the heart-wrenching news that Hugo, their guiding light and anchor, had departed from their midst.

Hugo's body was gently placed into the ambulance, his final journey beginning amidst the backdrop of an afternoon sun. The vehicle departed for the hospital, carrying with it the man whose passion for knowledge and quest for truth had touched the lives of many. For now, the circumstances surrounding his passing remained a mystery, but the world had lost a luminary, leaving behind a void that could never be filled.

Rodrigo dialed back Ana responding to her missed calls to inform about Hugo's departure from this world. "We have lost Hugo, it's a sad day for all of us", Asking Ana to convey the somber news to everyone at the office.

Ana sobbing on the other end of the line, Rodrigo, are you coming back to the office, we need to communicate the news to some of the guests who are scheduled for podcasts this week.

Rodrigo, I am coming back to the office in 30 minutes, let's discuss the next steps after I come back. We have many guest bookings scheduled over the next few weeks. We also need to convey the message to Veronica who is in Portugal right now. We will call her from the office. I am driving back from Hugo's home along with Antonio and will see you all soon. Even though Rodrigo's voice had a composure while speaking, he was trying hard to hold back tears and a wave of emotions at that moment.

Chapter 22

INSPECTOR CUNHA

The drive back from Hugo's Villa Carvalho, a journey of just thirty minutes, stretched into an eternity for Rodrigo and Antonio. The somber news of their beloved host's passing weighed heavily on their minds, casting a shadow over the familiar landscape that rushed by outside the car windows. The world seemed to move in slow motion, each moment a reminder of the profound loss they had just experienced.

There were only a few words exchanged between them during the drive back. The air inside the car was heavy with the absence of Hugo's infectious laughter, the witty banter, and the spirited discussions that had filled their days at the office. In the quiet of that moment, Rodrigo and Antonio both found themselves reminiscing about the jolly spirit that Hugo had carried with him, a spirit that had brightened even the dullest of days.

The familiar sights and sounds of Calangute, which they had often taken for granted, now held a different meaning—a poignant reminder of the void that Hugo's absence had created.

As they finally reached the office in Calangute, the weight of their grief was met by a collective sense of mourning. Ana, the ever-compassionate receptionist, rushed forward to embrace Rodrigo, her tears flowing freely as she sobbed, her heart breaking for the loss they all shared.

Around them, the entrance corridors were filled with nearly the entire team of fifty people who had gathered, waiting with abated breath to hear more about Hugo. Their faces were etched with sorrow, their hearts heavy with the news that Ana had conveyed before their arrival. In the midst of this sea of faces, Rodrigo and Antonio stood as bearers of the truth, their own grief intertwined with the collective mourning of their colleagues.

The office, once a place of intellectual exploration and camaraderie, had been transformed into a somber sanctuary of remembrance. The jolly spirit of Hugo, which had been a constant presence in their lives, now lived on in the memories of those who had been touched by his passion for knowledge and his zest for life.

Amidst the solemn atmosphere of the office, as the team gathered to mourn the loss of their beloved host, Rodrigo leaned in close to Antonio. His voice, soft but determined, carried a sense of purpose that cut through the grief that hung in the air.

"Antonio," he began, his words measured, "we still need to address the matter of those multiple hours of recording. It may hold some answers, or at least some clues, to what transpired." His gaze met Antonio's, a silent agreement passing between them.

Antonio nodded in agreement, his resolve firm. "You're right, Rodrigo. And we should also contact Inspector Cunha. He needs to be made aware of this recording."

With that, Rodrigo picked up his phone and dialed Inspector Cunha's number. After a brief exchange, he conveyed the urgency of the situation. "Inspector Cunha," he said, "we need you to come over to the office as soon as possible. We have a recording that spans from 7:30 pm on December 3rd until the morning of December 4th. The camera had been recording even when we glanced into Hugo's living room from outside, as indicated by the red blinking light."

Inspector Cunha acknowledged the request with a tone of appreciation. "Thank you for letting us know about the recording," he said. "The forensics team has already collected some evidence items from Hugo's home, including the camera, tripod, wine glass, and wine bottles. They will be subjected to analysis, and once the process is complete, they will be returned to the family."

As the call concluded, Rodrigo and Antonio knew that the investigation into Hugo's passing was far from over. The recording held the potential to shed light on the enigma that surrounded those final hours, and they remained resolute in their determination to uncover the truth, not only for their own peace of mind but also as a testament to the memory of their beloved host, Hugo.

Inspector Cunha's mention of the belongings to be returned to the family stirred an urgent reminder within Rodrigo. As the weight of their loss hung heavily in the room, he realized that it was his duty to reach out to Veronica, Hugo's wife, and convey the heartbreaking news.

As he pondered this somber task, Ana approached him, her eyes brimming with concern. She could see the turmoil etched on his face and sensed the gravity of the moment. Without a word, she stood beside him, a comforting presence in the midst of their collective grief.

Rodrigo, with a heavy heart, admitted, "I've tried to contact Veronica a couple of times, Ana, while we were driving back here, but she's not responding." His voice wavered as he spoke, the realization sinking in that conveying such news would be an ordeal in itself.

Ana's concern deepened, and she offered her support. "I also tried reaching her," she said, her voice gentle and empathetic, "but no luck. Hugo mentioned just a few days ago that Veronica was expected to return from Portugal on December 7th. Perhaps she will need to make some arrangements to return earlier."

Rodrigo nodded in agreement, his thoughts racing with concern for Veronica. "You're right," he said, "we need to give her time. In the meantime, we should start making funeral arrangements."

As the reality of the situation settled in, Rodrigo knew that the days ahead would be filled with difficult decisions and emotional tribulations. They would navigate this challenging chapter together, as a team and as a family, honoring the memory of Hugo and ensuring that his final journey was as dignified as the life he had lived.

In the dimly lit IT room, where countless hours of knowledge had been processed and shared, Rodrigo and Antonio had made the decision to delve more into the enigmatic recordings. With a sense of purpose and a touch of trepidation, they settled before the screen, watching as the digital timeline unfolded.

As they played back the recordings, a sense of intrigue and melancholy filled the room. The footage revealed the passage of time, with Hugo and Maria's presence casting shadows and echoes of stories from another era. Their voices and laughter filled the space, a testament to moments that could never be recaptured.

But as the playback continued, a sudden realization struck them both. The recording had abruptly stopped on December 4th at 12:30 pm, coinciding precisely with the time when the forensics team had been inside Hugo's residence. This was also confirming what Inspector Cunha told Rodrigo over the phone earlier about the forensics team retrieving the camera and other items as proof of evidence from Hugo's home.

Nearly an hour had slipped by as Rodrigo and Antonio immersed themselves in the recordings, attempting to decipher the mysteries that lay within. Their quest for answers had only just begun, and the enigma of Hugo's final hours remained a puzzle they were determined to solve.

As they contemplated this revelation, the hushed atmosphere of the IT room was interrupted by the arrival of Inspector Cunha, accompanied by another police officer. Ana, ever vigilant, entered the room to announce their presence, her expression a mix of anticipation and respect for the investigation that was underway.

The room, once a sanctuary of knowledge and discovery, had now become the epicenter of a complex and unfolding mystery. Rodrigo and Antonio turned their attention towards Inspector Cunha, their hearts heavy with grief and their minds resolute in their pursuit of the truth.

In the dimly lit IT room, where the glow of the screen illuminated the paused playback of the somber recordings that took place in Hugo's living room, Rodrigo and Antonio stood to welcome Inspector Cunha, accompanied by another uniformed police officer and Ana. Their expressions were a mix of respect for the investigation and the collective sorrow that had enveloped the office.

With a heavy heart, Rodrigo began to explain the perplexing situation to Inspector Cunha. "Inspector," he started, his voice tinged with both grief and urgency, "this morning, around 9:30 am, Antonio brought something unusual to my attention. We discovered a recording that was transmitted onto our office servers from Hugo's living room." Rodrigo's gaze locked onto the Inspector's, conveying the gravity of the situation.

Antonio continued, his tone measured, "The recording began around 7:30 pm on December 3rd, Inspector. In this recording, you'll notice Hugo seated on the sofa at one end, and Maria standing on the opposite end." He paused for a moment, letting the weight of the revelation sink in.

Inspector Cunha, who is Maria? Rodrigo responds, Maria is the name of the robot that you may have seen in the living room while you were at Hugo's house.

Rodrigo chimed in, his words laden with an eerie sense of discovery. "What makes this recording particularly strange, Inspector, is that Maria has been personalized with the voice of Veronica, Hugo's wife, who is currently in Portugal on the

Camino Portugués pilgrimage. She's expected to return on December 7th." Rodrigo's brows furrowed with concern as he continued, "We've been trying to contact Veronica, but she's not responding to our calls."

Inspector Cunha listened intently, his expression reflecting a mix of curiosity and concern. The unfolding mystery was unlike any he had encountered before, and the presence of the unexplained recording added another layer of complexity to the situation.

As Rodrigo, Antonio, and Ana stood before the law enforcement officers, they shared the puzzling circumstances surrounding Hugo's final hours. The enigma of the recording, Maria's personalized voice, and the absence of Veronica in their efforts to reach out to her created a web of unanswered questions that demanded investigation and understanding. The truth remained elusive, lurking in the depths of the recordings and the mysteries that shrouded Hugo's last moments.

Inspector Cunha had listened attentively to Rodrigo's brief, his expression a blend of curiosity and intrigue. Rodrigo's words had painted a peculiar picture of the recording, setting the stage for a perplexing mystery.

With a nod of understanding, Inspector Cunha turned his attention to Rodrigo and said, "Please, go ahead and start playing the recording from the beginning, from 7:30 pm on December 3rd." His voice carried the gravitas of someone ready to delve into the unknown.

As the playback commenced, Antonio swiftly initiated the sequence. The screen flickered to life, casting the scene of the living room. The voices of Hugo and Maria filled the air.

In the first few minutes, a curious detail caught Inspector Cunha's attention—a mention of the name Miguel. He furrowed his brow and asked Antonio to rewind the recording for further clarification.

As they listened again to Hugo's words, Inspector Cunha inquired, "Who is Miguel, Rodrigo?" His voice held a note of intrigue, eager to unravel this enigmatic thread.

Rodrigo's response was tinged with uncertainty. "We don't know, Inspector," he admitted, his gaze locked onto the screen. "It seems like Hugo is addressing Maria as Miguel. Throughout the recording, you'll hear Hugo responding to Maria as Miguel, and this reference repeats multiple times." He paused, pondering the peculiar conundrum. "We were guessing that the robot is called Maria by Veronica and Miguel by Hugo. But whenever Hugo has talked, it's always been with the reference of Maria. It's something we need to figure out—a perplexing piece of the puzzle."

As the playback continued, the room was filled with the resonant voices of Hugo and Maria, their dialogues punctuated by the enigmatic use of Miguel's name. Inspector Cunha's presence added a sense of gravitas to the investigation, and together, they ventured deeper into the realm of the inexplicable, in search of answers that remained just beyond their grasp.

Meanwhile, Inspector Cunha's phone rang with the name 'DCP Vivek Salve ji' as was saved in his contacts. Answering the phone, 'Jai hind sir, good afternoon', we are in the office of Hugo talking to the executive producer of the show Rodrigo.

Ho…, Ho…, Ho…., understand sir…., yes sir…., we will cooperate with them sir….when are they coming?.....okay sir….ends the call

Inspector Cunha turning to Rodrigo, that was our DCP sir Salve ji calling, we will be getting some help from multiple offices for investigation, from Delhi, Mumbai and Goa main office.

Let's continue with the playback, we were in the middle of Pedro and Ines story.

Rodrigo interrupting, there are multiple parts of 1-hour video recordings, Antonio and I have watched the playback. It seems Hugo gets up from the sofa about three times and each time brings a wine bottle, it's the same one 'Puerta del sol' reserve wine, and he sits back in the same position of the sofa with Maria standing on the other end of the sofa.

Then around 12pm, about 4 hours and 30 minutes later, he is absent from the recording, only Maria is standing at one end of the sofa. He returns back to the sofa in about five minutes around 12:05am and sits next to Maria with his left hand around her, there is fado being played in the background, Maria and Hugo never speak after that. This is the same position we found Hugo and Maria today, so there is no movement after 12:15pm, so the rest of the 12 hours of the recording since that time, it's the same position with nobody speaking.

As the playback of the recording unfolded in the dimly lit IT room, Rodrigo had meticulously instructed Antonio to playback the selected key sections for summary, highlighting the moments that held the most intrigue. The room was filled with the cadence of Hugo and Veronica's voices, their dialogues punctuated by the enigmatic use of names and the telling silence of the recorded hours.

One such segment occurred at the strike of the hour, around 12:00 am, where Hugo's summary had focused. The past four hours and thirty minutes had painted multiple tales of love, but now the segment around midnight had a vivid picture of the interaction between Hugo and Maria, as they shared a moment of intimacy while listening to the haunting strains of fado. What was particularly perplexing was that the same frame of the recording continued for the next twelve hours, with no words spoken—a frozen tableau that defied explanation.

The final twelve hours of the recording, showing Hugo and Maria in the same position, had only deepened the mystery, leaving Rodrigo, Antonio, and Inspector Cunha in a state of profound intrigue.

However, as they pondered the enigma before them, Inspector Cunha received a call from the coroner's team. His expression turned serious as he listened to the update, his features reflecting the gravity of the information being conveyed.

After ending the call, Inspector Cunha turned to the others and relayed the news. "The coroner and medical team have provided an update," he began, his voice steady but laden with the weight of the revelation. "Hugo's time of death was confirmed to be somewhere between 12:00 am and 12:30 am on December 4th."

The room fell into a contemplative silence, the implications of this revelation sinking in. The playback of the recording had corroborated the timeline of Hugo's passing, aligning with the mysterious hours they had just witnessed.

As they continued to unravel the mysteries within the recording, the confluence of time, silence, and unanswered questions cast a profound and haunting shadow over their investigation, urging them onward in their quest for understanding.

Inspector Cunha, his gaze fixed on Rodrigo, spoke with a measured tone, his words carrying the weight of yet another piece in the intricate puzzle they were trying to piece together. "We've also collected another piece of evidence today, its already been processed by our forensics team for fingerprints" he said, "a notepad that was found at Hugo's residence." His eyes held a glint of anticipation, as if he sensed that this notepad might hold a clue, a revelation, or a missing link to the enigma they were unraveling.

Cunha turned to the uniformed police officer who accompanied him and issued a request. "Could you please bring the notepad from our jeep?" he asked, his voice carrying an air of anticipation. The officer nodded in acknowledgment and stepped out of the IT room, swiftly making his way to the police vehicle.

A moment later, the uniformed police officer returned, holding a transparent plastic bag that cradled the notepad within. The bag was carefully sealed, preserving the potential evidence it contained. As he handed it over to Inspector Cunha, the room seemed to hold its collective breath, as if the notepad itself might whisper secrets of its own, waiting to be uncovered.

In that quiet room, with the notepad now in their possession, the investigators poised on the brink of another discovery, eager to examine its contents and decipher any messages it might hold—messages that could shed light on the mysteries of Hugo's final hours and perhaps bring them closer to unraveling the enigmatic recording that had captivated their attention.

Chapter 23

THE NOTEPAD

With the sealed plastic bag now in his hands, Inspector Cunha carefully unsealed the transparent plastic bag, handling it with the reverence of someone who understood the potential significance of the contents within. He then extended the notepad towards Rodrigo, a silent invitation for him to examine it.

"Please, Rodrigo," Inspector Cunha urged, "flip to the last written page of the notepad. That's likely to be the most recent of the notes Hugo made."

As Rodrigo turned to the last written page, roughly twenty percent of the notepad yet to be filled, his eyes fell upon five distinct bullet points neatly penned on the paper. Each point bore the imprint of Hugo's concise thoughts from which he could craft the most interesting questions to his guests on the show, but what intrigued him—and the others in the room— was the content of those notes.

Inspector Cunha leaned in, his gaze focused intently on the notepad, and he spoke in a voice filled with intrigue, "It's rather interesting, isn't it? Those five bullet points. The first three seem to talk about crime-related matters." He gestured to the first three points with a thoughtful nod. "But what's truly perplexing," he continued, "are the last two." He indicated the final two bullet points, his finger hovering over them. "They appear to be in slightly different handwriting."

He looked towards Rodrigo, his expression a mix of curiosity and anticipation. "Does that make any sense to you?" The question hung in the air, an invitation to unravel yet another layer of the enigma that surrounded them, as they sought answers in the cryptic notes left behind by Hugo.

- The human ingenuity for doing evil things always brings elements of surprises to investigations that involves learning something new and diving deeper into technological advances.

- Every society gets the criminals it deserves.

- Every society creates the criminals it deserves.

- In the symphony of their love, as their song played, the words remained constant, unaltered by the confines of different planes. Their souls, like distant stars, reached out toward each other, separated by the vast expanse of the universe yet eternally connected by the unbreakable thread of "Amor Eterno."

- True lovers, akin to rivers winding through the earth, possess an unwavering resolve to find their way to the vast expanse of the sea. It matters not that mortals may assign varied names to these boundless oceans; in the grand design of existence, the sea remains one, a testament to the timeless and unending nature of "Amor Eterno."

Rodrigo's voice filled the room, resonating with a blend of curiosity and intrigue as he read aloud the five distinct points scrawled within the notepad. His words carried an eerie resonance, as if the enigmatic notes held secrets that were just beyond their reach.

"1) The human ingenuity for doing evil things always brings elements of surprises to investigations that involve learning something new and diving deeper into technological advances."

"2) Every society gets the criminals it deserves."

"3) Every society creates the criminals it deserves."

Rodrigo paused briefly, allowing the weight of those first three points to settle in. The content bore a stark contrast to what followed, and the distinctiveness of the last two points had not escaped their notice.

"4) In the symphony of their love, as their song played, the words remained constant, unaltered by the confines of different planes. Their souls, like distant stars, reached out toward each other, separated by the vast expanse of the universe yet eternally connected by the unbreakable thread of "Amor Eterno.""

"5) True lovers, akin to rivers winding through the earth, possess an unwavering resolve to find their way to the vast expanse of the sea. It matters not that mortals may assign varied names to these boundless oceans; in the grand design of existence, the sea remains one, a testament to the timeless and unending nature of "Amor Eterno.""

The room fell into a contemplative silence, each person present pondering the implications of the notes. Rodrigo's voice, clear and measured, had laid bare the stark difference between the first three points, which seemed to delve into the depths of human darkness, and the final two, which radiated a sense of love and unity.

Intrigue hung in the air, and the question lingered: Was it the nature of the content—evil versus love—that had prompted the change in handwriting, or did these notes hold a deeper, hidden meaning that was yet to be unraveled? The notepad, with its cryptic messages, had added another layer of complexity to the enigma they were attempting to decipher, casting shadows of uncertainty over their quest for answers.

Rodrigo looking at Inspector Cunha, in fact I may have some explanation to the few bulleted points here in this notepad. Inspector Cunha with some curiousness on his face, unsure what to expect.

I called up Hugo yesterday, Rodrigo recalled his phone conversation with Hugo the previous night, in the twilight hours of December 3rd, around 7PM, I reached out to Hugo, inquiring about his readiness for the podcast scheduled for today, that was supposed to happen around 1pm. The theme of the discussion with the local technical guest Prof. Vikram Gore, living right here in Panjim Goa, the professor was planning to bring four of his peer faculty members and this was going to be panel discussion, the episode was going to be reflections on how technology influences the evolution of criminal activities in society, that was the planned focus of the discussion that Hugo would have been recording today. But ….

During our phone conversation, Hugo assured me that he had diligently prepared for the discourse, delving into the intricate connections between technology and the ever-evolving landscape of crime. He was planning to cover the profound impact of technology, both beneficial and malevolent.

Although I didn't need to remind Hugo, I was relieved to hear that he was ready. He emphasized the need to shed light on the darker aspects of technological innovation while offering potential solutions to these modern challenges. Mainly raising awareness and advocating for responsible technology usage.

Rodrigo looking at Antonio, can you ask Ana whether she can find Ashley. Turning his gaze towards Inspector Cunha, Ashley Fernandes is our research team lead. Hugo always worked closely with research team to imbibe more information prior to any episode recording, we can ask Ashley whether any of these points mean anything to her based-on discussions with Hugo.

Ashley enters the IT room along with Antonio who had gone to get her.

Rodrigo showing Ashley the notes on the last written page, we wanted to understand if any of the notes on this page mean anything based on your discussions with Hugo

Ashley carefully reading the written notes, The first three bullets seem to be related to the topic that was going to be discussed today. Oh I didn't realize Hugo was going with this angle during today's discussion, that's very innovative.

Rodrigo looking at Inspector Cunha, during our phone call we also discussed the sensitivity of the topic, how technology impacted homicide investigations. We had agreed to exercise caution, emphasizing the need to stay within the bounds of known uses of technology to avoid inadvertently providing criminals with ideas. I was very confident there would be a responsible discourse. We had wrapped our phone call in about 10 minutes, I guess….

As Rodrigo's eyes fell upon the words "Amor eterno" in the notepad, a spark of realization flickered in his mind. The Portuguese phrase, translating to "Eternal Love," held a significance that hadn't been apparent before. He turned to Inspector Cunha with a glint of having solved a piece of the puzzle, a sudden clarity dawning upon him.

"Inspector," Rodrigo began, his voice filled with a hint of excitement and newfound understanding, "remember the recordings we were watching? The first 4 hours and 30 minutes were filled with stories of eternal love, narrated by Maria in Veronica's voice." He paused, allowing the implication of his words to settle in.

"Maybe," he continued, "just maybe, the last two points in the notepad were written by Hugo during those 4 hours and 30 minutes. There might be something to be uncovered in that recording—whether Hugo writes something in the notepad or not." Rodrigo's gaze held a sense of determination, as if he had glimpsed a potential lead in their complex investigation.

He turned to Antonio, and inquired, "Antonio, do you think we could assemble some additional team members to start watching the recordings in detail? More eyes examining the footage might uncover clues that we've missed. It's a long shot, but it's worth exploring."

In that moment, as they contemplated the connection between the notepad and the recordings, the team's resolve to uncover the truth remained undiminished. The mysteries that had enshrouded Hugo's final hours seemed to be slowly unraveling, and with each revelation, they moved one step closer to understanding the enigmatic circumstances of his passing.

Amidst the lingering grief that hung heavily over everyone in the office, Antonio wasted no time in mobilizing the team. He had a keen sense that the clues they sought might be hidden within the 4 hours and 30 minutes of recorded footage, and there was no time to waste.

With a quiet determination, Antonio had already tasked several staff members with a vital mission—to delve deeper into the recording. The plan was straightforward yet effective: to divide the 4-hour-and-30-minute span into nine distinct segments, each lasting 30 minutes. Each of the nine teams would consist of two members, and they would be responsible for scrutinizing their designated segment for any hidden information, notes, or clues.

As the plan sprang into action, a sense of purpose filled the air. The teams huddled around individual desks, each member poised in front of a screen. One chair after another was pulled closer to watch the playback, and the office became a hive of focused activity.

In this moment, the collective grief was momentarily set aside, replaced by a shared commitment to uncover the truth.

The dedication and determination of the team members were a testament to their unwavering loyalty to Hugo and their relentless pursuit of answers. The enigmatic recording held their attention, as they embarked on a journey into its depths, hoping to unearth the secrets it held, and to bring clarity to the mysteries that had shrouded their beloved host's final hours.

The nine teams gathered with a collective focus, their eyes trained on the screens, ready to delve into the 30-minute segments of the recording they were tasked to view. As they embarked on this meticulous examination, they were transported into a world of captivating stories of eternal love, narrated by Maria in Veronica's voice. The echoes of Hugo and Veronica's voices reverberated in their ears, providing a poignant reprieve from the heavy weight of grief that had settled upon them.

Over the course of about 45 minutes, the team members meticulously watched and listened, their senses absorbed in the tales of love that spanned ages. Veronica's voice, reverberating through Maria, carried a hauntingly vivid presence that touched their hearts. For some, tears welled in their eyes as they witnessed Hugo's intimate glances at Maria, and a peculiar transformation began to take place—a few of them started to see Veronica within Maria, as if the lines between the two had blurred in the midst of the stories.

Yet, despite their emotional journey and the hope of finding clues, the recording had yielded no further insights. Hugo had not written anything in the notepad that rested on the coffee table beside the wine bottle and wine glass. They watched as Hugo lifted the wine glass multiple times for toasting, whether at the end of a story or in the midst of a particularly moving moment, sometimes pouring from the wine bottle to replenish his glass.

As the teams completed their detailed examination of the recording, they couldn't help but feel a sense of bittersweet nostalgia for the moments captured on screen—moments that showcased Hugo's love for storytelling and his profound connection with Maria. Though the recording had not provided the answers they sought, it had served as a testament to the depth of Hugo's passion and the enduring bond he shared with his beloved Veronica, a bond that transcended time and space.

Chapter 24

INVESTIGATIVE ENDEAVOR

As the evening sun began its descent over Calangute, casting long shadows and painting the sky in shades of orange, the office team members of Hugo's channel, along with Rodrigo, gathered to mark the end of a long and somber day. Grief had settled upon them like a heavy shroud, and the weight of Hugo's loss had taken its toll.

In the company of Inspector Cunha, they had pieced together some fragments of information, shedding light on the circumstances surrounding Hugo's passing. The clarity they had attained thus far included the approximate time of Hugo's death, around 12:15 am on December 4th. They had discovered that Hugo had been engaged in an intimate discussion with Maria, a discussion that bore Veronica's voice, an enigmatic twist that had left them bewildered as to why Hugo had pursued this recording in that manner.

Throughout the day, they had listened to 31 eternal love stories narrated by Veronica, stories that transcended centuries and had woven a tapestry of emotions within the hearts of those who had watched and listened. However, Veronica herself remained elusive in Portugal, refusing to pick up the phone and provide answers to their pressing questions.

In their quest for understanding, investigative teams had been dispatched, flying in directly from Delhi and Mumbai to Dabolim airport. Some of them had driven from the Panjim main office to join the efforts. Inspector Cunha had succinctly briefed the teams and provided them with a glimpse of the recordings, setting the stage for their own exploration.

Antonio, with his unwavering commitment to uncover the truth, had ensured that the 4-hour-and-30-minute recording was securely placed on a server. He had then furnished the credentials to the investigative teams, granting them access to this enigmatic piece of evidence.

As the sun dipped below the horizon, leaving behind a tranquil twilight, the collective resolve of the team remained unshaken. They were determined to uncover the mysteries that had shrouded Hugo's final moments, and to find answers that had eluded them thus far. The night held the promise of further investigation, of searching for the truth amidst the shadows and silence, as they navigated the labyrinth of clues and emotions that lay before them.

Chapter 25

FRONT DESK OF HOTEL

As the clock neared 8:45 pm on December 3rd, at the Parador de Santiago de Compostela. Veronica had requested a wake-up call, and the attentive front desk staff were committed to ensuring her evening plans went as smoothly as her pilgrimage had.

At the designated time, the front desk initiated the wake-up call, and the phone in Veronica's room began to ring. The soft chime resonated through the quiet space, a gentle reminder of the evening ahead. It rang once, twice, and then again, but there was no answer. Typically, even a deeply sleeping guest would stir after 15 rings, but as the phone continued to ring, there was an eerie silence from within the room.

Maria, the diligent front desk operator, noticed this unusual silence and grew concerned. It was clear that there was no response from Veronica's room, even after roughly 30 persistent rings. Something was amiss, and it was time to take action.

Maria swiftly notified her teammate, Carlos, of the situation. Together, they pondered the possible reasons for the lack of response. Carlos suggested that Veronica might have woken earlier than the scheduled wake-up call, possibly to prepare for her evening plans, which was not uncommon for travelers.

In a decision born of both caution and consideration, Carlos recommended waiting for another 10 minutes before attempting to reach Veronica once more. It was conceivable that she was already awake, perhaps taking a leisurely shower to prepare for the evening. The front desk staff understood the importance of respecting a guest's privacy and autonomy, and they were determined to strike the right balance between providing assistance and allowing Veronica the space she needed.

With a sense of responsibility and patience, as they assisted other travelers with their queries, Maria and Carlos monitored the passing minutes, ready to offer their assistance if needed, all while hoping that Veronica would soon answer the wake-up call, ensuring her evening in Santiago de Compostela would proceed as planned.

Ten minutes passed, and the clock in the front desk office at the Parador de Santiago de Compostela showed that it was now 9 pm. Maria, the front desk operator, knew it was time to follow up on the wake-up call for Veronica's room. Concerned by the continued absence of a response, she picked up the phone once more and dialed the number for Veronica's room, hoping for an answer this time.

However, as the phone on the other end of the line continued to ring without a response, Maria felt a growing sense of unease. It was becoming increasingly apparent that something was amiss. Veronica had requested a wake-up call, and the lack of any acknowledgment or reply was unusual.

With a sense of responsibility and a hint of worry, Maria made a swift decision. She called the housekeeping team responsible for Veronica's floor, requesting their immediate assistance. It was clear that they needed to check on the guest and ensure her well-being.

Moments later, a member of the housekeeping staff arrived at Veronica's door, accompanied by Maria. They knocked, their concern deepening as the seconds passed with no response from within the room. It was a tense moment as they waited for any sign of life from behind the closed door.

With growing trepidation, they decided to take action. The housekeeping staff assisted in unlocking the door, revealing what lay inside. As the door swung open, they were met with a sight that sent a shiver down their spines.

There, lying on the bed, was Veronica, her form still and unmoving. Her eyes were peacefully closed, facing the phone, on the screen of the phone, her touch had activated the display, revealing a picture of Veronica alongside a man they did not recognize as yet—it was none other than Hugo. However, neither Maria nor the housekeeper yet knew the identity of the man in the photograph, their primary concern at that moment being the safety of the guest who lay before them, unresponsive and still.

In the somber silence of Veronica's room at the Parador de Santiago de Compostela, Maria knew that the situation had taken a grave turn. Panic welled up within her as she realized that Veronica remained unresponsive on the bed, her eyes closed, oblivious to the world around her. Maria understood that immediate action was imperative.

With trembling hands, Maria reached for the phone and swiftly dialed Carlos's extension at the front desk. Her voice quivered as she explained the urgency of the situation, her words a desperate plea for assistance. She implored Carlos to send help to Veronica's room without delay, knowing that time was of the essence.

As the seconds ticked by, and with no time to spare, Maria knew that further action was required. She took a deep breath, her fingers trembling as she dialed the emergency number, 112, the lifeline that could bring swift assistance in times of crisis in Spain. Her heart raced as she recounted the details of the situation to the emergency personnel on the other end of the line. She explained the unresponsive guest, the repeated attempts to rouse her, and the deep concern that something was seriously amiss.

The voice on the emergency line assured Maria that help was on the way, their tone calm and reassuring in the face of uncertainty. In a mere matter of minutes, the first responders arrived at the Parador de Santiago de Compostela, their arrival marked by the sound of sirens and the urgency of their mission.

With practiced efficiency, the emergency personnel entered Veronica's room, their trained eyes assessing the situation. However, despite their best efforts, they too found themselves unable to rouse her, and the room remained shrouded in an unsettling stillness.

In those tense moments, hope and despair hung in the air, intertwined with a sense of helplessness. The presence of Veronica, lying unmoving on the bed, seemed to defy explanation, leaving all who witnessed it in a state of deep concern and uncertainty.

As the minutes wore on, a somber procession of forensics experts and detectives arrived at Veronica's room at the Parador de Santiago de Compostela, their arrival marked by an air of gravity and the hushed conversations that accompanied their presence. The initial assessment by the ambulance first responders had left them with unsettling questions, and they knew that a more thorough investigation was required to uncover the truth behind Veronica Carvalho's condition.

The paramedics, their expressions etched with solemnity, relayed their findings to the detectives. Veronica, it was tragically revealed, had succumbed to her death. The room, once a place of anticipation and plans, had become a scene of investigation and inquiry. The cause of her passing remained shrouded in mystery, and further analysis was deemed necessary to shed light on the circumstances that had led to this untimely tragedy.

Within the next 30 minutes, the team of professionals was prepared to leave, and Veronica's lifeless body was carefully placed in a bag, a poignant reminder of the fragility of existence. The ambulance stood ready to transport her to the nearest hospital, where the next steps in handling her remains and conducting a thorough post-mortem examination would take place.

Amidst the solemn proceedings, the detectives turned their attention to the personal belongings that remained in the room.

Veronica's phone, an unassuming device that had played a role in the unfolding events, drew their focus. With the benefit of biometric technology, they were able to unlock the phone, granting them access to its contents.

Julian, one of the detectives, scanned the call history on Veronica's phone, his eyes narrowing as he perused the list of recent calls. It was then that his attention was drawn to a particular entry—a recent call made to a name that seemed to hold significance. The name on the screen sent a shiver down his spine: Hugo. Julian was quick to make the connection based on the screen saver photo that bore the resemblance, as he thought, is this Hugo i will be calling. Julian was a subscriber to Hugo's channel and had watched multiple episodes of this famed host.

Julian, the detective knew that the unfolding investigation would require not only meticulous analysis but also a search for clues in the relationships and connections that had defined Veronica's life in her final moments. The hotel staff had informed him that Veronica had just checked in the afternoon after her Camino Portugues and had requested for a wake-up call.

With a sense of gravitas and a sense of urgency, Julian, the detective, dialed the number associated with the name "Hugo" that had been gleaned from Veronica's recent call log. The seconds ticked away as the phone rang on the other end, but there was no response. It was as if the call had vanished into the ether, leaving Julian with a growing sense of uncertainty.

As he stood in Veronica's room, his mind began to wander, contemplating the possibilities surrounding Hugo's whereabouts. He couldn't help but wonder whether Hugo had been traveling with Veronica, accompanying her on her pilgrimage along the Camino Portugués, although the hotel staff had briefed that Veronica had checked in alone. The lack of response on the other end of the line left a void in the narrative, and Julian was left to piece together the puzzle of their connection.

Drawing on the information available, Julian recalled that Hugo had been known to conduct his podcasts from Goa, India, where his studio was located. He often referred to it in his episodes, welcoming his guests with the phrase, "Welcome to our studio in Calangute, Goa." Many of his podcast guests had also praised the picturesque locale of his studio and office.

Considering the time difference between Spain and India, Julian realized that it was now past midnight in Goa. It was unlikely that Hugo would be readily available to take the call at this hour. With a sigh of resignation, Julian decided to postpone his attempt to reach Hugo until the following morning when the time zones would align more favorably.

Before ending his efforts for the night, Julian sent a text message to Hugo, introducing himself as a detective and urging him to contact him urgently regarding an incident in Santiago de Compostela, Spain. With this message sent into the digital ether, Julian hoped that it would reach Hugo and that the morning light would bring the answers and cooperation they needed to unravel the mysteries surrounding Veronica's untimely demise.

Chapter 26

JULIAN'S DECEMBER 4TH

Throughout the night, as the world around him slept, the face of Veronica remained etched in Julian's mind. He had encountered countless scenarios in his line of work, but each one carried its own unique weight, its own aura of mystery. The weight of the unknown, the haunting gaze of a life that had been extinguished prematurely, lingered in his thoughts.

With the first rays of dawn breaking through the curtains, Julian stirred from his fitful sleep. He knew that there was much work to be done, and he couldn't afford to let the specter of the previous night's discovery paralyze him. Rising from his bed, he checked his phone, a ritual that had become a daily routine, and he was met with a disheartening sight—there were no responses to his calls or text from Hugo.

Determined to unravel the mystery, Julian prepared himself for the day ahead. He knew that the key to understanding Veronica's story lay in the meticulous work of forensics, coroners, and the hospital staff. Their expertise and insights would be invaluable in piecing together the puzzle of her demise.

As he made his way to the police station, located in the historic Casco Antiguo, the old part of town, Julian's mind raced with questions. The city itself seemed to carry an air of ancient wisdom, its cobblestone streets bearing witness to centuries of stories and secrets.

To his surprise, as he entered the office around 8:30 am, Julian found the chief of police already present. His note from the prior night, hastily scrawled but filled with urgency, lay on the chief's desk. It had been a cryptic message: "There is some connection of Veronica to Hugo, who is the famous podcaster, YouTuber, and influencer on the internet." Julian knew that the chief would have questions, and together, they would need to navigate the complex web of connections that had brought them to this point.

With determination and the weight of responsibility on his shoulders, Julian knew that the day ahead held the promise of answers, but also the potential for deeper mysteries to unfold. The story of Veronica Carvalho and her connection to Hugo was a puzzle waiting to be solved, and he was prepared to unravel it, piece by piece, no matter where it led.

Julian sat across from the chief of police, ready to share the events that had transpired the previous night. The room bore witness to the weighty discussion that was about to unfold, and Julian began with a quick but concise summary of the unfolding investigation.

Julian recounted the initial steps they had taken upon their arrival at the Parador de Santiago de Compostela, where Veronica's lifeless body had been discovered. The grim scene had led to the involvement of forensics, coroners, and hospital staff, all working together to uncover the truth behind her tragic demise.

With a sense of urgency, Julian detailed how they had unlocked Veronica's phone, hoping to find some clues that might shed light on the circumstances surrounding her death. He mentioned that a call and a text message had been placed to a name listed in the recent call log of Veronica's phone— Hugo, about whom Julian had left a note for the chief citing he was a popular youtuber, podcaster and influencer on the internet. However, there had been no response from Hugo, leaving him with more questions than answers.

While Julian presented his account to the chief in Santiago de Compostela, on the distant shores of Goa, India, a parallel thread of the story was unfolding. Hugo's phone, a vital piece of the puzzle, had been collected by Inspector Cunha and was now safely secured in the evidence room, but the phone was completely out of charge waiting to be plugged in for revealing the phone calls and text from Spain. Inspector Cunha's investigation had led them to Hugo's office in Calangute Beach, where the recordings of his podcasts held potential clues that could help unravel the mysteries at hand.

In this intricate web of connections, Julian and Inspector Cunha were both diligently working toward a common goal— the truth. As the investigation continued on two continents, the elusive answers to Veronica's fate were still hidden, waiting to be uncovered within the echoes of recordings and the digital trails left behind. The story had much in store, and the path ahead remained shrouded in uncertainty and intrigue.

Chapter 27

VAGATOR ANJUNA STATION

As the night bore its tranquil spell on the coastal landscape of Goa, Inspector Cunha led the convoy of investigative teams back to the Vagator Anjuna police station. The journey was marked by a sense of purpose, as the officers from Delhi, Mumbai, and the main Panjim division gathered together, each with a determination to solve the puzzle.

At the station, they began the meticulous process of processing the evidence items collected from Hugo's residence. The forensics team had already processed the items collected from the residence, wine bottles and wine glass bore only the fingerprints of Hugo, reaffirming his presence in the intimate setting where his final moments had unfolded.

In one of the bags, among the collected evidence, rested Hugo's phone. Upon closer inspection, the team noticed that the phone was completely dead, its screen dark and unresponsive. With a sense of curiosity, they decided to charge it, connecting it to a power source.

As the phone came to life, the screen illuminating in the room, revealed a series of notifications that had gone unnoticed until now. Multiple missed phone calls and text messages had accumulated, and they were all from Spain, specifically from Santiago de Compostela.

The name "Julian" identifying himself as detective, asking Hugo to contact him urgently regarding an incident stood out among the text message, hinting at a connection that had previously eluded them. The discovery of these missed communications raised new questions and possibilities, their significance yet to be unveiled. Amidst the glow of the phone's screen, the mysteries surrounding Hugo's final hours, urging the investigative teams to delve even deeper into the enigma that had taken hold of their investigation and now with a connection to Spain and Julian.

Under the directive of DCP Salve, Inspector Cunha and the other members of the investigative team had awaited the arrival of the senior most member, Akash Tripathi, who had traveled from Mumbai to join them in their pursuit of answers. As the evening's shadows deepened and the room was bathed in the soft glow of ambient light, they observed the senior detective, Tripathi, poised to make a crucial call.

With a sense of anticipation hanging in the air, Akash Tripathi dialed the number for Julian in Santiago de Compostela. After a few tense moments, a voice on the other end of the line answered, "Hello, this is Julian."

Akash Tripathi, in his calm and authoritative tone, identified himself, "This is Akash Tripathi calling you from Goa, India. We noticed that you had called Hugo's phone and left a message mentioning an urgency regarding an incident."

Julian was sitting alongside the chief in the room of the Santiago de Compostela police station, their minds were consumed by the enigma that was Veronica's tragic story. This was a call they were expecting to get them some answers to the complex puzzle.

Senior Detective Akash Tripathi on the line, and both their hearts quickened, the urgency of their exchange palpable. Julian offered a concise summary of the events that had transpired with Veronica, the grim discovery at the Parador, and the attempts to contact Hugo, all the while conveying their condolences.

On the other end of the line, Senior Detective Tripathi paused, his voice weighted with somber news. He informed Julian that they too had news to share, and it was nothing short of heartbreaking. Hugo, the enigmatic figure whose connection to Veronica as a loving husband, had passed away just the day before, in the confines of his own residence. The news was a shock, a revelation that cast a pall over the ongoing investigation.

Julian listened in stunned silence as Senior Detective Tripathi explained that they had powered up Hugo's phone after his passing and had just found Julian's contact information amongst the missed calls and text message. The two detectives, separated by continents yet united in their pursuit of the truth, now faced the task of unraveling a double mystery—Veronica's tragic end in Spain and the circumstances surrounding Hugo's untimely demise in Goa.

A discussion ensued, lasting for nearly 20 minutes, as Inspector Cunha and other members of the investigative team in Goa eagerly waited to hear the details gleaned from the phone call to Spain. The conversation carried a weighty significance, as it held the potential to illuminate the intertwined fates of two individuals who had shared an intimate connection of loving wife and husband until a few hours ago. There were many pieces that were slowly coming together, but the full picture remained just beyond their grasp, waiting to be revealed through shared insights and collaborative efforts.

Under the moonlit night sky, Inspector Cunha and the investigative team prepared to make their way to Hugo's residence. The convoy of jeeps was ready, and the anticipation was palpable as they embarked on this significant journey.

As they approached Villa Carvalho, the scene that unfolded before them was both poignant and unexpected. A massive bouquet of flowers had been placed at the entrance to Hugo's driveway, surrounded by an array of flickering candlelights. The sight was a testament to the outpouring of grief and respect from those who had been touched by Hugo's life and work.

Close to a hundred visitors had gathered in the vicinity, even though the hour was late. They stood in quiet vigil, paying their respects to the beloved host whose voice had resonated in their lives for so long.

Inspector Cunha led the investigative team past the caution tape that had been placed at the entrance, signifying the official nature of their visit. As they entered Hugo's home, they were met by police officers who had been on vigilant watch throughout the evening.

One of the officers informed them that there had been a constant stream of visitors since the news of Hugo's passing had spread. The crowd had only recently started to dwindle, as the night had grown deeper. The scene bore witness to the profound impact Hugo had made on the lives of those who had followed his channel, and it was a reminder of the legacy he had left behind—a legacy that would be both cherished and investigated in the days to come.

The investigative team entered Hugo's living room and his residence with a sense of solemn purpose. Their trained eyes meticulously scanned every nook and cranny, taking in every minute detail of the surroundings. They paused for an extended moment near the sofa, where Maria was srill standing as they had observed in the recordings earlier at Hugo's office in Calangute. It was as if they were trying to recreate the scene, seeking any subtle clues or insights that might have eluded them on video.

In the present, Maria stood still by the side of the sofa, a silent witness to the events that had unfolded in this room. Hugo, after his passing, had been taken to the hospital for further examination, leaving behind an atmosphere of anticipation as everyone in the investigative team eagerly awaited the details of the examination. Hugo's death remained shrouded in mystery, and they were determined to uncover the truth.

Across the vast distance, in Spain, Julian also awaited news of Veronica's examination. Their worlds were connected by an incident that spanned continents, and the answers they sought were now intertwined. As the investigations on both sides progressed, the quest for clarity and closure drew them closer together, even as the secrets of the past and present continued to unravel.

Chapter 28

LEVELS & SOLITARY PRESENCE

In the vast and intricate landscape of human physiology, potassium (K), a humble element, plays a crucial role in maintaining the delicate balance that keeps our bodies functioning optimally. But like any good story, when potassium levels soar to excessive heights, chaos ensues, and the narrative takes on a dark twist.

Hyperkalemia - A Silent Threat, a medical term that might not ring a bell for most, yet it's a condition that poses a significant threat to the human heart. It's the presence of abnormally high levels of potassium in the blood. This element is essential for maintaining proper cell function, especially in muscle cells, including the heart.

The High Potassium Content has its links to heart failure. In our bloodstream, potassium levels are tightly regulated by various mechanisms. When the balance tilts towards excess potassium, the stage is set for a dangerous performance. Hyperkalemia becomes a ticking time bomb due to its potential to disrupt the electrical signals governing the heart's rhythmic contractions.

Potassium is crucial for the heart's electrical stability. It helps establish the resting membrane potential in cardiac cells, enabling them to contract in a coordinated manner. But when potassium levels rise, it throws this equilibrium into disarray. Excess potassium can interfere with the normal depolarization and repolarization processes, which are responsible for each heartbeat. As a result, the heart may start to exhibit erratic and potentially life-threatening rhythms, such as ventricular fibrillation.

The true danger of hyperkalemia often lies in its silent progression. Patients might not notice any symptoms until their potassium levels have reached a critical point. However, when symptoms do manifest, they can be subtle at first but may escalate rapidly.

Hyperkalemia can lead to muscle weakness, making even simple tasks like lifting objects or walking upstairs a herculean effort.

Can cause fatigue, a feeling of being exceptionally tired and lethargic, which can be mistaken for general exhaustion.

As the heart's electrical system becomes compromised, irregular heartbeats occur, signaling an impending cardiac crisis.

A feeling of tingling and numbness.

Shortness of breath occurs as the heart struggles to pump effectively, leading to inadequate oxygen delivery to the body. Hyperkalemia can sometimes affect mental clarity and cognitive function.

If the kidneys are not working well, hyperkalemia can culminate in cardiac arrest, a life-threatening emergency.

The high potassium content that leads to the risk of heart failure is a stark reminder of the delicate biochemical balance that sustains life.

On the first day, as the sun began its descent on the horizon, casting long shadows along the Camino Portugués, Veronica found herself in the last hour of her challenging hike from Porto to Vila do Conde. Her steps had become heavy, her legs ached, and the backpack on her shoulders felt like a burden she could hardly bear. She had pushed herself to the limit, and there was still about an hour of walking left for the day.

Just when she felt like she could hardly take another step, a gentle voice broke the silence that had enveloped her. An old man, with silver hair and a warm smile, had appeared from behind and started walking by Veronica's side.

"Hello there," he greeted her, his voice carrying a sense of kindness, camaraderie, sense of wisdom and experience, and a smile that was filled with energy.

Veronica, taken aback by the unexpected company, managed a tired smile. "Hi," she replied, her voice reflecting both exhaustion and gratitude for the companionship she was getting.

The man introduced himself as Miguel. He introduced as having been on the Camino multiple times, and it showed in the way he moved with ease along the path.

As they got into a conversation, Miguel's stories of his own Camino journeys were like a soothing balm for Veronica's weary soul. He spoke of the beauty of the landscapes, the kindness of strangers, and the profound sense of introspection that the pilgrimage offered.

Then, with a gesture of generosity, Miguel reached into his own backpack and pulled out an unopened, completely sealed packet of sports energy drink concentrate. The packaging gleamed in the soft glow of the setting sun.

"Here," he said, extending the packet toward Veronica. "This can help with some of the bodily pain and provide you with the energy you need. It contains essential electrolytes."

Veronica was touched by Miguel's kindness. She accepted the packet with gratitude, her eyes shimmering with appreciation.

"Thank you so much," she said, her voice filled with genuine appreciation.

Miguel smiled warmly. "It's my pleasure. Remember to follow all the instructions on the packet, take it every day in the morning and evening. It'll help replenish your strength for the journey ahead."

As they continued to walk together, the conversation flowed effortlessly between them. Miguel shared more insights about the Camino, offering tips and encouragement that seemed tailor-made for Veronica's journey.

Eventually, as they approached Vila do Conde and the sun dipped below the horizon, casting a warm, golden glow over the coastal town, Miguel mentioned that he needed to take a different route.

"Vila do Conde is just ahead," he said, gesturing toward the town in the distance. "I have to head in a different direction now. But I wish you all the best on your pilgrimage, Veronica. May your journey be filled with profound discovery and transformation."

Veronica nodded, her heart warmed by Miguel's kindness and wisdom. "Thank you, Miguel. You've been a true companion on this first day of my Camino."

With a final nod and a parting smile, Miguel bid her goodbye and turned down a separate path, leaving Veronica to continue her walk into Vila do Conde with renewed energy, a packet of electrolytes in her hand, and a newfound sense of camaraderie forged on the Camino.

Veronica's Camino Portugués from Porto to Santiago de Compostela involved daily twenty-plus mile treks through the picturesque Portuguese and Spanish countryside. She could complete her first few days on the camino with the assistance of sports energy concentrate in the morning and evening, this was a necessity to replenish her energy to cover the long days of walking. On the sixth day, Veronica thought she would add an additional dose of sports energy concentrate in the afternoon after lunch, clearly exceeding the daily consumption limit cited on the packet. Her first Whispers of Discomfort came on this sixth day of her journey when Veronica began to notice something peculiar. Her legs, accustomed to the relentless rhythm of the trail, were starting to feel heavy, as though laden with invisible weights. At first, she dismissed it as normal fatigue, part and parcel of the Camino experience. But as the days passed, her fatigue deepened. Her legs trembled slightly during ascents, and her usually brisk pace had slowed to a deliberate plod. Her fellow pilgrims, noticing her struggles, offered encouraging words and suggestions to ease her discomfort. She continued taking an additional dose clearly surpassing the daily limit consumption as listed on the packet.

Veronica pressed on as the days rolled by, undeterred by her body's protestations. The allure of the Camino, with its ancient churches, picturesque villages, and the promise of self-discovery, was too strong to resist. She had come so far and was determined to complete her pilgrimage.

Since the sixth day, each morning, afternoon and evening, Veronica would rehydrate and rejuvenate herself with a special electrolyte drink. This was a necessity for Veronica to even complete her daily walk, it was meant to replenish the minerals lost during the long hikes. But exceeding the daily consumption limit and unbeknownst to her, this concoction contained potassium supplements, which would inadvertently exacerbate her condition due to overconsumption beyond the daily limit, this acted as an immediate replenisher of energy but an accidental elixir.

On the ninth day, as Veronica approached Santiago de Compostela, her body delivered a clear message. Her heart, usually a steady drum, began to falter. She felt a strange fluttering sensation in her chest, like a bird trying to escape its cage. Her palms grew clammy, and her breath became shallow and erratic, the silent intruder was now revealing.

Veronica, determined to reach her destination, mistook these unsettling symptoms for the culmination of her physical exertion. She was just a stone's throw away from the Cathedral of Santiago de Compostela, the holy grail of her journey, and she couldn't bear to stop now.

With sheer determination and unwavering faith, she completed her pilgrimage, walking through the grandiose doors of the cathedral. But inside, amid the chants and prayers of fellow pilgrims, her condition had worsened. Unbeknownst to her, she had a condition of hyperkalemia. Her potassium levels had reached critical heights, endangering her heart's rhythm. The electrolyte drink, intended to sustain her, had inadvertently caused her downfall.

She had mistaken the symptoms of hyperkalemia for the strains of her pilgrimage, and in doing so, had walked dangerously closer to the precipice. The levels on the scale had already tipped.

On a celebratory note of having completed the Camino Portugues. Veronica indulged herself in a sumptuous lunch that was high in potassium content. The Spanish Galician cuisine known for its rich flavors and use of fresh ingredients, particularly seafood, wouldn't have done her any harm by itself, but Veronica's level had already tipped. Her lunch involved the most tastiest of food found anywhere in the world.

Sweet Potato and Lentil Stew: A hearty Galician-style stew with sweet potatoes, lentils, and leafy greens like spinach or Swiss chard, simmered in a flavorful broth.

Avocado and Mango Salad: A fresh salad with ripe avocados and mangoes, tossed with black beans and a zesty dressing made from vegetable juice and a hint of chocolate for depth.

Broccoli and Pumpkin Quiche: A savory Galician quiche made with a creamy mixture of broccoli, pumpkin, and baked beans, baked in a flaky pastry crust.

Papaya and Lentil Curry: A flavorful Galician curry with papaya, lentils, and a tomato-based sauce, served with white potatoes on the side.

Chocolate-Covered Banana Empanadas: A sweet twist on the traditional Galician empanadas, these are filled with chocolate-covered bananas and served as a delightful dessert option.

In the intricate tapestry of human anatomy, there existed another hidden marvel, this often is unnoticed until circumstances force its revelation. For the remarkable individuals born with only one kidney, life's journey begins with a unique narrative. The anatomy of these humans, an example of resilience, adaptability, and the discovery of a solitary kidney—an embodiment of the remarkable 1 in 1000 people of the world population impacted by renal agenesis.

For many born with just a single kidney, their condition remains an uncharted territory, a secret tenant dwelling quietly within. Unlike other congenital disorders that announce their presence with a noticeable mark, a solitary kidney is a stealthy anomaly. It often evades detection for years, sometimes decades, until fate intervenes.

There are numerous stories, one such story is of Alex Turner, a vibrant, active individual whose life was suddenly disrupted by a seemingly innocuous incident. While enjoying a friendly game of football with friends, a stray collision resulted in a sharp pain in his lower back. The excruciating discomfort led him to seek medical attention, fearing a minor injury.

The doctor ordered an X-ray to examine the extent of the injury. The image on the screen, however, revealed something far more profound than a mere sports injury. There it was, clear as day—a single kidney, alone in its glory, performing the Herculean task meant for two.

Alex's world momentarily stood still. He was living with a solitary kidney, a condition he had been blissfully unaware of until that very moment. The revelation opened a floodgate of questions and uncertainty.

Born with one kidney, or renal agenesis, as the medical fraternity termed it, is a marvel of a condition in itself, where one kidney fails to develop in utero. Fortunately, the human body is a marvel of adaptability. In most cases, a solitary kidney is fully capable of carrying out the tasks originally meant for two.

Life with one kidney might not be drastically different from having two, but it does come with a set of unique considerations. Individuals like Alex must be vigilant about their kidney health. Maintaining a healthy lifestyle, staying well-hydrated, and avoiding excessive alcohol and certain medications become crucial habits.

For some, this revelation can be life-altering, leading to newfound perspectives on health and well-being. It serves as a constant reminder of the resilience that resides within, hidden beneath the surface until called upon.

The stories of those living with one kidney often evolve into tales of inspiration, demonstrating the resilience of the human spirit. They learn to cherish the gift of life's adaptability, and in doing so, discover their own singular strength.

As Alex and countless others have realized, the singular kidney is not a limitation but a testament to the beauty of human diversity. Their journeys are marked not by their medical condition, but by the strength, courage, and adaptability that define their paths.

In the chapters of their lives, the solitary kidney is not a silent companion; it is a constant reminder of their singular strength—a testament to the remarkable resilience of the human body and spirit.

In the intricate narrative of life, Veronica and Hugo walked a unique path, bearing within them a singular secret, like hidden treasures waiting to be unearthed. Since birth, they had been entrusted with a solitary kidney, a condition medically known as renal agenesis. Unbeknownst to them, this enigmatic anomaly had nestled within their bodies, elusive and undetectable, quietly shaping the chapters of their existence.

Unlike many whose solitary kidney is unveiled unexpectedly, Veronica and Hugo's unique condition remained veiled in obscurity. Their solitary kidneys, like rare and precious jewels concealed beneath layers of rock, remained untouched by the probing light of medical scrutiny. For them, life's journey carried on, and the secret within lay dormant, its existence known only to the innermost chambers of their bodies.

As they traversed the meandering roads of existence, their hearts, bearing the solemn responsibility of sustaining their lives, occasionally stumbled in silence. Unbeknownst to them, the delicate balance of potassium in their bloodstream was a hidden specter, capable of orchestrating unexpected cardiac discord. Hyperkalemia, a treacherous condition that could tip the scales of life and death, lingered silently, masked by their solitary kidneys.

The undetected heart palpitations, the fleeting moments of breathlessness, the occasional fatigue that crept into their lives—these were not mere random fluctuations in the symphony of their existence. They were the subtle whispers of a condition lurking beneath the surface, a condition whose diagnosis remained obscured, hidden in the shadow of their solitary kidneys.

In the grand tapestry of life's uncertainties, the solitary kidney was a silent guardian and an elusive sentinel. Its existence held profound significance, akin to the undiscovered depths of human resilience. Veronica and Hugo, unknowing protagonists in this tale, were yet to uncover the profound meaning behind their singular kidneys.

Their journey was a testament to the unfathomable complexity of the human body, where mysteries lay concealed until life's unpredictable turns brought them to light. In the realm of their solitary kidneys and the shadowy specter of hyperkalemia, they moved forward, their hearts beating to the rhythm of life, oblivious to the narratives woven within their very beings.

Alcoholic cardiomyopathy, abbreviated as ACM, isn't a sudden tempest that sweeps through one's life with fury and haste. It's rather a gradual erosion, a quiet unraveling of the heart's resilience over the course of years. It's a story etched in subtleties, in the slow accrual of damage that goes unnoticed until it can no longer be ignored.

In the early days, the signs are mere whispers—nagging fatigue after a few drinks, an occasional flutter in the chest that can be shrugged off as nothing more than a fleeting discomfort. For Hugo, ACM took root in the mundane rituals of life.

Hugo had been a social drinker, nothing more. An occasional glass of wine with friends, a celebratory toast at family gatherings—it was all part of the fabric of his existence. He had never seen himself as a heavy drinker, never crossed the line into the realm of excess. Yet, his heart bore the weight of the choices.

It was the subtle transformation of heart muscle that was the hallmark of ACM. Over the years, as alcohol coursed through his veins, his heart had undergone a metamorphosis. It had stretched itself, trying to accommodate the demands of his lifestyle. But the heart was not an infinitely elastic organ, and as it expanded, it grew weaker, like a rubber band stretched beyond its limit.

The damage was insidious, unfurling in the hidden chambers of his heart over the past few months since August of this year. Scar tissue formed, replacing healthy muscle. The walls of his heart thinned, and its pumping ability diminished. Blood, the life force that once coursed through his body with vitality, now moved sluggishly, unable to meet the demands of his organs.

The symptoms crept up on Hugo gradually. At first, it was just the shortness of breath during the brisk evening walks in the garden—a minor annoyance that he chalked up as a long tiring day at work. Then came the persistent fatigue, as if a weight pressed down on his shoulders with every step he took.

Nights were punctuated by the erratic rhythm of his heart, the steady beat of his own mortality.

Hugo, a podcaster, influencer and YouTuber, had made his mark on the digital landscape. When his subscribers had surged past the impressive milestone of 5 million, he had enthusiastically decided to take his operations to the next level. Thus, an office had sprouted in the sun-kissed coastal town of Calangute, Goa. What had started as a two-person endeavor along with Veronica had blossomed into a thriving hub, housing a dedicated staff of 50 individuals.

In the world of digital content creation, Hugo's ascent was nothing short of meteoric. Over the course of multiple years, the subscriber count had skyrocketed from that initial 5 million to an impressive 20 million. It was a remarkable journey, though slightly more gradual than the anticipated trajectory of 50 million subscribers that Hugo had envisioned, considering the exponential growth he had witnessed while operating his podcast from the humble confines of his home in Vagator.

The earnings generated by Hugo's podcast, however, were not sufficient to sustain such a sizable staff. Yet, Hugo's heart was as big as his ambitions, and he never once contemplated trimming the workforce. He cared deeply for the team that had grown alongside him, recognizing their unwavering dedication and the indispensable role they played in his success.

But, as is often the case in the tumultuous world of content creation, success came at a cost. The pressure to deliver, to meet the ever-increasing demands of a burgeoning audience, weighed heavily on Hugo's shoulders. It was a burden he bore willingly, but it took a toll on him nonetheless.

To cope with the mounting stress, Hugo had turned to a modest indulgence—two glasses of wine, imbibed approximately four times a week. It seemed a harmless ritual, a means of unwinding in the midst of chaos. However, as the months passed, those glasses of wine unwittingly sowed the seeds of his undoing.

Alcoholic cardiomyopathy (ACM), a condition Hugo had scarcely given thought to, seized the opportunity to infiltrate his weakened heart. Over the course of just four months, his heart deteriorated further, exacerbated by the alcohol he had turned to as solace.

The once vibrant and ambitious Hugo found himself ensnared in a cycle of stress and self-medication, a silent struggle that mirrored the quiet unraveling of his heart. The very passion that had propelled him to great heights now threatened to consume him.

Hugo's story was a poignant reminder of the price one could pay for ambition and empathy. As he faced the consequences of his choices, both professional and personal, the walls of his office in Calangute bore witness to the dedication of a man who had cared too much to let go, even when it meant sacrificing his own well-being.

Hugo should have visited his doctor for a regular checkup, but the busy schedules at work made it tough. It was a journey marked not by dramatic crescendos but by the quiet ebb and flow of life, by choices made without heed to their consequences.

In the months that had passed, ACM had etched its presence into his being, changing the shape of his heart and the course of his life. Hugo's story was one of many, a testament to the relentless passage of time and the impact of seemingly small decisions.

Hugo's life had not been ordinary, it was remarkable existence that unfolded in a sleepy town of Vagator, Yet, as life often reminds us, the mundane can give way to the extraordinary in a heartbeat, or in Hugo's case, a heart that was far from ordinary.

Alcoholic cardiomyopathy, they called it—a condition that whispered of shadows cast by wine-soaked glasses and the subtle erosion of one's own vitality. A condition where the very essence of life seemed to lose its rhythm, much like the way Hugo's heart had.

For him, not being a heavy drinker, no reveler of raucous nights. Even though his vice lay in moderation, a glass or two of wine, savored three or four times a week. Yet, even such measured indulgence had its price, a lesson life had been weaving for him in the secret chambers of his heart.

It wasn't just the wine, though. Destiny also, it seemed, had its hand to play. Born with a solitary kidney, Hugo carried within him an added burden, one that conspired with his habits to deepen the chasm of his misfortune.

The heart, that faithful sentinel of life's relentless march, had begun to betray its master. It swelled, not in joy or love, but in response to the insistent pressures of maintaining his office staff intact, stretching himself thin and wide on finances, like an ageing balloon straining to hold its breath. With every beat, it grew weaker, less capable of the vigorous task it had so diligently performed for decades.

245

As the days turned to weeks and the weeks to months, the damage was insidious, creeping into the very core of his being. His heart, once a steady drumbeat, had faltered into a discordant rhythm, like a tired musician stumbling over the notes of a familiar tune.

The body, in its infinite wisdom, requires a steady supply of oxygen to function, to thrive. But Hugo's heart was failing, inch by inexorable inch. Its pumps had grown feeble, unable to propel the crimson river of life with the vigor it demanded. The result was a slow suffocation of his body's cells, a silent cry for help that went unanswered.

The whispers of a solitary kidney and the echoes of measured indulgence had conspired to mold his heart into something unrecognizable, something fragile and frail.

And so, Hugo's life as it unfolded, a tale of a heart transformed by the alchemy of choices made and circumstances bestowed, where heart, like lives, reshaped by the unlikeliest of forces.

Chapter 29

CORONER'S REVELATION

Detective Julian: (knocking on the office door of the coroner): Dr. Stevens, Got your call, this is Julian. Got those autopsy results on Veronica's case?

Dr. Stevens: (Opening the door) Julian, come in. Yes, I've just finished examining the findings. Have a seat.

Detective Julian: Thanks, Doc. What did you find?

Dr. Stevens: Well, it's not a straightforward case, Julian. The cause of death was indeed hyperkalemia-induced heart failure. Her potassium levels were off the charts. But here's the tricky part - the time of death falls between 8:30 pm and 9:00 pm on December 3rd.

Detective Julian: (Frowning) That's a pretty wide window. Anything more specific?

Dr. Stevens: Unfortunately, no. The condition of the body made it hard to pinpoint the exact moment. It appears she may have been sleeping while the body tried to fight for some time before it became fatal.

Detective Julian: (Rubbing his chin) That doesn't make sense. We know from the hotel staff that she was perfectly fine when she checked into the hotel after completing her camino portugues pilgrimage yesterday. What could've caused such a sudden spike in potassium levels?

Dr. Stevens: (Pausing) That's the curious part, Julian. It seems the presence of undigested food in her stomach played a significant role, but it's hard to conclude this could have been the only cause of an unusually high amount of potassium-rich food in her system, enough to trigger hyperkalemia.

Detective Julian: (Raised eyebrow) So, she ingested something right before her death that caused this?

Dr. Stevens: It's a possibility, but I can't say for sure. The hyperkalemia could've been building up for some time. Her solitary kidney probably exacerbated the condition, making it more critical.

Detective Julian: (Nodding) This is getting complicated. Thanks, Doc. I'll need a copy of these findings for our records.

Meanwhile, Julian comes back to Police Department – to meet the Chief at the Office.

Detective Julian: (Knocking on the Chief's door) Chief, got some news on Veronica's case.

Chief: (Motioning him in) Julian, what have you found?

Detective Julian: The coroner's report is in. It's hyperkalemia-induced heart failure, Chief. The time of death falls between 8:30 pm and 9:00 pm on December 3rd.

Chief Anderson: (Frowning) That's a broad timeframe. Any leads on what might've triggered it?

Detective Julian: It gets murkier, Chief. There was a substantial amount of potassium-rich food found undigested in her stomach. But as per Coroner, its highly unlikely that the food she ate was something that caused this. The solitary kidney probably made it worse. She may have ingested something else to make it worse.

Chief Anderson: (Deep in thought) This is quite the puzzle, Julian. We need to figure out what she ate and where she got it. We also need to establish her whereabouts in that time frame. Get a team on this, and let's unravel this mystery.

Detective Julian: (Nodding) I'm on it, Chief. We'll get to the bottom of this. I will head over to forensics evidence room to check on the items we collected from Veronica's room.

Forensics Evidence Room

Detective Julian: (Examining the bagged evidence) Alright, let's see what we've got here. (Notices a bag containing a sports drink concentrate) Huh, what's this?

Forensics Technician: (Examining the label) This is a a sports drink concentrate. We gathered some information about this, it's an Electrolyte replenisher, available at various stores in Portugal and Spain. It's a product readily available over the counter.

Forensics Technician: (Glancing towards Julian, holding a piece of paper in the form of a bookmarker): "Julian, we found this book-marker style note along with packet, usually the inspirational notes that can be shared instead of greeting cards, so it appears like a gift from someone.

Detective Julian: (Examining the note and reading it loudly):" Rivers, gracefully converge into the boundless expanse of the sea, the destinies tied together envelope into the embrace -- Miguel"

Detective Julian: Yeah, this does sound like a philosophical quote in the form of a bookmarker sold at stores. This quote seems to give credit to Miguel.

Detective Julian: (Picking it up) Let's call the coroner. I want to know if this thing could've had anything to do with Veronica's hyperkalemia.

Coroner's Office - Over the Phone

Detective Julian: (On the phone) Dr. Stevens, it's Julian from the police department. I was in your office earlier today, we found a sports energy drink concentrate in Veronica's room. Could something like this induce hyperkalemia?

Dr. Stevens: (Over the phone) Sports energy drink concentrate, you say? It's possible, Julian. Some of these products can contain high levels of potassium. Can you bring it over? We can check the contents to be sure.

Coroner's Office - Julian In-Person

Detective Julian: (Entering the coroner's office, holding the sports energy drink concentrate in a plastic bag) Dr. Stevens, here it is.

Dr. Stevens: (Taking the concentrate and examining it) Thank you, Julian. (Opens the bottle and takes a small sample)

Detective Julian: (Curious) So, what do you think? Could this be the culprit?

Dr. Stevens: (Examining the contents) Well, Julian, this sports drink concentrate is packed with magnesium, potassium, and sodium—electrolytes that athletes and marathoners often use to recover after a race. In high quantities, especially if consumed frequently, it could potentially disrupt the electrolyte balance in the body and lead to hyperkalemia.

Detective Julian: (Realization dawning) Veronica was probably drinking this during her Camino Portugués pilgrimage. She probably thought it would help her stay hydrated and replenish lost minerals. But over the course of her journey, it might have caused her potassium levels to spike.

Dr. Stevens: (Nodding) That's a plausible scenario, Julian. It's crucial to remember that while sports energy drinks can be beneficial for some, excessive or inappropriate consumption can lead to unexpected health complications.

Detective Julian: (Resolute) Thanks, Doc. This could be a significant lead. She must have consumed this concentrate excessively during her pilgrimage. It might be the missing piece in this puzzle.

As Julian left the coroner's office, he couldn't help but marvel at the unexpected twist in Veronica's case. A simple sports energy drink concentrate, taken with the intent of staying energized during her journey, had unknowingly become a key element in the investigation. The mysteries surrounding her tragic demise had slowly unraveled, one piece at a time.

Coroner's office - Goa India

Detective Akash Tripathi: (raising an eyebrow) "This way to the coroner's office, Inspector Cunha?"

Inspector Cunha: (nodding) "Yes, Detective Tripathi, right this way. The coroner has some crucial information for us."

The group of detectives follows Inspector Cunha through a sterile hallway, the fluorescent lights overhead casting a stark glow on the linoleum floor. They arrive at a nondescript door marked "Coroner's Office." Inspector Cunha knocks lightly and then pushes the door open.

Coroner Dr. Patel: (standing up from a desk cluttered with paperwork) "Gentlemen, welcome. I'm Dr. Patel, the coroner. Please, have a seat."

Detective Ramirez: (whispering to Detective Vasquez) "This place always gives me the creeps."

Dr. Patel: (clearing his throat) "I understand, Detective. Now, I have the preliminary findings on Hugo's cause of death."

Detective Akash Tripathi: (leaning forward) "Please, go on."

Dr. Patel: (consulting his notes) "Hugo's death was caused by alcoholic cardiomyopathy, or ACM. It's a condition where heavy alcohol use weakens the heart muscle, ultimately leading to heart failure."

Detective Vasquez: "ACM? But wasn't Hugo more of a social drinker?"

Inspector Cunha: (nodding) "Yes, that's what we thought too, but it seems there's more to the story."

Dr. Patel: (continuing) "Indeed. The autopsy revealed that Hugo consumed a significant amount of alcohol on the evening of December 3rd. Specifically, he had consumed approximately three bottles of wine.".

Detective Ramirez: (whistles) "Three bottles? That's not social drinking; that's a party."

Dr. Patel: (continuing) "Besides that, Hugo seems to have been born with a solitary kidney that worsens the body conditions."

Detective Akash Tripathi: (rubbing his chin) "So, if he consumed that much alcohol on the 3rd, and with solitary kidney, seems like his heart condition worsened significantly."

Dr. Patel: (nodding) "Exactly, Detective. We estimate that Hugo's time of death falls between midnight and 12:30 AM on December 4th. It seems his heart just couldn't handle the strain."

Detective Akash Tripathi: (Making a mental note for further investigation) "We need to find out from Rodrigo whether Hugo was concerned about anything related to work that would be a cause for stress"

Detective Akash Tripathi: (looking at Dr. Patel and nodding) "This is tragic. We will get to the bottom of this."

Detective Ramirez: (grimacing) "It's a sobering reminder that even seemingly harmless habits can have dire consequences."

Detective Akash Tripathi: (sighing) "Thank you, Dr. Patel, for your thorough examination and prompt findings. We'll need the official autopsy report for our investigation."

Inspector Cunha: "Yes, we have to find out if there were any external factors involved as well. We will need to get report from the forensics team as well about the findings from collected evidence."

The detectives exchange nods of agreement and file out of the coroner's office, the weight of their new knowledge hanging heavily in the air.

Phone Call from Spain to India – as detective Julian needs to convey Veronica's coroner report to senior detective Tripathi.

Detective Julian: (Dialing the number, waiting for the call to connect)

Senior Detective Akash Tripathi: (Answering) Akash Tripathi here. Who's calling?

Detective Julian: (Clearing his throat) Sudeep, it's Julian from Santiago de Compostela, Spain. I've got some updates on the Veronica case.

Senior Detective Akash Tripathi: (Curious) Julian, good to hear from you. What's the latest?

Detective Julian: We've wrapped up the coroner's report and forensic analysis on Veronica's case. The coroner's autopsy indicates her time of death was somewhere between 8:30 pm to 9:00 pm on December 3rd.

Senior Detective Akash Tripathi: (Thoughtful) That's a pretty good narrow window. Anything else?

Detective Julian: Well, the other part. There were no fingerprints other than Veronica's found in her room from the evidence we collected. So, no foul play involved.

Senior Detective Akash Tripathi: (Raising an eyebrow) Okay, Julian. What's the cause of death?

Detective Julian: (Pausing for effect) Hyperkalemia, Sudeep. High potassium levels. But here's the kicker – Veronica had a condition of solitary kidney that exacerbated the hyperkalemia, leading to cardiac failure.

Senior Detective Akash Tripathi: (Surprised) A solitary kidney? That's a rare condition. It must have played a significant role in her death. Tell me more about this hyperkalemia.

Detective Julian: (Explaining) Hyperkalemia occurs when there's an excessive amount of potassium in the bloodstream. In Veronica's case, it seems she ingested a sports drink concentrate, loaded with potassium, and other minerals during her Camino Portugués pilgrimage, we found an almost 90% consumed packet. Her solitary kidney might have struggled to filter it out effectively.

Senior Detective Akash Tripathi: (Deep in thought) So, a seemingly innocuous sports energy drink concentrate could have caused this? It's a piece of the puzzle we couldn't have foreseen.

Detective Julian: (Resolute) It's an unexpected twist, but it brings us closer to understanding what happened to Veronica that night. Since we can't dig deeper into her pilgrimage of the past 9 days to find out how frequently she consumed this concentrate.

Senior Detective Akash Tripathi: (Determined) Agreed, Julian. We'll keep our eyes peeled for any leads on this end.

As the conversation came to a close, Detective Julian and Senior Detective Akash Tripathi understood that the pieces of this intricate puzzle were slowly assembling together into place. The unexpected revelation of Veronica's solitary kidney seemed like a common thread between Veronica and Hugo leading to their tragic demise.

Detective Julian, sat in the forensics office, continued poring over the evidence collected from Veronica's room.

As Detective Julian meticulously examined the contents of Veronica's backpack in the evidence room, his eyes fell upon a folded piece of paper tucked away between a few items in one of the inside pockets. He carefully retrieved it, unfolding the document to reveal a two-page report dated June 3, approximately six months prior. The report was from Dr. Aditi Sharma in Goa, and its contents would soon illuminate a significant aspect of Veronica's life.

The report detailed a disheartening medical diagnosis. It stated that Veronica faced formidable challenges in her desire to become pregnant. The shape of her uterus posed complications that rendered even procedures like Intrauterine Insemination (IUI) or In Vitro Fertilization (IVF) impossible. It was a heavy blow to her hopes of conceiving a child of her own.

As Julian continued to read, the report unveiled another layer of complexity. It mentioned an issue related to Veronica's age, indicating that her ovaries were not producing eggs in sufficient quantities for surrogate pregnancy to be a viable option. This revelation compounded the difficulties that Veronica and her partner, Hugo, faced in their quest to have a child together.

The weight of the information sank in as Julian absorbed the implications. Veronica had been grappling with profound challenges on the path to parenthood, challenges that transcended the ordinary hurdles faced by many. It was a poignant reminder of the deeply personal struggles and setbacks that often remained hidden beneath the surface of even the most seemingly ordinary lives.

 The smartphone's recent call history had gotten him connected to the police detectives in Goa, now Julian was curious to find the clues to Veronica's daily conversations after she had arrived in Portugal to start her Camino Portugues pilgrimage.

As he navigated through the phone's call history, the digital record of conversations hinted at the relationships and interactions that had filled Veronica's days. Two names, in particular, caught his attention as he scrutinized the entries.

The first was Hugo's number, a name he was well acquainted with by now. Julian noted with interest that Veronica had been in frequent contact with Hugo. Her phone log revealed a consistent pattern of communication, almost like clockwork. She had called Hugo twice every day, their conversations spanning about 15 minutes each time. Morning and evening, it seemed they had made it a routine to connect, sharing moments of their lives.

The second name was Ana Da Costa, a name unfamiliar to Julian until this moment. Yet, it was evident that Ana held a significant place in Veronica's life. The call frequency and duration were remarkably consistent, almost mirroring her contact with Hugo. Ana received calls from Veronica almost every day, particularly in the evening, with their conversations lasting about 5 minutes each time.

Julian couldn't help but wonder about the nature of these calls and the relationships they represented. Hugo, presumably her partner or spouse, appeared to be an integral part of her daily routine. Ana, on the other hand, was more enigmatic, a figure who shared daily conversations with Veronica but remained a mystery to the detective.

As he continued to sift through Veronica's digital footprint, Julian knew that these calls might hold the keys to understanding her life, her relationships, and perhaps even the events leading up to her untimely demise. Each entry in the call history was a piece of the puzzle, waiting to be examined and fitted into the broader narrative of Veronica's story.

As senior detective Akash Tripathi was trying to connect all the dots before heading to sleep.

Detective Julian: (Dialing Akash's number, waiting for the call to connect)

Detective Akash Tripathi: (Answering immediately as the screen flashes 'Julian Spain' as saved on the phone), Akash Tripathi speaking.

Detective Julian: (Urgently) Akash, it's Julian from Spain. I've got some crucial updates on Veronica's case.

Detective Akash Tripathi: (Attentive) Julian, go on. What have you found?

Detective Julian: We've discovered a medical report from Goa dated about six months ago. It's from Dr. Aditi Sharma, and it states that Veronica couldn't become pregnant, not even through IUI or IVF, due to complications with her ovaries.

Detective Akash Tripathi: (Surprised) That's a significant finding, Julian. It explains a lot about her personal situation. Anything else?

Detective Julian: Yes, there's more. I found a name, 'Ana Da Costa,' in her call history. Veronica had been talking to her almost every day for the past ten days, probably since her arrival in Portugal. I have a hunch that Ana might hold some clues about Veronica's recent life.

Detective Akash Tripathi: (Taking notes mentally) 'Ana Da Costa.' We need to look into this further. Good catch, Julian. Anything else we should know?

Detective Julian: (Pausing) Not at the moment.

Detective Akash Tripathi: Thanks for the update, Julian, seems like several pieces are coming together. Keep me posted on any developments, Julian.

As the conversation ended, both detectives knew they were inching closer to unraveling the complexities of Veronica's life. The medical report and the enigmatic figure of Ana Da Costa had injected new vigor into their investigation, and the visit to

Hugo's office in Calangute loomed as the next day would dawn for detective Tripathi and team.

Chapter 30

VISIT TO INDIA

Chief Anderson: (Looking at Detective Julian) Julian, I've been reviewing the progress on the Veronica case. It's clear that there are elements to this that go beyond our jurisdiction.

Detective Julian: (Nodding) Yes, Chief. The trail has led us to India, to Goa specifically.

Chief Anderson: (Pausing) I understand the importance of this case, Julian. The circumstances are unique, and it's crucial that we get to the bottom of it. Not just for Veronica's family but for the safety and peace of mind of the pilgrims on the Camino de Santiago.

Detective Julian: (Resolute) I couldn't agree more, Chief. We need to bring closure to this and ensure that those embarking on the pilgrimage feel safe amidst some of the chaos such news may cause.

Chief Anderson: (Sighs) Very well, Julian. I'm giving you permission to travel to Goa, India, and continue your investigation there. Coordinate with Detective Akash Tripathi and the local authorities. I trust you to represent our department and bring this case to a resolution.

Detective Julian: (Grateful) Thank you, Chief. I'll do everything in my power to find the answers we seek.

Chief Anderson: (Serious) Just remember, Julian, this case carries a lot of weight. The eyes of many are upon it, and the impact of your findings could be far-reaching. Exercise discretion and diligence.

Detective Julian: (Determined) I will, Chief. I won't rest until we uncover the truth.

With the Chief of Police's permission granted, Detective Julian's path was now clear. He was ready to embark on the next phase of his journey, one that would take him to India in search of answers and, ultimately, the closure that Veronica's case demanded.

A couple of days later, Detective Julian stood somberly beside the carefully prepared casket that held Veronica's body. The arduous journey ahead weighed heavily on him, both emotionally and logistically. Accompanied by the responsibility of bringing Veronica home, he was prepared for a long and complex journey with multiple connections.

The journey began at Santiago de Compostela, where Julian and Veronica's remains were bound for Madrid, the first of several connections. From Madrid, they boarded a flight to Doha, Qatar, a bustling hub that connected them to the next leg of the journey. The onward flight took them to Mumbai, India, where the final leg awaited.

Upon landing at Mumbai's Chhatrapati Shivaji International Airport, Julian felt the weight of the past few days and loss of some hours due to time difference settle upon him. He had traveled thousands of miles, crossing borders and time zones, to fulfill the solemn duty of accompanying Veronica's body on its journey home. Her final destination was Goa, specifically Dabolim, where she would be reunited with her homeland and her people.

Waiting at Dabolim Airport was Senior Detective Akash Tripathi, a familiar face to Julian, and Inspector Cunha, who were leading the investigation on the Indian side. As they exchanged nods of recognition, the gravity of the task at hand hung in the air. Together, they would carry out the next phase of the investigation, pursuing the elusive answers that lay at the heart of Veronica's mysterious death.

With Veronica's body safely in the ambulance, the trio made their way from the airport to a nearby hotel. As they navigated the bustling streets of Goa, Julian couldn't help but reflect on the winding path that had brought him here—a path marked by unexpected twists and turns, but one that had led him to this moment of convergence, where the pursuit of truth and justice would continue on foreign soil.

After a long and exhausting journey that spanned continents and time zones, Detective Julian along with Senior detective Akash Tripathi and Inspector Cunha, finally arrived at the hotel in Vagator, Goa. The ride from Dabolim Airport to their destination had taken nearly an hour, navigating through the vibrant and bustling streets of Goa. The weight of the past few days, coupled with the emotional toll of the investigation, had left him physically drained, yet determined to continue his quest for answers.

Upon arrival, Julian found himself amidst the Indian detective team led by Senior Detective Akash Tripathi. It was a moment of convergence, where the investigations from two corners of the world would merge in pursuit of the truth about Veronica's demise and an even stranger thing about Hugo's demise around the same time.

As they settled into the hotel, Detective Tripathi, considerate of the long and tiring journey Julian had just undertaken from Santiago de Compostela to Goa, suggested, "Julian, you must be exhausted from your journey. We've made significant progress in the last 30 hours that it took for you to travel here. Why don't you take some rest, and we can catch you up on the investigation later?"

Julian, however, had a different perspective. His determination to uncover the truth about Veronica's death burned brightly. He replied, "Thank you, Akash, for your consideration. But I've had enough rest on the plane. I want to hear more about the investigation, the progress you've made, and where we stand now."

Senior Detective Akash Tripathi nodded, acknowledging Julian's commitment. The two detectives were now united by a common goal—the pursuit of justice for Veronica and the need to untangle the intricate web of events that had led to her tragic demise.

The hotel room in Vagator, Detective Akash Tripathi sat across from Detective Julian, the room filled with other detectives and Inspector Cunha, a palpable sense of anticipation. Julian leaned forward, his eyes locked onto Akash's, eager to hear what the Indian detective had uncovered.

Detective Akash Tripathi: (Clearing his throat) Julian, let me bring you up to speed on the investigation. First, the forensics team has confirmed that Hugo's Villa Carvalho home carries four distinct fingerprints, which belong to Ana Da Costa, Rodrigo Esteves, Veronica, and, of course, Hugo himself. It's an intriguing mix of people connected to this case.

Detective Julian: (Raising an eyebrow) Ana's fingerprints in Hugo's home? That's unexpected. What's the significance?

Detective Akash Tripathi: Initially we weren't entirely sure, but it was a piece of the puzzle we couldn't ignore. Now, let me tell you about our questioning of Ana and Rodrigo at the office in Calangute.

Detective Julian: Please, go on.

Detective Akash Tripathi: Rodrigo Esteves, who is the executive producer of the channel told us that Hugo's channel had been facing some financial challenges recently. Rodrigo was considering reducing the workforce to alleviate some of the financial strain, but Hugo was vehemently opposed to the idea. Rodrigo mentioned that Hugo cares deeply about the entire staff and their well-being. In his words, Hugo couldn't even think in his dreams of reducing the staff. Instead, he insisted that they produce more episodes and content to release, with the aim of attracting more subscribers and viewers.

Detective Julian: (Frowning) So, financial troubles were weighing on Hugo's mind. That could have added stress to the situation.

Detective Akash Tripathi: Indeed, it's a possible factor. Now, let me tell you what we learned from Ana. About six months ago, Veronica confided in her. It turns out Veronica had been grappling with an issue related to her inability to become a mother due to her uterus complications. She couldn't undergo IUI, IVF, or even use her eggs for surrogacy.

Detective Julian: Remember the medical report that I found in the backpack of Veronica, and we spoke about on the phone, it makes sense, that explains the medical report I found. But why would Veronica share this with Ana?

Detective Akash Tripathi: (Continuing) Veronica had been trying to get a promise from Ana. She wanted assurance that Ana would assist and maybe asking her to take care of Hugo in case she wasn't around. It appears she was deeply concerned about her husband's well-being and wanted to ensure he would have support even if she couldn't provide it herself.

As the details of the investigation unfolded, Julian couldn't help but feel that they were getting closer to untangling the web of relationships, financial pressures, and deeply personal concerns were coming into focus, painting a more intricate and potentially revealing picture of Veronica's life and the events that had led to her tragic demise. The pursuit of truth continued, with each revelation bringing them closer to the answers they sought. He was already feeling glad that Chief

Anderson had approved his travel to India, he was eager to learn more about Ana and Hugo's relationship after what detective Tripathi had disclosed just now.

Chapter 31

ANA DA COSTA

In the bustling office of Hugo's media production company, Veronica had been a force to be reckoned with, skillfully managing various aspects of the business. However, as the staff had grown over the years, the need for additional support became evident. This led to the hiring of Ana, a receptionist, approximately five years ago.

Ana's arrival at the office had been a notable event. During her interview with Hugo, Rodrigo, and Veronica, something curious had been observed. Both Hugo and Rodrigo had remarked on Ana's striking resemblance to Veronica. They found similarities in her facial looks and features, which had not gone unnoticed during the interview process.

Ana had seamlessly integrated into the team, taking on the vital role of receptionist based on her qualifications from previous employer. Her presence had become indispensable to the entire office, ensuring smooth operations and making her a familiar face to all who entered.

Ana's charm and grace had not gone unnoticed among the staff members. Many of them had developed crushes on her, finding her both professionally competent and personally enchanting. However, Ana remained steadfastly professional in her interactions, not giving any of her admirers a second glance.

It was only a secret that only Ana knew in her soul, she admired Hugo, the charismatic leader of the company, and had always held deep respect for his dedication and commitment to the business. Her admiration for him had remained steadfast over the years, a sentiment that had not gone unnoticed by those who worked alongside her.

As the layers of Veronica's life and the dynamics within the office continued to be unraveled, the presence of Ana Da Costa had emerged as a significant piece of the investigation.

Ana Da Costa, a woman of Portuguese ancestry with a heritage rooted in Goa for the past four generations, was a central figure in the investigation. Her connections to Veronica and Hugo's life had raised intriguing questions about her role in the unfolding events.

During the interrogation with Detective Akash Tripathi, Ana revealed that she had spoken to Veronica almost every day during Veronica's Camino Portugués pilgrimage. Veronica had been a source of guidance and encouragement for Ana, often advising her to visit Hugo at their home. As a result, Ana had been to Hugo's residence approximately three times in the past 11 days. On some occasions, she brought along egg puff pastries from the renowned Siolim Bakery, a local favorite, knowing that Hugo enjoyed them immensely.

However, when the interrogation took a more serious turn, Detective Tripathi posed the most pressing question: had there been any romantic or intimate relationship between Ana and Hugo during Veronica's absence?

Ana's response to this question had been emotionally charged. She broke down, her tears flowing freely as she vehemently denied any such involvement. She sobbed as she explained to Detective Tripathi that she adored Hugo and Veronica as a couple and would never do anything to disrupt their relationship. Her deep admiration for the couple, it seemed, was a wellspring of genuine emotion that transcended any romantic intentions.

As the investigation progressed, Ana's unwavering devotion to Hugo and Veronica became increasingly evident. Her presence at their home and the emotional connections she had forged with them were clear, although it had added layers of complexity to the case. Detective Julian and Detective Akash Tripathi found themselves convinced with the honest answers they were getting from Ana.

The meticulous work of the forensics team had left no stone unturned in their efforts to gather evidence from Hugo's home. Fingerprints and DNA samples had been carefully collected and analyzed to shed light on who had been where in the residence.

The results of their investigation were clear and precise. In the intimate bedroom quarters of the home, the fingerprints and DNA samples pointed solely to the presence of Hugo and Veronica. It was a confirmation that the bedroom had been a private sanctuary for the married couple, untouched by any other individuals.

In the living room, where the dynamics had been more complex due to Ana's presence, the evidence aligned with her testimony. The fingerprints and DNA samples collected in this area correlated with Ana and Rodrigo, corroborating Ana's account that her visits had been confined to the living room, respecting the sanctity of Hugo and Veronica's private space.

The garbage bins also told a similar story. Among the remnants of discarded items, the forensics team had discovered evidence that aligned with Ana's testimony. Crisp egg puff crusts, remnants from the pastries of Siolim Bakery, were found. This finding served as confirmation that Ana had indeed visited Hugo's home with pastries, as she had claimed during the interrogation. Her motives for these visits were rooted in concern for Hugo's well-being, following Veronica's advice and ensuring that he was okay.

As the pieces of the puzzle fell into place, the investigators were gaining a clearer understanding of the events that had transpired. The evidence collected from the home and the garbage bins formed a cohesive narrative that aligned with Ana's testimony. However, there were still lingering questions and complexities to untangle in the investigation, as they delved deeper into the intricate web of relationships surrounding Veronica and Ana.

The next day after his arrival in Goa, Julian accompanied Tripathi to Hugo's office in Calangute, Detective Akash Tripathi and Detective Julian had some more questions as they resumed their interrogation with Ana Da Costa. It was a crucial session, and they hoped to uncover more details that might shed light on the intricate dynamics within the case.

As the questions flowed, Ana hesitated for a moment before coming forward with another revelation, one that added depth to the complex narrative. She disclosed that a couple of months ago, Veronica had taken her out for an extended coffee session, during which Veronica had confided in her about her profound inability to bear children. She had explained that she couldn't undergo IUI, IVF, or surrogacy due to her physical condition. Till now, only the detectives were aware of Veronica's condition through the medical report that Julian had uncovered in the backpack.

It was during this intimate conversation that Veronica had shared more about her relationship with Hugo. She revealed that Hugo, a man who deeply loved children, had been incredibly supportive throughout their journey. Hugo had reassured Veronica that having children wasn't the only measure of happiness in their marriage, emphasizing that their togetherness was what truly mattered.

Veronica, however, had been particularly inquisitive during that conversation, probing Ana with questions about her feelings toward Hugo. Veronica seemed determined to understand Ana's perspective, consistently asking whether Ana had any romantic interest in Hugo.

Ana's response had been clear and heartfelt. She admitted that while she had a genuine liking for Hugo, it was a respectful admiration and nothing more. What she truly cherished was the unique bond shared by Hugo and Veronica as a couple. Ana had deep respect for their relationship and had never entertained the idea of pursuing anything beyond friendship.

This revelation added another layer to the intricate relationships within the narrative. Veronica's deep concerns about her own inability to have children and her interest in Ana's feelings for Hugo hinted at the complexities of her emotional state. As the interrogation continued, Detective Akash Tripathi and Detective Julian were beginning to piece together a deeper understanding of the individuals involved and the challenges they faced in their personal lives.

As Detective Julian and Detective Akash Tripathi delved deeper into the investigation, a crucial detail came to Julian's mind like a bolt of lightning. He remembered an aspect of Veronica's phone that they hadn't yet explored—the entirety of the notes application. While they had been focused on recent call history, emails, and calendars.

With this newfound realization, the detectives rushed back to the station where all the evidence collected from Veronica's room had been meticulously stored since Julian's arrival in Goa. Time was of the essence, as the contents of the note's application, if it contained anything to begin with, maybe would hold some potential to shed light on the true nature of Veronica's intentions and her feelings towards Hugo and Ana.

Upon retrieving the phone and accessing the notes, there were about close to fifty separate filings in the notes application, amongst these separate titled notes they discovered a collection titled "Novenas for Camino" - nine novenas, each with two distinct parts. The first part of each novena was a heartfelt plea for the Lord's blessings upon Hugo, while the second part was meant for both Hugo and Ana. These novenas were a testament to Veronica's deep care for the two people she wished would get closer together in their hearts.

As the detectives read through the novenas, the words on the screen spoke of Veronica's desires and hopes, serving as a powerful testimony to her love, sacrifice and selflessness. The notes application would play a pivotal role in verifying Ana's honesty and in understanding the depth of Veronica's feelings and wishes for Hugo and Ana.

The second part to the nine novenas that Veronica had recited on her Camino Portugues pilgrimage at the end of each day before she would talk to Ana.

1. **Novena for Unity:** "Heavenly Father, as I walk this path of faith and endurance, I pray for the unity of hearts between Hugo and Ana. I will not be around to witness it, I ask that You bless their connection, allowing their souls to find solace and companionship in one another. May their bond be a source of strength and support in times of need."

2. **Novena for Trust:** "Lord, instill in me the trust to believe in the goodness of others. May Hugo and Ana trust in the intentions of each other, finding comfort and solace in their growing connection. Let their trust be the foundation of a beautiful relationship."

3. **Novena for Acceptance:** "Dear God. If it is Your will that Hugo and Ana find happiness together, Get them to embrace each other with grace and understanding and accept the changes with an open heart."

4. **Novena for Forgiveness:** "Lord, if there are any hurts or misunderstandings between Hugo and Ana, I ask for Your divine assistance in forgiving and letting go. May forgiveness pave the way for new beginnings and harmonious relationships."

5. **Novena for Blessings:** "Heavenly Father, I seek Your blessings for Hugo and Ana. Shower them with happiness, love, and all the beautiful things life has to offer. May their journey together be filled with joy and fulfillment."

6. **Novena for Selflessness:** "Dear Lord. May Hugo and Ana's connection, if it blossoms, be rooted in kindness, compassion, and consideration for each other's well-being. May they find in each other a source of selfless love."

7. **Novena for Joy:** "Dear Lord, may the prospect of a loving relationship between Hugo and Ana bring joy to their lives. Let happiness fill their hearts as they discover the beauty of companionship and love."

8. **Novena for Graciousness:** "Help me to be gracious, God, in all circumstances. Whether I am here or not, may I extend kindness and goodwill towards Hugo and Ana as they explore the possibilities of their connection."

9. **Novena for Divine Will:** "Above all, Lord, I pray for Your divine will to guide the paths of Hugo and Ana. Let Your wisdom and grace prevail in their lives, leading them toward the destiny You have ordained."

As Veronica embarked on her Camino journey, her heartfelt novenas carried her deepest hopes and wishes. These prayers, uttered with sincerity and devotion, were a testament to her love and selflessness, a beacon of light to illuminate the paths of those she cared about.

Detective Tripathi and Julian approached the investigation with a meticulous and clear objective: to understand Maria, the robot, and find any information stored within her. After perusing the online resources along with some technical help, they discovered the creator of Maria was 'Masqueda Corporation'. They identified the contact details for the manufacturer.

Without delay, Detective Tripathi made a formal request to the corporation, explaining the significance of the case. To his relief, Masqueda Corporation was forthcoming and showed no hesitation in supporting their investigative endeavors.

The corporation sent them a detailed instruction manual, brimming with technical details, pointing them specifically to sections that would be of immediate interest in the investigation for retrieving the activity.

One particular instruction stood out: a directive to connect Maria to a computing device using a USB Type-C cable. The reference immediately reminded Julian of the ubiquitous and universality of chargers used for Phones.

With the manual in hand and a laptop ready, along with help from technical staff, they connected Maria, the process was straightforward. Once connected, they were immediately in access of a series of files stored within Maria.

Upon a careful review, they found a match. One particular file contained content that was eerily similar in sort of caption form, matching to what they had seen in the recording related to their case. The detective understood, there was similarity and alignment between the text form and speech form: Maria used this exact text to produce speech, using the technique of Text-to-Speech (TTS) and in doing so, she synthesized the distinct and personalized voice of Veronica, adding another layer of explanation to solve the mystery they were dealing with.

As the detectives delved deeper into the file's content, they summarized between themselves as it became evident that Maria's role was pivotal in the entire sequence of events. The precise replication of Veronica's voice was no accident; it was a deliberate act of mirroring, synthesizing of voice, resulting in the uncanny vocal reflection they had observed.

The clarity of this finding was monumental for Detective Tripathi and Julian. The pieces of the puzzle now fit seamlessly. With this newfound evidence, the investigation was indeed taking a decisive turn, bringing them a step closer to resolving the mystery that had seemed so elusive.

Maria, in her robotic precision, had inadvertently played a vital role in providing the closure Detective Tripathi and Julian had been relentlessly seeking. Their journey through the technological intricacies had finally borne fruit, painting a clearer picture of the events that transpired.

On December 11th, one week after the fateful events that had brought Detective Julian, Detective Akash Tripathi, and their team together to investigate the tragic deaths of Hugo and Veronica, the investigation was drawing to its conclusion. The past week had been a whirlwind of fast-paced events, as they meticulously gathered evidence, interviewed witnesses, and uncovered the intricate details of the couple's lives.

As the pieces of the puzzle fell into place, the bright minds of the detectives and their team members reached a consensus that shed light on the mysterious deaths of Hugo and Veronica. It became evident that their demise was not the result of foul play or any malicious intent. Instead, it was a tragic case of accidental death, marked by a series of fateful circumstances.

One significant revelation that had come to light was that both Hugo and Veronica shared a unique birth trait—they each had a solitary kidney. Veronica had been aware of her solitary kidney due to medical tests that had been conducted in her pursuit of understanding her capability of becoming pregnant. On the other hand, Hugo had been unaware of his own solitary kidney. It was almost as if destiny had played a role in their union, as Hugo's deep love and commitment to Veronica had led him to join her in the realm, united in both life and death.

The conclusion of the investigation left the detectives with lingering questions and a sense of wonder about Veronica's intentions and actions leading up to her tragic passing. Despite being aware of her solitary kidney, had she knowingly consumed a sports energy concentrate that was high in potassium, fully aware of the risks of hyperkalemia. The possibility hung in the air, casting a shadow of uncertainty over her motivations.

As the detectives reflected on the evidence and the details that had emerged during the investigation, they couldn't help but contemplate the significance of the two-part novenas. The first part had been dedicated to praying for Hugo, while the second part had been intended for both Hugo and Ana. It raised the question: had Veronica orchestrated this journey as a means of bringing Hugo and Ana closer together, even if it meant removing herself from their future.

It was evident from the testimony they had gathered that Hugo's love for Veronica was profound and unwavering. He had shown unyielding commitment to their relationship, even in the face of financial challenges and personal difficulties. It seemed unlikely that he would willingly agree to anything that would separate him from Veronica.

Veronica's motivations remained a mystery, a complex enigma that the detectives couldn't fully unravel. Her actions and intentions, whether driven by selflessness or a deeper desire to see Hugo and Ana together, left them with a sense of wonder and admiration for the depth of human emotions and the complexities of love.

In the end, the detectives could only speculate about Veronica's true intentions, but one thing was certain—her legacy would forever be intertwined with the love story that had unfolded, leaving an indelible mark on the hearts of those who had known her and the investigators who had uncovered the truth of her extraordinary journey.

The investigation had unraveled the sequence of events that had led to the tragedy. Hugo's overconsumption of wine had ultimately resulted in a fatal condition known as acute cardiomyopathy (ACM), a condition that had likely been exacerbated by his solitary kidney. The couple's destinies had intertwined in a way that defied explanation, leading them to a realm where they would be together for eternity.

With this understanding, the investigation was brought to a close, and the detectives and their team could only reflect on the poignant and tragic love story that had unfolded before them—a love so deep that it transcended even the boundaries of life and death.

Meanwhile, Veronica harbored a secret ambition, one that had been brewing in the recesses of her mind for quite some time. It concerned the future of their podcast, which had hit a plateau in terms of its subscriber base. The need for a breath of fresh air and a new direction had become increasingly evident.

Veronica was just waiting to complete her Camino Portugués and return back to Goa, India, to initiate a catalyst. Veronica recognized that Ana possessed a unique combination of looks and charm that had the potential to rejuvenate the podcast's appeal. Moreover, Ana's perspective would bring a different and complementary dynamic to the discussions that unfolded when Hugo and Ana engaged with their guests.

However, Veronica had chosen to keep her idea a closely guarded secret. She had yet to utter a word of her plan to Hugo, who remained unaware of the exciting prospect Veronica had in mind. Veronica understood the delicate nature of this proposal and the potential impact it could have on the podcast's future. Therefore, she intended to discuss her vision with Hugo at the right moment, presenting it as a thoughtfully considered proposal rather than an impulsive decision. The fate of their podcast hung in the balance, and Veronica was determined to navigate this pivotal moment with care and discretion.

Chapter 32

VERITAS UNVEILED FANS

In the golden embrace of the Goan sun, Detective Julian's journey from Spain traversing the miles to join forces with Detective Akash Tripathi in pursuit of truth had finally concluded.

Julian recalled their journey that felt like their own embarkation of a ritualistic pilgrimage through four key locations, tracing the intricate threads of the case until its conclusion on December 11th. These places were the anchors of their quest, each revealing a fragment of the enigmatic puzzle they were piecing together.

The first among these inquiry setting was the Office in Calangute. Within its walls, the detectives navigated the labyrinthine corridors of clues, bearing witness to secrets whispered in hushed tones among the staff members, testimonies they had etched in ink, and revelations that hung heavy in the air as their interrogation had progressed. The office was a gateway to understanding Hugo and Veronica's world, and it bore the weight of their life's intricacies.

Then, there was Hugo's Villa Carvalho, a place that stood as both a mausoleum and a shrine. It was here that the essence of Hugo's existence lingered, even after his departure from the realm of the living. Each day, as Detective Julian had arrived at the villa's gates along with detective Tripathi, he couldn't help but marvel at the devotion Hugo had inspired. Candles burned with fervor, their flames dancing in homage, and flowers adorned the pathway, vivid tributes from admirers who continued to be drawn to the enigmatic aura of the man. The offerings were meticulously cleared each day, but like the tides, they returned in even greater numbers, a testament to the indelible mark Hugo had left on the hearts of those who revered him.

The police station, with its stoic walls and echoing chambers, served as the crucible of justice. It was here that Julian worked intimately with the Indian team on evidence that was collected, witnesses were questioned, and the foundations of truth were laid bare. The station bore witness to the diligence of the detectives, where the puzzle pieces of the case were methodically arranged, step by step, in pursuit of answers.

Amidst this fervent quest, Detective Julian found respite in the hotel where he rested each night. Here, in the quietude of his temporary sanctuary, he contemplated the myriad complexities of the investigation. The room, a haven of solitude, absorbed his thoughts, offering a moment of introspection amidst the whirlwind of emotions and inquiries that defined this chapter of his life.

And so, as the days melded into one another, Detective Julian's gaze often turned towards Hugo's Villa Carvalho. It was a place where the profound impact of a couple's life was laid bare, a place where candles and flowers served as an enduring testimony to a man whose legacy transcended the boundaries of time. In this foreign land, amidst the mysteries and revelations, Detective Julian's journey unfolded, leaving footprints on the sands of time and a heart forever touched by the stories he had uncovered.

Detective Tripathi, accompanied by Detective Julian, took to the podium in front of a gathered group of journalists and reporters. The press interview marked the conclusion of a week-long investigation into the mysterious demise of Hugo and Veronica, an investigation that had spanned continents and uncovered a complex web of events.

In their somber summary, the detectives provided a clear account of the circumstances surrounding the deaths of Hugo and Veronica. According to the coroner's report, their lives had slipped away almost simultaneously, despite being on opposite sides of the world. Veronica had drawn her final breath in Santiago de Compostela, Spain, at a time between 8:30 pm and 9:00 pm local Spanish time. Hugo, on the other hand, had succumbed to the hands of fate in Vagator, Goa, sometime between 12:00 am and 12:30 am Indian time. The synchrony of their passing was underscored by the 3-hour and 30-minute time difference between Spain and India.

The cause of death for Veronica was determined to be hyperkalemia, a condition marked by high levels of potassium in the blood. For Hugo, the culprit had been acute cardiomyopathy (ACM), a sudden and severe heart condition that had tragically ended his life.

Throughout the investigation, detectives from Spain and India had collaborated closely, sharing information and insights across continents. Their dedication and unwavering pursuit of the truth had illuminated the intricate details of this complex case, ultimately leading to a conclusion that provided some closure to the enigma that had gripped them all.

Detective Tripathi and Detective Julian, having just summarized the investigation's findings, opened the floor to questions from the gathered press. A reporter from the 'Goan Herald,' representing the inquisitiveness of many, was the first to speak.

Reporter: "We have heard there was a recording of 4 hours and 30 minutes where Hugo is discussing with Maria, and the coverage goes until the final moments. How was this useful in the investigation, and can we get that recording released?"

Detective Tripathi: "Yes, the recording played a crucial role in our investigation. The cutting-edge technology of Maria had been personalized to have the voice of Veronica, as a team we went through the recording which captures the evening of Hugo and it was instrumental in shedding light on the events. However, as for the release of the recording, it's important to note that it is now the property of the 'Veritas Unveiled' channel. Decisions regarding how and when to make it available would need to come from their office."

The response left a sense of anticipation among the press, the press wondered about the recording that held the potential to reveal further details about the enigmatic circumstances that had surrounded Hugo's final moments and the viewers wanted to watch the recording as well. Yet, the detectives had made it clear that the decision rested with the channel, leaving the fate of the recording in their hands.

The press conference continued, with a myriad of questions directed at the detectives, seeking further insights into the investigation. One journalist inquired about the collaboration between Detective Julian and the Indian detectives.

Journalist: "Julian, can you tell us how it was collaborating with Indian detectives in this investigation?"

Detective Julian: "Collaborating with Indian detectives in this investigation was a seamless process. Both sides worked closely and efficiently, sharing all the information in a timely manner. This collaboration played a pivotal role in reaching all the conclusions we have presented today within the span of just one week."

The reporters continued to probe for more details, and another question was directed at Julian regarding the condition in which he had found Veronica's body in Santiago de Compostela.

Journalist: "Julian, could you tell us in what condition you found Veronica's body in Santiago de Compostela?"

Detective Julian: "Veronica's final moments were marked by a sense of serenity and peace. Her body was found lying on the bed, and she was looking at a photo of 'Hugo and Veronica,' taken at the São João Goan festival, earlier in the year and we found many other photos on Veronica's phone from this festival. This photo served as a screensaver, and it was a poignant moment—a snapshot frozen in time amidst the tranquility of her surroundings."

As the detectives provided these insights, the press continued to capture the intricate details of an investigation that had crossed continents and unfolded like a complex mystery. The collaborative efforts of the investigators had brought them closer to the truth, even as they grappled with the enigmatic circumstances of the case.

Meanwhile the detectives tackled other questions deftly-Had Veronica completed the Camino Portugues pilgrimage? Was Veronica's hyperkalemia condition exacerbated due to her condition? Did Hugo and Veronica know about their solitary kidney conditions?

As the press interview concluded, and the detectives stepped away from the podium, they left behind a story that spanned oceans and continents—an inexplicable tale of two souls, Hugo and Veronica, whose lives had been interwoven in ways that transcended time and place. Julian found himself contemplating the complexities of their final moments and the efforts to unravel the mysteries surrounding their deaths.

In a moment of introspection, Julian couldn't help but reflect on the intricate nature of life and death. He realized that, in many ways, it was easier to provide explanations for the circumstances of death—such as the causes and timing—than it was to capture the essence of the lives that had been lived. The human experience, filled with its joys, sorrows, connections, and mysteries, an intricate tapestry woven with countless threads, and trying to describe it all in the face of mortality. Julian carried this contemplation with him—a reminder that while death may have its answers, the stories of those who had passed on were often far more intricate and elusive.

The most poignant and unforgettable memory etched in Detective Julian's heart was the solemn funeral of Hugo and

Veronica, a final chapter in the story of their intertwined lives. The caskets, holding their embalmed bodies, were carried on a somber journey from Vagator to the Siolim cemetery—a Goan town where their love had first taken root during the vibrant Sao Joao festival.

The funeral procession was a testament to the profound impact that Hugo and Veronica had on the lives of those who had known them. It was a procession of epic proportions, allowed by the state, and it stretched for a mile, meandering through the winding roads. Thousands of mourners, with heavy hearts and tear-filled eyes, gathered to pay their respects to the departed souls.

The procession was not merely a physical journey but a symbolic one—a final farewell to two individuals whose love story had captured the hearts of many. Along the route, people stood in silent reverence, lining the roadsides to watch the procession pass by. It was a moment of collective mourning, a poignant reminder of the love and legacy that Hugo and Veronica had left behind.

Finally, as the procession reached its destination, Hugo and Veronica were laid to rest side by side in the Siolim cemetery. In death, as in life, they remained inseparable, their souls finding eternal companionship in the peaceful embrace of the earth. It was a fitting conclusion to a remarkable love story—a love that had transcended the boundaries of time and continued to touch the hearts of all who had been a part of their journey.

In the serene Siolim cemetery, where Hugo and Veronica found their eternal rest side by side, a creative tombstone was erected to honor their enduring love story. Carved from the resilient stone of time, it stood as a testament to their unwavering devotion and the profound impact they had on those who knew them.

The tombstone bore the names of Hugo and Veronica, etched in elegant, flowing script, a mirror of their love that had transcended the confines of mortality. Beneath their names, a heartfelt inscription captured the essence of their extraordinary journey:

"Here lie two souls, forever entwined in love's embrace, Hugo and Veronica, whose love knew no bounds or space. In life and death, they found their destiny's call, Together they rest, as love's eternal thrall."

At the center of the tombstone, a sculpted heart, intertwined with ivy and roses, symbolized their enduring love, an emblem of passion and devotion that could not be extinguished even by the passage of time.

Surrounding the heart, delicate engravings depicted scenes from their shared life—moments of joy, laughter, and the warmth of their companionship. It was a tribute to the vivid tapestry of their existence, a collage of memories that would forever live on in the hearts of those who visited their final resting place.

As the sun cast its gentle rays upon the creative tombstone, it served as a beacon, inviting all who came to pay their respects to reflect on the profound love story of Hugo and Veronica. Their legacy would endure, not only in the stone and engravings but in the hearts and memories of those who cherished their remarkable journey of love.

The day after the funeral, Julian glanced at some of the headlines in the top newspapers available in print and online:

- **"A Tale of Love and Mystery: International Detectives Unearth the Extraordinary Saga of Hugo and Veronica"** Front Page Headline of Goan newspaper -

In a stunning revelation, detectives from two nations uncover a love story that transcends life and death, as Hugo and Veronica find their final resting place side by side.

- **"The Enigma Unveiled: Hugo and Veronica's Funeral Draws Thousands in Tribute"** Front Page Feature of national newspaper -

The funeral procession of the beloved couple, Hugo and Veronica, captivates the nation, as a remarkable love story comes to its poignant conclusion.

- **"From Investigation to Inspiration: The Incredible Saga of Hugo and Veronica"** Front page Feature and detailed follow up of events in national newspaper -

Join us as we delve into the detective work that uncovered a tale of love, sacrifice, and destiny, uniting hearts across borders.

- **"Love Beyond Borders: India and Spain Collaborate to Honor Hugo and Veronica"** Follow-up Article

Explore the heartwarming collaboration between international investigators as they piece together a love story that defied all odds.

- **"Eternal Love: Hugo and Veronica's Tombstone Chronicles Their Timeless Bond"** Follow-up Special

Witness the artistic tombstone that immortalizes the enduring love of Hugo and Veronica, leaving an indelible mark on history.

- **"The Final Chapter: Siolim Cemetery Welcomes Hugo and Veronica, United in Eternity"** Follow-up Feature

Visit the tranquil Siolim cemetery where two souls, brought together by destiny, rest in eternal togetherness, captivating the hearts of all who pay their respects.

Julian appreciated the coverage as he sipped his coffee at the hotel's breakfast buffet, he thought deeply as his mind raced through the past few days, these newspaper headlines and articles paying apt tribute to a love story that unfolded against all odds, honoring the dedication of detectives who unearthed the remarkable tale of Hugo and Veronica—a story that will continue to inspire and resonate with people across India and beyond.

Julian also made a trip to the 'Chapel of Our Lady of the Mount' in Arambol, Goa—a place imbued with profound significance in Hugo and Veronica's lives. About 15 years ago, Hugo and Veronica had exchanged their vows and celebrated their marriage.

Julian followed a road that wound its way up the hill, leading to a flight of steps that ascended to the church. The chapel was a gem of its own, nestled atop a wooded hill, its elevated location offering a breathtaking panorama that extended over the serene waters of the Mandovi River. From this vantage point, the view was nothing short of magnificent. Old Goa lay sprawled before him, its historic buildings and church spires seemingly rising out of a lush sea of palm trees— a testament to the enduring Portuguese influence on the region.

The 'Chapel of Our Lady of the Mount,' originally built by Afonso de Albuquerque and completed in 1519, had a timeless quality that made it the perfect setting for reflection and remembrance. Its hallowed halls seemed to echo with the prayers and memories of generations gone by. Today, it served as a place of solace, where Julian could pay tribute to the lives of Hugo and Veronica.

As the sun began its descent, casting a warm and golden glow over the ruins of Old Goa, Julian stood in silent contemplation. The chapel's solemn ambiance lent itself to thoughts of both joy and sorrow, a place where the memories of the past were held in reverence. Here, amidst the serene beauty of Goa, Julian found solace in watching the sunset—a poignant reminder of the fleeting nature of life and the enduring power of love.

Following the solemn funeral of Hugo and Veronica, the offices of "Veritas Unveiled" in Calangute were closed for a four-day period of respite. Rodrigo, deeply affected by the recent events and the exhaustive investigation, had made the thoughtful decision to grant his dedicated staff some time off to be with their families. It was a time for reflection, healing, and coming to terms with the loss they had all experienced.

For Rodrigo, these days were also an opportunity to contemplate the future of "Veritas Unveiled" channel. With the weight of recent events bearing down on him, he sought clarity on how to proceed. The channel had been an integral part of his and Hugo's shared vision, and he was determined to honor that vision while moving forward.

As Rodrigo found solace in this brief respite, he decided to spend some time scrolling through the messages posted on the channel's social media sites. It was a heartwarming and overwhelming experience. Thousands of viewers had come forward, conveying their condolences and sharing in the collective grief that had touched so many. Among the messages, a common request stood out: the viewers were yearning to see Hugo's last recording, the 4 hours and 30 minutes that had been mentioned during the detectives' press conference and covered in articles both in print and online.

The outpouring of interest and the desire to hear Hugo's voice one last time moved Rodrigo deeply. It was a testament to the connection Hugo had forged with the channel's audience, and it reaffirmed the importance of sharing this final recording with those who had been touched by his work. He had watched poignantly the recording where Maria in the voice of Veronica narrated love stories to Hugo. With a newfound sense of purpose, Rodrigo began to consider how to fulfill this heartfelt request from the viewers to carry forward the legacy of "Veritas Unveiled."

With a sense of purpose and determination, the staff of "Veritas Unveiled" returned to their office after four days of rest and reflection, ready to carry forward the legacy that Hugo had left behind, yet unsure what they would be hearing from Rodrigo their executive producer.

Rodrigo, gathered everyone together to share the path forward and the exciting news that Hugo's final recording of 4 hours and 30 minutes would soon be made available to their eager viewers.

Rodrigo addressed each team member, assigning them specific roles and responsibilities in this new chapter.

Ashley Fernandes, the researcher, was tasked with delving into the stories and their respective locations around the world, ensuring that the content they were about to release would be well-informed and captivating.

Sunil Gupta, the visual editor lead, was entrusted with the vital task of crafting and polishing Hugo's recording, with the goal of readying it for release within a tight two-week timeframe.

Vishal Sen, the audio and sound lead, was called upon to enhance the background audio and sound quality, ensuring that the content would be a delight to the ears without a glitch.

Antonio Batista, the IT team lead, was given the crucial responsibility of making sure that every team member had access to the content and that the IT team was on standby to assist in the preparation process, despite the short timeline.

Priscila Silveira, the marketing manager, was charged with creating compelling promotional videos to build anticipation for the upcoming content release.

Rebecca Silvestri, the social media manager, was tasked with strategically promoting these promotional videos across various social media channels, harnessing the power of digital outreach.

Olivia Posada, the guest booker, was encouraged to plan and secure guest speakers for future episodes, ensuring that their schedules were locked in for upcoming episodes and facilitating post-episode follow-ups to gather esteemed guest comments.

With each team member's role clearly defined, the "Veritas Unveiled" team embarked on this new journey with a sense of purpose and unity, determined to continue Hugo's mission of unveiling truths and sharing stories with their dedicated viewers.

As the dedicated staff of "Veritas Unveiled" worked tirelessly to process and prepare Hugo's final recording for release, something incredible began to happen. The channel experienced an unprecedented surge in subscribers, with the number steadily climbing. In just a mere two weeks, the subscriber count had doubled, reaching a remarkable 40 million subscribers. It was a staggering rate of growth, surpassing any the channel had seen in recent years.

The catalyst for this rapid expansion was the captivating and enigmatic love story of Hugo and Veronica, which had garnered widespread media coverage. Their tale of love and mystery had struck a chord with audiences, and people from around the world were drawn to the channel to explore their story.

As the new subscribers joined the "Veritas Unveiled" community, they also began to explore the channel's extensive archive of older episodes. The rich content, filled with knowledge and information, satisfied their thirst for insights and enlightenment.

Word of mouth played a significant role in spreading appreciation for the channel, as viewers shared their newfound discovery with friends and family. Rodrigo watched with joy as the channel's reach expanded, knowing that this surge in subscribers would enable them to comfortably meet their financial obligations to the dedicated staff.

The growth was a testament to the enduring impact of Hugo's work and the channel's commitment to unveiling truths and sharing knowledge with a global audience. It was a bittersweet moment, with Hugo's absence keenly felt, but his legacy and the channel he had built continued to thrive and flourish.

Priscila Silveira, the marketing manager of "Veritas Unveiled," wasted no time in fulfilling her role in the team's plan. Within a week, she had meticulously prepared promotional video content for the upcoming episodes. The team had decided to break down the 4 hours and 30 minutes recording into a series of nine episodes, each lasting 30 minutes.

Priscila's promotional videos were likely filled with tantalizing glimpses of what the viewers could expect in this upcoming series. They were designed to pique the audience's curiosity and anticipation, enticing them to eagerly await the release of each episode.

As the team worked diligently to ready Hugo's final recording for its debut, Priscila's efforts in marketing and promotion played a vital role in building excitement and engagement among the channel's ever-growing audience. The countdown to the release of the series had begun, and the viewers could hardly wait to uncover the truths and stories that lay within.

Rebecca Silvestri, the social media manager of "Veritas Unveiled," wasted no time in amplifying Priscila's promotional videos for the upcoming release of the series of nine episodes. Across all the channel's social media platforms, Rebecca shared these enticing teasers, sparking excitement and curiosity among the audience.

As the promotional videos made their way onto the digital landscape, viewers from around the world engaged with the content, leaving their thoughts and comments.

Rodrigo scrolled through some of the subscriber comments that surfaced on various social media platforms:

- User_latch_2011: "I can't believe we're finally getting to hear more of Hugo's wisdom! Can't wait!"
- TravelEnthusiastically_99: "The stories and insights on this channel are always mind-blowing. Ready for the new series!"
- CuriousCatLady: "I've been binge-watching older episodes in anticipation. This is going to be epic!"
- FilmyBuff23: "Hugo's legacy lives on! The world needs more content like this."

- InquisitiveMind_767: "That teaser gave me chills. Hugo's last recording is going to be a treasure trove of knowledge."
- thousands of more comments bore a common theme of – 'awaiting the release of content.'

Rebecca's adept management of the channel's social media presence not only built anticipation for the upcoming series but also fostered a sense of community among the viewers. Their comments and interactions showcased the eager anticipation for Hugo's final recording and the channel's commitment to unveiling the truth and sharing stories that resonated deeply with its audience.

Earlier in the year, a significant decision was taken by Hugo and Veronica. They had decided to entrust their cherished residence, 'Villa Carvalho,' along with the official trademark controls of the 'Veritas Unveiled' channel's content, to a trust. The sole responsibility for this trust had been placed in the capable hands of Rodrigo, a decision that had taken Rodrigo somewhat by surprise but had left him deeply appreciative of the trustful gesture made by Hugo and Veronica.

As Rodrigo held the trust papers in his hand, he couldn't help but reflect on the profound sense of responsibility that came with this role. He understood the weight of preserving and extending Hugo's legacy, a legacy that had touched the hearts and minds of millions of viewers around the world. Hugo had always been passionate about his work, and the channel's dedicated workforce had been like a family to him.

Now, with the anticipation growing around the release of the new content and the surge in subscribers eagerly engaging with older episodes, the future of 'Veritas Unveiled' was starting to look exceptionally promising. Rodrigo was determined to honor Hugo's memory by not only preserving the channel but also exploring new ideas and avenues that would keep the office workforce thriving and continue the mission of unveiling truths and sharing knowledge with the world.

The trust placed in Rodrigo was a testament to the unwavering faith that Hugo and Veronica had in him and in the enduring impact of the channel they had built together. It was a responsibility Rodrigo was ready to embrace, knowing that the channel's journey was far from over and that Hugo's spirit would live on in the stories, wisdom, and discoveries yet to be unveiled.

Rodrigo's mind was teeming with innovative and resourceful ideas on how to preserve and celebrate the enduring love story of Hugo and Veronica. Their home, 'Villa Carvalho,' held a treasure trove of memories and sentiments that Rodrigo believed could be transformed into a lasting tribute to their remarkable bond.

In his role as the trustee for Villa Carvalho, Rodrigo decided to take the first step toward this vision. He applied to the appropriate offices in Panjim with a heartfelt proposal: to rename the residence 'Amor Eterno,' which meant 'Eternal Love.' This new name would not only encapsulate the essence of Hugo and Veronica's love but also serve as a fitting dedication to their enduring legacy.

Furthermore, Rodrigo requested special permission to open 'Amor Eterno' to guided tours. He envisioned that these tours would offer visitors a glimpse into the intimate world of Hugo and Veronica, allowing them to explore the beautiful home where this extraordinary love had flourished. The income generated from these tours could then be used to support the channel and its mission, ensuring that Hugo's vision continued to thrive.

With 'Amor Eterno,' Rodrigo aimed not only to preserve the memory of Hugo and Veronica but also to share their extraordinary love story with the world. It was a heartfelt tribute that would allow their legacy to live on, inspiring others with the power of love, dedication, and the pursuit of truth.

Rodrigo's entrepreneurial spirit was alive and well, and his mind was constantly on the lookout for new opportunities to expand the 'Veritas Unveiled' channel and secure its future. As he pondered the possibilities, one particular idea sparked his interest, and he decided to take action.

Rodrigo also reached out to Masqueda, the renowned Japanese manufacturer known for its cutting-edge technology, particularly in the field of robotics. He presented a compelling proposal to Masqueda, suggesting that his channel could become the sole dedicated reseller for their advanced robotic products in several countries around the world. Rodrigo believed that these robots could be integrated into the channel's offerings, enhancing its content and engagement with viewers.

Furthermore, Rodrigo shared this innovative concept with his research team, who were always eager to explore new avenues. He discussed the idea of marketing the robots as not just technological marvels but also as personalized companions. One intriguing feature Rodrigo proposed was the ability for the robots to adapt their voices to match those of their buyers, offering a unique and personalized experience, similar to how Maria was personalized with Veronica's voice, this would be an additive feature provided by the channel for people that were not so tech-savvy and would appreciate the assistance of a hands-on crew from the channel that would be dedicated to their service.

With multiple opportunities lining up in his mind, Rodrigo was determined to seize the moment and explore these potential ventures. He understood that the channel needed to evolve and diversify to continue thriving in the ever-changing landscape of media and technology.

Rodrigo's proposal to the Japanese robot manufacturer had not fallen on deaf ears. In fact, he received a positive and enthusiastic response from the company. They recognized the tremendous potential of collaborating with the 'Veritas Unveiled' channel, which boasted a staggering 45 million subscribers. For the Japanese manufacturer, this partnership was an opportunity to work with a digital influencer who had a significant presence in the online world. Rodrigo was excited to see the rise in subscribers who had grown from 40 million to 45 million in just a matter of 4 days.

The prospect of leveraging the channel's vast reach and influence to promote their innovative robotic products was an enticing one. Rodrigo's vision and dedication to expanding the channel's horizons had opened doors to exciting new possibilities. This collaboration had the potential to bring advanced technology to a global audience, and both parties were eager to embark on this journey together.

Meanwhile Ana, who had a deep connection with the content that Hugo had generated for the channel over the years. She had immersed herself in the channel's 1359 episodes, absorbing the knowledge, the stories, and the wisdom shared by Hugo and his guests. As she delved into this vast repository of information, Ana found herself not only learning but also preparing herself for what lay ahead.

In her quiet moments, Ana would revisit some of the iconic episodes, positioning herself in front of the camera. She would repeat some of the insightful and thought-provoking questions that Hugo had posed to his guests. It was as if she was rehearsing, internalizing the essence of Hugo's interviewing style, and gaining a deep understanding of the art of conversation.

Ana's dedication and self-confidence were steadily growing with each episode she revisited and each question she repeated. She knew that she was standing on the threshold of a new chapter in the channel's journey, and she was determined to carry forward Hugo's legacy with grace and authenticity. As she continued to hone her skills, Ana was preparing herself to step into the spotlight and continue the channel's mission of unveiling truths and sharing knowledge with the world.

Ana, the ever-confident and fearless receptionist at the 'Veritas Unveiled' office, had always been the first point of contact for a diverse range of people, inquiries, and situations. Her role had made her adept at handling various aspects of communication and interaction with grace and composure.

Over time, she had developed her skills and grown more self-assured.

With a burning desire to contribute more to the channel and take on a more prominent role, Ana had been practicing and preparing herself for a significant step. In fact, she had practiced many times in front of the mirror asking the question to Rodrigo –"Rodrigo, Do you think I could get an opportunity to host a future episode for the channel?"

Gathering her courage, in the office, she approached Rodrigo, the channel's leader, with a heartfelt request. Her voice steady and her determination unwavering, dressed in a beautiful red floral dress, she had noticed this dress had got a glance from everyone in the office when worn in the past, wearing white heels, with one of the hands placed on her hip with confidence, she asked Rodrigo the question.

"Rodrigo," Ana began, "I've been thinking about something, Do you think I could get an opportunity to host a future episode for the channel?"

Ana's question hung in the air, her eyes reflecting her eagerness and determination. She was ready to step out of the shadows and into the spotlight, ready to take on new challenges and make her mark on the 'Veritas Unveiled' channel.

Rodrigo listened attentively to Ana's request, and her enthusiasm was unmistakable. He welcomed her initiative with an encouraging smile and a sense of excitement for what the future could hold. While he was confident in Ana's abilities, he also understood the collaborative nature of their work at 'Veritas Unveiled.'

In response, Rodrigo expressed his appreciation for Ana's proactive approach and her readiness to take the lead in various aspects of the channel's production process. He explained that hosting an episode would involve working closely with other team members, each of whom played a crucial role in creating and releasing episodes. He listed the key team members Ana would collaborate with, emphasizing the importance of teamwork and synergy: You will be working very closely with Ashley Fernandes – Research team lead, Vishal Sen – Audio & Sound lead, Priscila Silveira – Marketing manager, Rebecca Silvestri – Social media manager, Sunil Gupta – Visual editor lead, Antonio Batista – IT Team lead (Local & Cloud), Olivia Posada – Guest Booker

Rodrigo assured Ana that he would take a couple of days to discuss her request with the other team members and gather their feedback. He recognized the significance of her aspirations and was committed to fostering an environment where team members could explore new opportunities and contribute to the channel's growth.

Ana was thrilled with Rodrigo's response, knowing that he would initiate discussions with the team members on her behalf. She had been contemplating how to approach the others, and Rodrigo's support gave her confidence and hope. For Rodrigo, this was an exciting development, as it marked the beginning of a plan for the channel's continued success and evolution.

Meanwhile the editing team had worked on the first episode and ready for review, So the team gathered eagerly in the office conference room, their anticipation palpable in the room. It was time to watch the first episode that they had meticulously prepared.

The unique name chosen for this inaugural episode, one that would not only captivate the audience but also set the tone for the upcoming eight episodes, was "Eternal Embrace: Love Stories Across Time." As the episode commenced with this evocative title splashed across the screen, it promised an enchanting journey through the ages, exploring the enduring power of love.

The scene on the screen unfolded, with Hugo seated on the dark brown living room sofa on one side and Maria, the robot, standing on the other end. Maria began to speak, her voice personalized to sound like Veronica's, as she delved into the enchanting tales of eternal love that spanned centuries.

The detectives had shared with Ana, Rodrigo, and other team members the notes they had found on Veronica's phone, which detailed the nine novenas she had been praying during her pilgrimage. In order to determine if any of them had suspicions or insights based on Veronica's prayers, the detectives had been very transparent once all the feedback had been from the team. This information in the notes of Veronica was an integral and a valuable piece of the puzzle in understanding the enigmatic circumstances surrounding Hugo and Veronica's deaths, mainly it had been instrumental in clearing the suspicion of involvement from anyone at the office.

After watching the emotionally charged episode, Ana couldn't help but feel deeply moved, and tears welled up in her eyes. Her heart was touched by the profound stories of love presented in the episode. Ana had an idea that she wanted to share with the team. She mentioned that Veronica had prayed nine novenas, each with its own set of prayers, during her Camino Portugués pilgrimage. Coincidentally, they were planning to release a total of nine episodes. Ana suggested that they include this connection in the introduction of each episode, with a subtitle reflecting the novena for that particular episode.

The team embraced Ana's suggestion, recognizing the beautiful symbolism it carried. So, they decided to add subtitles to each episode based on the novenas. For example, the first episode, "Eternal Embrace: Love Stories Across Time," would have the subtitle "The Novena for Strength, Unity, and the Camino of Faith" as a tribute to Veronica's spiritual journey.

The highly anticipated day had arrived for the release of the first episode. By this time, the number of subscribers had swelled to an impressive 50 million, this was such an amazing jump of subscribers from 20 million where it stood on December 3rd. The entire team gathered in the conference room, their anticipation palpable in the air, as they eagerly awaited the response from viewers once the episode left their hands and was released on the channel into the vast digital world. They knew that in just about an hour, the first reactions and responses would begin pouring in, and they couldn't wait to see how the audience would receive it.

As the first hour rolled by since the release of the episode, there were already half a million views on the video, and the comment section was buzzing with activity:

- "This is such a beautiful tribute to Hugo and Veronica's love story. I'm in tears. 🩶 "
- "I've been a long-time subscriber, but this episode is next level. Loved Veronica's voice, first time!! Can't wait for the rest!"
- "Veronica's voice is so captivating! Can't stop listening to her."
- BookLover27: "The novena prayers in the intro gave me chills. What a wonderful touch!"
- "Hugo and Veronica's story is like a real-life fairy tale. Can't wait to watch all nine episodes!"

The team couldn't help but smile as they read these comments, knowing that their hard work was resonating with the audience and that Hugo and Veronica's legacy would live on through their channel.

The day after the release of the episode, as everyone gathered in the office, the team was elated to see the incredible response. The statistics showed that about 4 million people had viewed the episode within the first 16 hours of its release, which was an extraordinary achievement for the channel. What made it even more special was that nearly 25% of the viewers had left comments, showing high engagement.

The subscriber count had skyrocketed to 55 million within a single day after the release of the first episode, a remarkable feat that left everyone in awe. It was clear that the channel had gained popularity not only in India but also in countries like Portugal, Spain, Italy, France, the USA, the UK, Australia, New Zealand, Fiji, and many others around the world.

The team couldn't have asked for a better start to this new chapter, and they were excited to continue sharing Hugo and Veronica's love story with their growing global audience.

Veronica had always been an avid reader, and she harbored a desire to appear as a guest on Hugo's show. The idea had been a topic of discussion between Hugo and Veronica over the past few years, but they couldn't quite pinpoint a specific topic that would suit the show. However, it was nothing short of a miracle that Veronica and Hugo had now engaged in a conversation, and even though it was mediated by Maria, their chosen topic was one that they would have never anticipated in their wildest dreams – love stories.

Hugo had mentioned the name of Miguel during the recording, the editing team had cleverly given an introduction earlier in the episode by referencing Miguel, which in Portuguese translates to 'who is like God,' it struck a powerful chord with viewers. Many viewers were moved by this choice, and it provided an explanation for Hugo mentioning Miguel's name, some of the comments from viewers specifically highlighted this connection, expressing their appreciation for the profound reference. Few comments from viewers:

- "The reference to Miguel at the beginning is so poignant. It reminds us that love, in all its forms, is a divine gift."

- "This channel always surprises me with its depth. The mention of Miguel as 'who is like God' is so fitting for this conversation about eternal love."

- "Wow, the introduction gave me chills. 'Who is like God' - it perfectly captures the essence of this beautiful dialogue."

- "The grace of God indeed shines through this episode. Miguel, a name that embodies the divine nature of love."

- "I teared up when they mentioned Miguel. It's like a reminder that love is a divine blessing."

- ....

The comments kept coming in from viewers as the engagement showered the channel with lots of confidence on approaching the release of other episodes, the reference to Miguel added a spiritual dimension to the episode and resonated deeply with the audience, creating a meaningful and emotional connection.

Rodrigo was thrilled to see the subscriber base growing and the older episodes acting as a filler for viewers as they waited for the new episode to be released.

Meanwhile as the days rolled by, the rest of the episodes were ready for release, the team was energized with the response they were getting for just a single episode. The team just had to follow the strategic cadence for timed release of these episodes.

The rest of the episodes had the same main title, and there were new subtitles for each of the episodes based on the novenas:

1. Subtitle - Episode 1: "Novena for Strength, Unity, and the Camino of Faith"

2. Subtitle - Episode 2: "Novena for Protection, Trust, and the Pilgrimage Within"

3. Subtitle - Episode 3: "Novena for Love's Distance, Acceptance's Grace"

4. Subtitle - Episode 4: "Novena for Patience's Journey, Forgiveness's Healing"

5. Subtitle - Episode 5: "Novena for Guidance on the Camino to Blessings"

6. Subtitle - Episode 6: "Novena for Hope's Light, Selflessness's Gift"

7. Subtitle - Episode 7: "Novena for Understanding Across the Miles, Joy's Arrival"

8. Subtitle - Episode 8: "Novena for Gratitude's Reflection, Graciousness's Practice"

9. Subtitle - Episode 9: "Novena for Reunion's Promise, Divine Will's Guidance"

The other episodes were rolled out every week.

With the release of each episode in the "Amor Eterno" series, the channel's subscriber count continued to surge. Starting at 55 million after the release of the first episode, the channel's popularity grew exponentially, with an increase of at least 5 million subscribers each week.

As the day arrived for the release of the final 9th episode in the series, the subscriber count had soared to an impressive 98 million. The overwhelming response and unprecedented growth of the channel's viewership were a testament to the captivating stories of love, the innovative use of technology, and the enduring legacy of Hugo and Veronica. "Veritas Unveiled" had truly become a global phenomenon, captivating the hearts and minds of viewers around the world.

As the final 9th episode of "Amor Eterno" was released, the culmination of this unique project that had brought together four key participants as evident to the viewers: Miguel, Maria the robot embodying Veronica's voice and presence, Hugo the charismatic host of "Veritas Unveiled," and, of course, Veronica's voice emanating through Maria.

This extraordinary combination sparked diverse perspectives and takeaways among viewers, each with their unique interpretations and beliefs. The comments poured in, reflecting various viewpoints:

- "The presence of Miguel, 'who is like God,' in this episode is deeply moving. It's as if divinity has arrived in Vagator, Goa."

- "Maria is a testament to human ingenuity and technological advancement. Hugo's vision to use her for these love stories is commendable."

- "I can't help but think of the sacrifice in love as I watch these episodes. It's a reminder that true love knows no bounds."

- "This series highlights the power of feminism. Veronica's voice through Maria is like a symbol of strong, empowered women."

- "Love is undeniably tragic, but it also brings hope and meaning to our existence. This episode beautifully captures that essence."

- ......

The viewers' comments encompassed a wide spectrum of perspectives, from the spiritual and divine to the technological and innovative. "Amor Eterno" had touched the hearts of its audience, leaving them with a profound appreciation for the complexity and beauty of love in all its forms.

Chapter 33

AMOR ETERNO

In Vagator, Goa, nestled amidst the familiar swaying palms and the timeless whisper of the Arabian Sea, stood Villa Carvalho. Once, the private sanctuary of Veronica and Hugo, two souls entwined in an eternal love story. But now, its name had transformed, echoing the spirit of their romance. It was known as 'Amor Eterno', a Portuguese phrase that resonated through the corridors of time: 'Eternal Love'

Guides in vibrant sarongs led groups of tourists through the hallowed grounds of the villa. They spoke with a gleam in their eyes, each word a testament to the now legendary story that had unfolded within these walls. Hugo, the famed podcaster, whose words transformed into stories and ideas into inspiration. His subscribers had swelled to record numbers, but it was not just his voice that echoed; it was the love story that had unfolded beneath this sun-kissed roof.

As visitors strolled through the villa's lush gardens and elegantly furnished rooms, they marveled at the tangible traces of a love that transcended time. The couple's photographs, captured in moments of laughter and tenderness, adorned the walls like living memories. Veronica's paintings, a testament to her artistic prowess and the depths of her love, adorned the living spaces with vibrant colors and emotion.

Maria, the robot, stood sentinel by the living room sofa, a silent guardian of memories. Visitors, like curious pilgrims, stepped into the hallowed space where Hugo had once recorded his final words. It was as if they had entered a museum, a sanctified enclosure, preserving the essence of a bygone era.

The dark brown sofa, once the comfy seating upon which Hugo had sat to prepare for his stories, was now a relic of his creative haven. Veronica and Hugo had spent their time on this sofa for countless evenings and days. Cordoned off for reverence, it seemed to hold the echoes of their laughter, the weight of their contemplative moments, and the warmth of their conversations. Like a sacred artifact, it remained untouched, a testament to the man and woman whose voice had resonated within these walls.

Bookshelves, lined on the walls behind the sofa, untouched now, held the tomes that had been Hugo's and Veronica's companions in countless adventures of the mind. They, too, were shielded from the touch of time, a testament to the knowledge that had shaped his words and thoughts.

Orchids, once meticulously cared for by Veronica, bloomed in their pots, now the fifty orchids replaced by the thirty-one unique ones, an allegory of saintly blessings, enduring love and beauty. Their delicate petals whispered stories of love that transcended time and adversity, much like the love between Veronica and Hugo.

But it was the wall behind Maria that bore the inscription of their immortal love story. In bold letters, a sign read 'Meu amor e eterno,' a Portuguese phrase that carried the weight of eternity: 'My love is eternal.' It was a declaration etched into the very soul of the room, a reminder that love, once ignited, never truly extinguished.

As visitors gazed upon this scene, they were enveloped by the aura of the living room. It was a place where time stood still, where the past and present merged, and where the eternal nature of love was palpable. Maria, the silent observer, seemed to observe not just the physical artifacts but also the intangible essence of a love story that would forever remain etched in the annals of history.

Couples from all corners of the world made a pilgrimage to 'Amor Eterno' to take pictures of the sign 'Meu Amor e Eterno & Maria' seeking the inspiration of Veronica and Hugo for their own love stories to flourish. They believed that the aura of this place, infused with the essence of an eternal love, held the power to ignite their own passions and cement their bonds.

Underneath the azure Goan skies, newlyweds exchanged vows, hoping to replicate the profound connection that Veronica and Hugo had shared. They stood beneath the ancient Gulmohar tree in the villa's courtyard, where the couple had shared their love for each other countless times, the whisper of the breeze seemed to carry the blessings of the past.

The evergreen Gulmohar tree in the courtyard, with its vibrant crimson blossoms and lush emerald foliage, forming a dense and cooling canopy, providing a protective embrace from the goan sun, stood as a testament to all the visitors and their wishes. Its flowers, like fiery sparks of beauty amidst a sea of green, each petal a delicate masterpiece, a velvety flame, their fiery red-orange hue intensifying in the goan sun, bursting forth in clusters, forming a radiant canopy beckoning the visitors from afar, who made videos and posted reels with recordings of birds seeking solace among the leafy boughs, their melodious songs harmonizing with the rustling of the Gulmohar's leaves in the gentle breeze providing solace in the sweltering heat.

Rodrigo also played a pivotal role in forging a meaningful partnership with local artisans, one that would not only preserve the memory of Hugo and Veronica but also benefit the channel and the talented craftsmen of the region. Together, they embarked on a creative endeavor to fashion memorabilia that bore the emblematic 'Amor eterno', etching the likenesses of Hugo and Veronica onto wooden canvases and other forms of artistry.

In the quaint entrance area of the villa, where the soul of the place met the anticipation of the visitors, a small gift shop had been established. Here, amidst the rustic charm of Goa, tourists could find these lovingly crafted memorabilia, each piece a labor of devotion, skill, and reverence for the enduring love story of the villa's former residents.

The 'Amor eterno' logo, with its profound message of everlasting love, graced these creations, turning each piece into a poignant memento of the love that had blossomed within the villa's walls. Carvings of Hugo and Veronica in wood and various other artistic expressions bore witness to their tale, inviting visitors to take a piece of their love story home with them.

For the channel, this endeavor was more than just a tribute; it was a source of additional revenue, allowing them to continue sharing their stories and experiences with a wider audience. It was a reminder that love had the power to inspire not only emotions but also creativity and commerce.

Simultaneously, for the local artisans, it was an opportunity to showcase their talent to a global audience, a means to sustain their craftsmanship and heritage. The partnership was a harmonious blend of tradition and modernity, where the past met the present in a celebration of love and creativity.

As visitors perused the offerings in the gift shop, they became part of this narrative, taking home a piece of 'Meu Amor e Eterno' and contributing to the legacy of Hugo and Veronica. In every purchase, there was a shared connection, a recognition of the enduring power of love and the collaborative spirit that transcended boundaries, just as the memorabilia transcended time.

The legend of Villa Carvalho, now 'Amor Eterno,' had become a timeless allegory of love's enduring power. It was a place where love transcended the bounds of time, a testament to the belief that true love was eternal and could inspire generations. As the sun dipped below the horizon, its last rays kissed the villa's façade, casting a warm, golden glow upon the hallowed ground where Veronica and Hugo's love continued to bloom, inviting others to find their own eternal love stories amidst its storied walls.

After the visit to 'Amor Eterno,' tourists embarked on a poignant journey to further deepen their connection with the timeless love story of Hugo and Veronica. Their next stop was the 'Chapel of Our Lady of the Mount' in Arambol, Goa, perched majestically overlooking the serene Mandovi River. It was here, in the embrace of nature's grandeur, that Hugo and Veronica had exchanged their vows and pledged their love for all eternity. The chapel stood as a silent witness to their sacred union, a place where love had found its highest expression.

Another destination on this heart-touching touristic expedition was the Siolim Cemetery, where the couple had been laid to rest side by side, forever together even in death. As visitors approached their resting place, the guides extended a gentle offer: would they like to purchase flowers to pay their respects? Many visitors accepted, recognizing the symbolic beauty of this gesture.

And so, a phenomenon unfolded daily at the cemetery. Visitors, clutching stems of vibrant blooms, stood before the graves of Hugo and Veronica. As they whispered their own words of love, remembrance, and gratitude, the gentle Goan breeze would play its part. Every now and then, wind gusts would sweep through, causing the flowers resting on the graves to shift and sway, as if touched by an invisible hand.

It was a heartwarming spectacle, a dance of nature that seemed to invoke the spirits of Hugo and Veronica. The sight brought smiles to the faces of all who bore witness to this delicate display. In the tender breeze of Goa, amidst the rustling leaves and the distant murmur of the river, visitors felt a profound connection to the couple they had come to honor. It was as if Hugo and Veronica were taking a sweet, ephemeral whiff of the flowers offered by those who still cherished their love story.

In those moments, amidst the quiet serenity of the Siolim Cemetery, visitors found the courage to express the sweetest and most genuine sentiments to their loved ones. The atmosphere was infused with love, gratitude, and a poignant reminder that true love, like the wind's caress, could touch the heart even in the most ethereal of ways.

Meanwhile at the Office in Calangute, it had been almost a course of three months since December 3rd. It was time for a new face to be introduced as host to the podcast. Afterall, it had to match Hugo's legacy, who was the podcast's seasoned host, and expertly curated a collection of 1359 episodes, each filled with profound insights and captivating interviews.

Each of the episodes in the 'Amor Eterno' series had an attach rate of 85% with the viewers. Now the number of episodes that Hugo had released for the channel stood at 1368 after the release of the 9 episodes.

Finally, the day had arrived for a significant shift in the show's dynamics. The studio buzzed with excitement as Ana Da Costa, the new face of Veritas Unveiled, prepared to take her seat in front of the microphone. The guest awaiting her across the table was none other than a famed spiritual guru from India, a luminary revered by seekers of truth worldwide. The channel was starting this episode recording with the subscriber count of 105 million.

Ana Da Costa, with her Portuguese ancestry of four generations in Goa, embodied a unique blend of cultures and histories, making her the perfect choice to carry forward the podcast's legacy of exploring diverse spiritual perspectives.

As Ana settled into her chair, she exuded an air of confidence and grace that seemed almost magnetic. Her attire was a testament to her captivating presence. Draped in a resplendent red sequin saree, its shimmering fabric caught the studio lights, creating an aura of regal elegance. She paired this with a sleeveless black blouse that offered a striking contrast, emphasizing her poised and powerful demeanor.

Ana's flowing hair cascaded over one shoulder, cascading like a dark brown monsoon waterfall, while the other shoulder bore the weight of her saree's intricate folds. It was as though she carried not just her family's rich history but also the wisdom and beauty of her ancestral land while the camera frames captured her looks.

As the recording lights blinked to life, Ana began her conversation with the spiritual guru. The studio was hushed in anticipation, for this was not just a new chapter for Veritas Unveiled but a vibrant, multicultural dialogue that promised to transcend boundaries and unveil the profound truths of the human spirit.

Chapter 34

EPILOGUE - BALANCE OF A SEESAW

In the grand theater of the universe, the seesaw of life is a perpetual motion, its fulcrum marked by birth seated on one end and death seated on the other. As we traverse our life's existence, this fulcrum shifts, and the end representing death gradually ascends. When the end of death rises high enough, we collectively come to acknowledge it as the culmination of an individual's destined journey on this earthly plane. But the ceaseless oscillations of the seesaw will continue in another plane, as we navigate the intricate balance between the emergence into life and the eventual return to the great unknown, our existence is marked by the inexorable rise of that solemn end. Life's seesaw teeters gently between birth and death, an eternal oscillation that defines any individual's journey.

In the grand theater of earthly existence, life unfurls like a seesaw, an eternal dance between the zenith and nadir, where each ephemeral moment engraves its enduring signature upon the fabric of the soul. These waves of experience merge into the ever-flowing river of time, thrusting us unyieldingly toward loftier aspirations.

Upon this seesaw, a symphony of emotions serenades our inner being. Laughter dances with tears, bliss and pain take their turns upon the stage, and we learn to soar with wings fragile as gossamer, only to be gently returned to earth in love's capricious embrace. Amidst this kaleidoscope of sensation, we glimpse fleeting beauty, savor the sweet taste of grace, and unearth hidden reservoirs of strength, clutching to faith even in the darkest of hours. It is upon this precarious fulcrum of existence that we dare to dream of a brighter morrow.

Yet, as we traverse the seesaw of life, we must not succumb to the vertigo of despair or melancholy. For these dizzying highs and plunging lows, these tumultuous swings, are not malicious tormentors but steadfast guides. They mark our path, illuminating the contours of our being and the boundless potential within.

As we ascend to the zenith, we must resist the blinding allure of hubris, for the peaks remind us of our achievements and the heights we are capable of scaling. When we descend into the depths, we must not surrender to the abyss of despair, for the valleys teach us resilience and the art of ascending once more.

In this ceaseless rhythm, we find our purpose. Life's undulating cadence does not exist to confound or extinguish our inner flame; it is a guiding hand, propelling us toward the discovery of our true path, helping us unearth the unique imprint we are meant to leave upon the world.

So, when you find yourself upon the seesaw of life, remember that the highs and lows are not adversaries, but companions, mentors, allies. They unveil the brilliance of your spirit and beckon you toward your destined summit. Embrace the swaying journey, find your equilibrium, and allow the seesaw to transport you toward the profound revelation of your purpose.

The solemnity of All Saints' Day, a Christian celebration held on November 1st, stands as a testament to the veneration of countless unknown and uncanonized saints within the Church, those whose virtuous lives have not been individually commemorated with feast days. The origins of this sacred day are shrouded in the mists of time, a testament to its ancient roots.

The concrete evidence of the November 1st date for this celebration and the expansive concept of honoring all saints, whether canonized or martyred, can be traced back to the reign of Pope Gregory III, who held the papal office from 731 to 741. During his pontificate, he dedicated a chapel within the hallowed walls of St. Peter's Basilica in Rome, a place of divine reverence, on November 1st, specifically to honor all saints.

The Feast of All Saints serves as a poignant reminder of the countless faithful individuals who, while not officially recognized through canonization or beatification by the Church, have nonetheless contributed to the noble tapestry of Christian faith. It is a day dedicated to celebrating the unsung heroes of faith, those whose lives of devotion and virtue have often gone unnoticed by the broader world.

These unsung heroes, now enjoying their eternal reward in the presence of the divine, remain deeply concerned about the earthly realm they left behind. The saints in heaven are entrusted with a sacred task—that of intercession. While God, in His infinite wisdom, is fully aware of our needs and could certainly listen to our prayers without intermediaries, He chooses to involve the saints in our lives.

The saints, those who have gone before us, act as powerful intercessors. They stand as conduits between the earthly and the divine, bringing our prayers before God's throne and, in return, delivering His boundless grace to us. In this way, they play an active role in God's divine plan for the world.

Through their intercession, the saints become participants in the ongoing dialogue between humanity and the Creator. They are the bridges that connect our hearts to the divine, the advocates who plead on our behalf, and the witnesses to our earthly struggles and triumphs. Their lives of faith and virtue serve as an enduring source of inspiration for believers, guiding them on their own spiritual journeys.

On All Saints' Day, as the faithful gather to honor the memory of these unsung heroes, they do so with the understanding that the saints, though they have departed this world, remain eternally connected to the living through the bonds of faith and intercession. In celebrating their lives, believers reaffirm the timeless truth that the communion of saints is a living reality, a testament to the enduring power of faith, and a source of solace and inspiration for all who seek to walk in the footsteps of the holy.

The feast of All Saints serves as a radiant tapestry of holiness, showcasing its manifold facets in a diverse array of saints. It reminds us that holiness knows no boundaries of age, wealth, occupation, or circumstance. Among the saints, we find the rich and the poor, the young and the old, the warriors and the peacemakers, the hermits and the organizers of charities, parents and celibates, scholars and those who couldn't even read. Every era has borne its own saints, and ours is no exception. The struggles they faced may have changed with time, but the heroes, the champions of faith, continue to walk among us. It is an integral part of our Catholic teaching that every one of us is called to aspire to sainthood.

What we celebrate on this hallowed day is, at its core, holiness—a manifestation of God's own holiness. The saints, far from being superhuman beings with supernatural powers, were good and virtuous individuals who exemplified holiness through their actions. They were not exempt from human frailty; rather, they were marked by their virtues. They dwelt in heaven, yet they were formed here on earth. They remain close to us when we seek their intercession. Saints are not mere statues to be venerated; they are biographies to be emulated. They stand as true champions of faith, exemplifying the possibility of a holy life.

For many, there exists a misconception of what a saint represents. Some envision saints as individuals who never sinned throughout their lives—constantly shining with unwavering virtue, possessing unyielding willpower, humility, and purity. They are seen as beings who never lost patience and always placed God and others above themselves. This, however, is a fallacy. It suggests that saints were inherently holy from birth, born saints. In reality, saints became saints; they underwent a profound conversion, a transformation of heart that translated into a transformation of life. This metamorphosis did not transpire overnight; rather, it resulted from a protracted and often arduous struggle. To become a saint is to become authentically oneself—a process that unveils the true self, often concealed beneath layers of folly and pretense.

Sainthood is not a lofty rank reserved for a select few but a universal call extended to everyone. Saints serve as our role models, demonstrating through their lives that Christ's holy love, mercy, and boundless forgiveness can be embodied by ordinary individuals from all walks of life and across all epochs. Saints are the heavenly mediators who intercede on our behalf before Jesus, the sole mediator between God and humanity. Those who placed their trust in Christ and lived lives of extraordinary faith serve as instruments through which God performs miracles in our world today. Today, we pray to the saints, both canonized and uncanonized, beseeching them to intercede for us, that we may lead faithful lives.

The Church's message on this day is clear: God's call to holiness is universal. It beckons each of us to dwell in His love and to manifest that love in the lives of those around us. Holiness finds its kinship in the word "wholesomeness." We grow in holiness when we lead lives characterized by integrity, truth, justice, charity, mercy, and compassion, sharing our blessings with others.

Sainthood is not an unattainable ideal; it is a noble aspiration that we can realistically strive for. Pope Francis aptly observed, "Holiness of life is not the privilege of a chosen few; it is the obligation, the call, and the will of God for every Christian." Today, as we celebrate All Saints' Day, let us be inspired by the multitude of saints who have walked the path of holiness before us and remember that, by God's grace, we too can embark on this sacred journey.

In the annals of time, there exists a venerable adage, passed down through generations like a cherished heirloom, that speaks to the intricacies of human identity. It proclaims that within each of us, there dwell three distinct facades, each veiled in varying degrees of secrecy.

The first of these visages is the façade we present to the world at large, a public mask artfully crafted to navigate the labyrinthine streets of society. This is the face we wear when we interact with strangers, an amalgamation of pleasantries, societal norms, and the expectations that society has cast upon us.

The second face, more intimate and vulnerable, is reserved for those we hold dear, our closest confidantes, the family and friends who have journeyed alongside us through the labyrinth of life. Here, we peel away the layers of pretense, revealing the genuine self beneath, a self-forged through shared experiences, laughter, tears, and an unspoken understanding.

Yet, it is the third face, the most enigmatic and clandestine, that holds the truest reflection of our essence. This is the face we reveal solely to ourselves, the mirror through which we glimpse the depths of our desires, fears, and innermost secrets. It is the face that gazes back in moments of solitude, where the unadorned soul meets the unvarnished truth.

But the heart of this ancient wisdom lies not only in the revelation of these three faces but in the profound union of two souls. It posits that true, enduring love, the kind that transcends the bounds of time and mortality, is achieved when lovers choose to unveil their third faces to one another. In this sacred exchange, they lay bare the most authentic aspects of their being, entrusting their deepest vulnerabilities and aspirations to the other's care.

To the rest of the world, their love story may appear to unfold with swiftness and mystique, as if it were a fleeting whisper in the winds of existence. Yet, to these lovers, it is a narrative of fulfillment and completeness, an epic saga played out in the hallowed chambers of their souls. Through the shared revelation of their third faces, they discover a profound and eternal connection, a love that defies the constraints of time and leaves an indelible mark on the tapestry of their existence.

In this, they find not merely a life lived, but a life lived to its fullest, a life colored by the hues of authenticity, vulnerability, and boundless love. It is a testament to the enduring power of the human heart, capable of forging a love that stands as a beacon of light in the midst of life's intricate and ever-unfolding tapestry.

In distant corners of the world, under the same moon's gaze, in Santiago de Compostela, Spain, and Vagator, Goa, India, two souls named Veronica and Hugo. They lived their lives, each with their unique dreams and stories, and it seemed to the world that their fates converged in a manner both sudden and mysterious, for they departed from this world at the age of 40.

To the world, their passing might have appeared as a mere coincidence, an intricate dance of time and circumstance. Yet, the truth lay in the depths of a connection forged beyond the boundaries of ordinary existence. Veronica and Hugo had dared to reveal most of their third secret faces to each other, sharing the most authentic and intimate facets of their souls. This revelation transcended the constraints of time, and in doing so, they achieved a remarkable equilibrium in the seesaw of love.

Their story stood as an exemplar, a beacon in a world often preoccupied with wealth, fame, age, and the distances that divide continents. It whispered a profound truth to those willing to listen: that the essence of life lies not in the material wealth we amass, the accolades we accumulate, or the years that pass us by, but in the depth of connection we forge with another soul.

Yet, as their earthly journey concluded, a question hung in the air, a question that tugged at the very fabric of existence: Does the love story between Veronica and Hugo continue in a different realm?

It is a question that transcends the realm of the tangible, one that probes the mysteries of the afterlife, the enigmatic spaces beyond our understanding. In the tapestry of human existence, love has often been considered a force that defies the boundaries of time and mortality. It is the stuff of myths and legends, a theme that has woven itself into the collective consciousness of humanity.

So, as Veronica and Hugo departed this earthly realm, perhaps their love story found new chapters, written in the ethereal ink of the unknown. In the grand symphony of existence, their love may continue to resonate, an eternal melody that sings of the profound connection they shared, an echo that whispers to those who wonder whether love, in its purest form, can transcend even the boundaries of life and death.

Growing up in a quiet 1970s small town nestled on the border of the vibrant state of Goa, I found myself crossing the state line at least once a month, if not more frequently. Those Goan towns and beaches, etched in my memory, continue to evoke a deep sense of nostalgia to this day.

Among the many enchanting spots, Vagator Beach held a special place in my heart. I can vividly recall those lazy days, lying on the golden sands with a simple coconut material mat beneath me, the raised sand forming an improvised pillow. Each morning, the tranquil beauty of the sunrise greeted me, accompanied by the rhythmic sounds of paddleball being played on the beach.

One of the most cherished memories from those Goan escapades was the early morning breakfast at Mr. Fernandez's modest beach shack. His egg omelets were a culinary delight, and the simplicity of his offerings was a stark contrast to the grandeur of the ocean that stretched endlessly before us. Lunch and dinner often consisted of thick-grained rice paired with yellow lentil dal, a humble yet comforting combination that brought warmth to our souls amidst the vast expanse of the ocean.

The natural world around us added to the charm of those days. A fresh water stream meandered along the hills, and it became a part of our daily routine to indulge in a refreshing shower under its gentle flow after our time spent in the warm embrace of the sea.

In those moments, as I reminisce about the simplicity and beauty of that bygone era, I am transported back to a time when life was unhurried, and the world seemed to pause, allowing us to savor the joys of nature, friendship, and the simple pleasures of life by the sea.

Since those idyllic childhood days spent on the Goan beaches, a burning desire has resided within me—a yearning to pen a novel that serves as a heartfelt ode to the rich tapestry of Goan history and the enchanting towns and beaches that held such significance in my youth.

With every passing year, the memories of those sun-kissed shores, the laughter of friends, the flavors of Mr. Fernandez's dishes, and the gentle embrace of the sea have grown more precious. It is as if those days etched a deep impression on my soul, an indelible mark that can only find release in the written word.

The lure of Goa, with its amalgamation of cultures, its colonial history, and its pristine natural beauty, has continued to beckon to me. The desire to explore its hidden corners, unearth its stories, and bring to life the vibrancy of its towns and beaches in the pages of a novel has remained a constant companion on my creative journey.

In crafting this novel, I hope to capture not only the essence of a place but also the essence of an era—the cultural traditions that weave nostalgia of a time when life was simpler, when the ocean whispered secrets, and when history danced on the shores of Goa. It is my dream that this simple tribute will transport readers to that magical world, where the past and the present converge, and the heart finds solace in the beauty of words and the power of memories.

ACKNOWLEDGEMENTS

For my family: Especially my wife of 28 years, who has showered unconditional love and enriched my life with two boys who are a source of joy. May we travel together for as many miles that are left for us in this beautiful journey of life.

For the Reader: Thank you for purchasing the book and wishing all the best on your journey towards using the contents of this book.

ABOUT THE AUTHOR

Rajeev Nalawadi is not your typical author. He's a man of many facets, a blend of technological genius and an adventurous spirit that knows no bounds. With a marriage spanning 28 years, Rajeev and his wife, Roopa, have built a life together in the picturesque town of El Dorado Hills, California.

Rajeev's zest for life is evident in his diverse array of passions. First and foremost, he's a globetrotter with a wanderlust that has taken him to more than 75 countries across the world. What sets him apart is his unique penchant for exploration – he's not content with just seeing the sights; he prefers to get behind the wheel and drive through foreign landscapes, making every corner of the world his own. Whether it's navigating the bustling streets of Japanese cities like Kyoto, Tokyo, Osaka, Nagoya or cruising through the serene countryside of Tuscany, Rajeev's love for travel knows no boundaries.

But that's just the tip of the iceberg. Rajeev is equally enthralled by the great outdoors. Hiking is one of his cherished pastimes, and you can often find him conquering challenging trails in Sierra Nevada mountains and forging new paths in the wilderness of Pacific Crest trail (PCT). His connection with nature is amplified by his love for dogs, which he considers not just pets but cherished companions on his adventures.

When he's not globe-trotting or conquering hiking trails, Rajeev indulges in his other passions: cars and technology. He possesses an innate fascination with both, from the sleek lines and raw power of automobiles like Lamborghini to the ever-evolving world of cutting-edge technology.

Academically, Rajeev is a powerhouse. He holds a master's degree in computer science from Florida Atlantic University, which laid the foundation for his illustrious career. Later, he delved deeper into the realm of emerging technologies by earning a post-graduate degree from the prestigious Stanford University, specializing in Energy and Emerging Technologies.

Professionally, Rajeev's journey has been nothing short of remarkable. With 28 years of experience at industry giants IBM and Intel, he has been at the forefront of technological innovation. As an AI Technologist and Architect, he has steered the development of a wide spectrum of products, ranging from Cloud computing to cutting-edge Client platforms and everything in between. His contributions have consistently pushed the boundaries of what is possible, often leading to "State of the Art" advancements in both software and hardware technology.

Rajeev's impact extends beyond the corporate realm. He is the proud holder of an impressive 30 patents, spanning across a diverse range of products. These patents are a testament to his unwavering commitment to innovation and his ability to transform abstract ideas into real-world solutions.

In the pages of his books, Rajeev Nalawadi combines his rich experiences, from traversing the globe to driving technological progress. With a unique blend of adventure and intellect, he invites readers to embark on a journey of discovery, one that explores the farthest reaches of the world and the depths of cutting-edge technology. His storytelling prowess is just as impressive as his technical expertise, making his books a thrilling and enlightening experience for readers of all backgrounds. So, whether you're an adventurer at heart, die-hard romantic, mystery fan or a tech enthusiast, Rajeev's works promise to be an exhilarating and intellectually stimulating ride through the worlds he knows best.

Rajeev can be reached through any of these mediums:

Email - lifesmagicaljourneys@gmail.com

Website - https://rajeevnalawadi.com

Website - https://lifesmagicaljourneys.com

www.ingramcontent.com/pod-product-compliance
Lightning Source LLC
Chambersburg PA
CBHW050921030726
47503CB00007BB/2408